OF
GODS,
HUMANS
AND
BEASTS

THE HORSE SACRIFICE
AND OTHER STORIES

ARNOLD WISHMAN

OF GODS, HUMANS AND BEASTS
THE HORSE SACRIFICE AND OTHER STORIES

iUniverse books may be ordered through booksellers or by contacting:

iUniverse
1663 Liberty Drive
Bloomington, IN 47403
www.iuniverse.com
1-800-Authors (1-800-288-4677)

ISBN: 978-1-5320-9738-6 (sc)
ISBN: 978-1-5320-9739-3 (e)

Library of Congress Control Number: 2020911062

Print information available on the last page.

iUniverse rev. date: 06/17/2020

CONTENTS

Preface ix

The Curious Birth of a Gentleman God................................1
King David, the Great Patriarch..................................... 15
Why Good Women Are Stoned....................................43
How Ramji Got the Beard 53
How Supreme Court Played Spoil-sport 71
Sweet Balls For A Man-God...79
The Great Horse Sacrifice 89
The Purpose of A Prayer.. 111
The Ghost Who sighed 119
A Sam D'Cruz Terror Story..137
The Tragic End of a Love Affair............................. 169
Remembering Father Thomas 179
Four Days of Terror...187
Thingamajig – An Old Soldier's Tale..............................243
How Jesus Saved Mrs. Frankson.................................261

These stories are dedicated
To all women and men who were sacrificed, persecuted,
tortured, decapitated, drowned, burnt alive, whipped,
stoned, amputated or otherwise inflicted with perilous
mental and physical agony in the name of their faith
or for the lack of it.

Religion is based mainly upon fear. Fear of the mysterious, fear of defeat, fear of death. Fear is the parent of cruelty, and therefore it is no wonder if religion and cruelty have gone hand in hand.

- Bertrand Russell

PREFACE

This book of stories is about faith and violence, both of which more often than not go together.

That said, not all stories in this book are violent or terror-filled. The reader will find an occasional humorous sketch to relieve tension. However, some stories do depict extreme violence perpetrated by God on man, man on his neighbor, the powerful on the helpless, a mob on the lone. They might not all appeal to the conventional concept of how a story should run.

Apart from scriptural and widely published episodes of historical significance, personal names, specific instances and locations mentioned are purely fictional. The extremes of human cruelty, such as piercing the eyes of alleged criminals and filling the holes with acid have happened in real life; so have mob violence and the corrupt ways of those in authority. However, any resemblance to a real-life event or person as depicted in my stories is entirely unintended; if anything, it should be attributed to the realism I ventured to instill into my work. If someone feels that I blasphemed a scripture or a sacred episode described in it, he or she should once again read that particular part of the scripture to which, though quite unconventionally in a book of short stories, I have made references in footnotes.

There are many to whom I am indebted for the making of these stories and for their compilation in the form of a book. Among them my Wife who advised me to write stories rather than criticize religious superstitions and cultural cruelty on my blogsite and has been extremely patient, the media who publish my posts and blogs without curtailment, my Daughter who painstakingly and meticulously makes arrangements for my comfort and privacy while I keep chipping and scraping on my work, my Son who has been an inspiration and a role-model since the day he was born, my Grandson who expresses amazement at the description of events and believes that I am a gifted writer and my Granddaughter, who rarely reads my work and passes no comments but compliments my style with polished imitation.

I am grateful to iUniverse for readily coming forward to publish this book. Of them, I must specially mention Marvin Maxwell, Vinnia Alvarez, Gil Maley and Monica Mars for their patience and perseverance; for sending out a long chain of words of encouragement, and for bearing up with my stubbornness and temper tantrums. My friend Reed Samuel deserves a special word of thanks for coordinating the production; Tim Galvin for directing the designs of the cover as well as the interior of the book. I am deeply grateful to the editorial board of iUniverse for some excellent suggestions to improve the format and content as well as for valuable advice for forestalling any risk of litigation or fraudulent claims. Needless to say, the publishers are in no way responsible for the contents. Much gratitude is also due to my talented artist-friend Amrita Paintal who readily agreed to create sketches for my website to promote the book. I must not forget to acknowledge the value addition provided by those who liberally gave their critical views, whether for or against, after reading the pre-print version.

Hong Kong,
March 2020

It is in the nature of women to seduce men; hence wise men should never let down their guard in the company of women

- Manu Smriti 2: 213

THE CURIOUS BIRTH OF A GENTLEMAN GOD

East of the Arabian Sea, Gods were a Trinity of three distinct and discrete Males unlike the Trinity towards the West, who was just one Person with a thrice-split Personality. Among the three-some Trinity was Vishnu who created Brahma. This latter God, Brahma, created the rest of the universe, and then rested on a lotus that had sprung forth from the naval of Vishnu. The third God Shiva, who was self-born, bore the responsibility to wreck the entire creation four billion and a few million years later so that Brahma, as ordained by Vishnu, could rework his architectural plans for a fresher creation. It was a perfect arrangement by which the universe ticked on like clockwork.

Having done the creation with the dexterity of a master craftsman and the tempo of the *Big Bang*, Brahma left the maintenance to Vishnu, who did the job with the competence of an amateur motor mechanic. Most godly days and nights, Vishnu lay on His side, head propped up by his right arm, on the coiled serpentine body of *Ananta, a* massive multi-headed anaconda whose name meant the Infinite One. Vishnu the omnipotent and Ananta his cuddly bed, together rested right in the middle of an ocean of milk that never curdled.

Devas or demigods who resided in the stratosphere above the clouds enjoyed the status of being the most-favoured tribe of Vishnu. Like the solitary and jealous God across the Bay, the multitude of demigods were a jealous lot; very possessive of their divine status, superior caste and golden skin. They thrived on burnt offerings and peace offerings that came from the pious human priests who lit fires in their honour and sent up Vedic chants along with the sweet aroma of burnt flesh and layers of fat. When thus satiated, the gods would send down timely rains and other good tidings to the human world. No matter what *devas* did, or didn't, Vishnu loved them and would incarnate at the drop of his gold crown to rescue them from any trouble.

Now and then, Sage Narada, the divine gossip who roamed the three worlds – heaven, earth and *Patal* the underworld – scavenging for juicy news, waded the sticky ocean of milk and reported trouble in the realm of Vishnu's favourite tribe. Thereupon, a furious Vishnu would take a couple of decades to incarnate as some kind of an animal, a dwarf or a handsome prince. The prince thus incarnated would take another couple of decades to grow into adulthood and, after much drama that called for a long epic to describe, would annihilate the trouble- maker. That's the way justice worked then; that's the way justice works today. It takes twenty to forty years in the spiritual land of Vishnu-worship to dispense justice. More often than not, those who were sentenced to hang would up and hang themselves simply from the boredom of listless waiting.

The equivalent of Amalekites and Canaanites who once lived across the bay were the dark-skinned *Rakshasas* or demons. The demons, like the Canaanites, were cousins of the gods, but their born enemies. Vishnu, who carried all kinds of weapons of torture[1] was openly and fiercely on the side of gods and, like the God across the Western Bay, was not averse to lying, cheating or breaking His covenants with the demons to help gods.

Realizing the futility of resting their hopes on the treacherous and patently biased Lord Vishnu, the demons turned their piety and prayers towards Lord Shiva, the God of annihilation. True to the ways of their God, the demons set up devices to destroy things that belonged to the gods – smashing their thrones and carriages, beating them up in streets, stealing their wives, even attacking the throne of King Indra himself. Thus, the demons came to be called *Shiva-sena*, army of Shiva, which thrives till today. Sadly, Lord Shiva was to encounter many troubles on account of his affinity for the wily army of demons named after him.

Among the most determined demons was the one called *Bhasmasura*, or Ash-Demon, aptly so named by his parents of great foresight. Ash-demon loved to play deadly pranks on gods. Later, having lost interest in merely harassing the cowardly gods, he made up his mind to go in for serious stuff – mischief on none but a God, one among the Trinity. To achieve that ignoble aim, he stood in penance for a dozen years, standing only on the toes of one leg, stretching a hand upwards pointing towards heaven, eating nothing, and fervently chanting the name of Lord Shiva.

Ash Demon's unflinching piety and obstinate austerities apart from celibacy, which is normally unheard of among the demon tribes, raised the temperature in Mount Kailas, later renamed Mount Everest by impious British colonialists, where Shiva resided with his wife and two children – Muruga and Ganesha - who were conceived in ways that avoided conception by entry or exit from the only unholy part of his divine wife – the vagina.

In the icy mountains of Kailas, the heat generated by

---

[1] In Sanskrit, *Sarva-praharan-ayudha*. Sarva=entire; Prahrana=torture; Ayduha=weapons.

Ash-demon's austerities became so unbearable that the snow melted into glaciers and glaciers into rivers which flooded the plains below, drowning humans, cattle and spotted deer essential for hunting by kings and for sacrifice by Brahmin priests. Unable to bear the heat, Shiva's normally cool wife Parvathi demanded that her dear Lord meet the *tapaswi* (heat-generator) post-haste and restore the air-conditioning of the icy mountain peak.

Thus hen-pecked, Lord Shiva, despite his premonition of impending danger, appeared before the demon who had his one hand and one leg raised, eyes closed, mouth chanting "*Om Nama Shivaya*" as a Bollywood actor would chant when he had to prove his patriotic piety for a role in a movie that would be produced with an eye on tax exemption by the nationalistic government.

"Relax, and open your eyes," said Shiva in his thunderous growl. "*Devotee*, I am here. Ask for your boon". The sound echoed from the mountains all around, making the earth tremble.

Ash-Demon's raised leg and hand dropped in the tremour. He opened his eyes and, overjoyed, prostrated and touched the Lord's feet.

"Now that you have appeared before me, what other boon can I ask for?" He said with a modesty that did not ring true.

The Lord, who was a scholar in astrology and had written a treatise on that scientific subject in his biography named *Linga Purana[2]* did not miss the ominous signs that were playing in the sky and all around him. Donkeys brayed, wolves howled eerily, Saturn moved to the zone of Jupiter, animal bones and blood rained down from the clouds – all terribly foreboding and portending trouble even for a member of the Trinity of Gods.

---

[2] *Crudely translated, Linga Purana means Historic record of the Penis. Over the centuries, and due to overuse, the word lingam has come to mean a pillar-like statue of Shiva. The spiritually knowledgeable describe lingam with the relatively respectable word, Phallus, instead of Penis.*

Unlike the God to the West of Indian Ocean who broke his covenants time after time with one excuse or another, even unlike His Brother-God Vishnu, Shiva was made of sterner divine substance. He offered no excuse, and never broke a covenant. Nor did he say "I broke the covenant because you served another God." Serving other gods was OK with the True Trinity of Gods because service rendered to any smaller god would eventually land up at their feet, just as a chunk of the bribe paid to a lowly traffic constable would end up in the election funds of the minister of transport.

"Don't beat around the bush. Tell me what it is that you've been raising the temperature of my abode incessantly for the past twelve years. The ice has melted, even I had trouble negotiating the glaciers and the floods; my third eye can see that far, far away to the East and the West, the sea-level is rising. So, hurry and make your wish," Said the Lord.

"I ask for very little, my Lord," said the Ash-Demon in fake humility. "I am not asking for mountains of gold, a huge palace, or the kingdom of those treacherous demigods and their king Indra."

He paused for effect before dropping the bombshell.

"The simple boon I plead for is this, my Lord. My name is Ash-Demon, as you very well know, so named by my parents of great foresight. All that I ask is that whomever I touch on the top of his or her head, he or she should instantly burn to ash – irretrievably."

Lord Shiva ignored the tingle he felt through His vertebral column that ran from the nape of his neck where a hooded cobra had taken residence, all the way down to the back of His universally venerated *lingam*.

"That's a stupid request, but I'm not surprised that you demons are always out to cause destruction. Your devotion to me is laudable, but you need to ask for something more reasonable," said Lord Shiva, his heavy baritone tapering to a pitch of abject plea.

"I don't need to remind you, my Lord, that in this land of spirituality, Gods are not like the God on the other side of the Bay. A covenant is a covenant. I did the penance; you owe me my prayer."

The Lord knew that he had no alternative. If he rejected the demon's prayer, the demon would go back on his penance, causing global warming and setting his own home at Mount Kailas on the boil. On the other hand, where would this idiot get a chance to touch the top of anyone's head other than on one of his wives or concubines?

"So be it," said Shiva, taking a long breath and recovering some of the harsh bass of his voice. "True, we Gods this side of the Bay do not break our covenants under any excuse. My Partner Vishnu might cheat you demons once in a while, but wouldn't dream of breaking a covenant. I do neither. I will grant your worthless prayer. If you place the palm of your right hand on anyone's head, he or she will burn into ash. Irretrievably."

Having said that, Lord Shiva had a premonition that it was a terrible boon, but he could do nothing about it.

Ash demon hopped up and down in sheer delight. "Thank you, Lord, thank you so much. That's the best boon you granted to anyone as far as I know."

"That's it for now. Now you go your way, and I go back to my abode," said Lord Shiva, while beginning to chant the vanishing *mantra.*

"Not so soon, dear Lord, not so soon. I need to test this boon before I let you go. Let me touch the crown of *your* head."

There lay what came to be known as Lord Shiva's conundrum. The Trinity of Gods – Brahma, Vishnu and Shiva – were indestructible. Among them, Shiva happened to be the most powerful. Legends abounded to show that the other two members of the Trinity together do not measure up to Lord Shiva's huge *lingam*. He was the destroyer, who could not be destroyed.

But a boon by Him was irreversible. If the demon touched His head, He had no way but to turn to ashes, irretrievably.

Not destructible, but would be destroyed. Couldn't die, but would be incinerated.

This was no easy Rubik cube. This was no Newton's Conundrum that arose when he propounded the law of gravity, which went like this: Stars are massive bodies that are stationary. By his own equation for two bodies of mass, the force is such that they should fall into each other, no matter how distant, at some point of time, committing suicide like forlorn lovers.

Stars should fall into each other and destroy themselves. But they didn't seem to fall into each other and destroy themselves. Instead, they kept revolving around each other like romantic characters in a Hindi movie. That was the riddle Newton went to his deathbed with, leaving the solution to God. Two hundred years later, a man named Edwin Hubble burst the bubble of that riddle.

Being God, Lord Shiva knew there was no solution for his riddle, and there would be no Hubble to find one. Anyways, He didn't want to risk finding out if there was a solution to his predicament. So, He took the next best step.

He ran with one of his hands held up, palm spread out to protect the top of his head. He ran faster than any Usain Bolt of his time.

Ash-demon felt cheated when he was denied the most sacred ash of Lord Shiva. So, he ran after Him with his right hand stretched out to touch the Lord's head at the first opportunity.

Lord Shiva could have just vanished, which was within the

power of any God. But that would only make him a laughing stock in the eyes of the other two members of the Divine Board.

"You not only ran, he-he-he but also vanished in fear of a mere demon," Brahma would say. Vishnu would smirk as usual, not wanting to strain himself with a loud laughter.

Moreover, Shiva was not sure if the demon knew the vanishing *mantra* as well. As in any terror movie, the dead could see the dead, the vanished could see each other as if in plain daylight.

So, the great Lord Shiva ran around the earth, around the moon, around the sun, around the three worlds that consisted of the Earth, Heaven and *Patal* – a deep underground world built by his friend and junior accomplice *Yama, the* demi-god of death, where he housed sinners and fierce beasts together in a Colosseum of colossal dimensions. Shiva tried hard to hide within the rings of Saturn, another friendly junior god, but found himself too lustrous, despite his dark complexion, to escape notice. Wherever He went, the demon kept right after Him.

Lord Shiva racked His divine head covered with dread-locks while flashing across the galaxies, but could not divine a solution to the riddle. Will He die although a God should not die? Will the boon fail although a God's boon could never fail?

Thankfully, while on the run like lightning, He remembered his companion God, Lord Vishnu, who had a solution for every riddle, and who used to play with a Rubik cube when not fondling his beautiful masseur of a wife Lakshmi or engaged in the act of reincarnating himself to a man or beast to kill some enemy or another of the gods.

The Trinity of Gods were far ahead of their times. They needed no visible instrument of communication. The divine telepathy was very powerful and had the bandwidth of several Terra-bits and a speed several times that of light.

On that telepathy circuit Lord Shiva pleaded, without letting up on His speed, thus: "Brother Vishnu, Are you there? Please forget our rivalry and do something. I'm in deep cow-dung. Help me."

Lord Vishnu received the message in the divine language of Sanskrit. He, being the God of wisdom as well, knew that what Shiva got himself into was not holy cow-dung, but real, unholy demon-poop. So, he telepathized back:

"You're indestructible. Why are you worried?"

"Please, this is no time for devilish jokes. You know that my boon is irreversible and irreconcilable."

"Oh, yes. Let's not wait till the stars hit each other to find out what would happen. Here I come," said Lord Vishnu, giving the much-needed solace to Lord Shiva.

Now there must have been a distance of some 2000 cubits between the running Lord and the chasing demon, and their rapid footsteps were resounding like thunderclaps across the three worlds. Lord Shiva turned a corner and, for a few moments, was out of sight.

Not to worry, the demon soon came up and turned the corner.

Lord Vishnu had once again donned the looks and shape of Mohini, the one who bewitched the entire demon-tribe some eons before to cheat them out of their due share of the Elixir of Life. What Ash Demon saw in a fleeting vision was the prettiest and the sexiest woman he had ever set eyes upon. He stopped in his track and stepped back while Lord Shiva ran and ran and disappeared over the edge of the Milky Way.

Moon-like face. Kohl-lined Lotus-petal eyes. Cherry lips, teeth like beads of pearls. Voluptuous breasts that thrust out pink nipples with purple halos like a challenge. Belly flat like a banyan-tree leaf. Wide hips. Smooth, elephantine thighs suggestive of immense pleasure within. Carved calves.

Ash-demon did not notice the disappearance of his prey. The

beauty in a flimsy topless bikini hit him like a flash of light in the eyes of a running hare. Blinded for a moment, he felt delirious and nearly drained. His twelve-year-long abstinence seemed like taking its toll.

There was no time for preliminaries because the urge to put his hand on Lord Shiva's head was still in the back of his mind. Could also be that he was born in the subcontinent where none did believe in too many preliminaries and kissing was considered a blasphemy against culture.

"Please, oh please, you heavenly beauty, let me hold you," he pleaded

"You look as though you need more than a hold. You can make love to me if you promise to be faithful ever after," said Mohini, for that was Vishnu's trans-gendered name.

"I promise. This very moment."

"Well, you know how we make a solemn promise. This side of the Bay, one doesn't put his hand under the thigh of the other and promise on his balls as they do across the Bay[3]. Place the palm of your right hand on top of your head and swear that you'd always be faithful."

The demon, in his delirious ecstasy, placed his palm over his head and said: "I swear…"

Boom. There fell a heap of ash where the wily Ash-demon had been standing. Shiva's boon, he should have known, did not exempt his own head.

"Your riddle is solved; You're safe," called out Mohini, Lord Vishnu in fancy disguise, over the divine telepathy.

"I hope You aren't fooling me the way you fool demons," called back Lord Shiva, panting like an old steam engine. "If You truly solved it – huff-huff – tell me how you managed to do it"

---

[3] "So the servant put his hand under the thigh of Abraham his master and swore to him concerning this matter." (Genesis 24:9 NIV

"Come back and look," said Lord Vishnu, wanting to impress his Trinity-partner with His yet unheard-of makeup artistry.

Shiva walked back gingerly, still riddled and hence cautious, till He saw the beautiful Mohini, fit to walk any heavenly ramp and gather any number of wolf whistles. A heap of ashes lay in front of the beauty queen.

Now Gods are special. When they make up as females, they don't just take a close shave, put on a wig, plant coconut shells under their blouse and dab on lipstick. They become females all the way, I mean all the way, including the double-X chromosomes as well as the bodily fittings and all the crevices and cleavages that go with them.

Lord Shiva forgot his promise of fidelity to Parvati.

Lord Vishnu, now Mohini the perfect female with feminine ways, felt enamoured of the rough-and-tough macho look of Lord Shiva.

Sparks flew. As they show in romantic movies, creepers swayed, moon showed through the leaves of a tree-branch, a pair of pigeons French-kissed while romantic music played in the background. Two dozen belles, all decked in gold and roses, danced in well-rehearsed, perfectly synchronized steps against a background where stars twinkled like neon lamps. An invisible band played semi-classical romantic music in the background.

Lord Shiva's *lingam* performed well; soon thereafter Lady Vishnu secretly carried a baby bump for several thousand years. Finally, at the right opportunity in the 11th Century of the Common era, Vishnu delivered a bony boy by the banks of River Pampa below the South-West mountains of India, and abandoned him at the foot of the *Sabari* Hill. A local warlord picked up the child and named him Bell-neck because Vishnu had the foresight to tie a small bell round the baby's neck for future identification.

Vishnu's attempt at hiding his shame had failed. A wily

South-Indian sage known as *Guru-Swami* divined the cause of the child's birth the moment he set his eyes on him.

"This is a special God," he announced. "Ayya-Appa, Gentleman God for us all. His father is Lord Shiva, his Mother none other than Lord Vishnu.".

Since no lightning struck and killed Sage Guru-Swami who composed several rhymes in Sanskrit to prove the point, the masculine world agreed that what he said was the divine truth, hence not blasphemy. The females, true to tradition were allowed no say in the matter.

Little Bell-neck grew up to be a big God in his own right under the care of a human king who adopted him. Since his birth was from the union of two male Gods, it was rumoured that Lord Bell-neck despised women, swore himself to eternal celibacy and wished all female devotees out of his precincts. The Guru-swamis ruled that if Lord Ayyappa had anything to do with a real female, He would break the holy tradition of unisexual reproduction set up by his parents – Father Shiva, Male and Mother Vishnu, Male.

Thus, the young Gentleman god sits atop a hill, listening to deafening eulogies by millions of men who barge into his private life in the cooler months, but never getting to see a youthful female form he could hope to fall in love with.

The righteous will rejoice when he seeth the vengeance; He will wash his feet in the blood of the wicked.

Psalms 58:10-11 KJV

"For thou shalt worship no other god: for the LORD, whose name is Jealous, is a jealous God:"

Exodus 34:14, KJV

KING DAVID, THE GREAT PATRIARCH

When the people of Israel, feeling rudderless and anchorless, demanded that they, like all other people in the rest of the world, be given a King, God was furious; he asked, "What the f**ks am I here for?" or in even harsher words to that effect. However, He noticed the feeling of helplessness in the face of His favorite Prophet Samuel who led the hordes without being a king himself. So, finally, God relented. The nomadic Israelites would at last have a king to lead them.

God, in his omniscient and inscrutable mind, chose Saul, a low-grade Benjaminite. Saul was the tallest and best-looking among young men at the time. God convinced Samuel, who presumably felt peeved for not being selected for the role, that the young man would be best suited to rule his favorite tribe of Israelites and to cause enough bloodshed all around. To soothe the democratic sentiments of all Benjaminite's, lots were drawn, and, with a sleight of hand that held many miracles in the sleeves, God ensured that the name of Saul came up. Thus, young Benjaminite was divinely anointed as the king to the satisfaction of all. He was also made a Prophet next only to Samuel.

To God's jubilation, Saul harassed, killed and looted Moabites, Ammonites, Edomites, Aram Rehob and the kings of Zobah, the Philistines, and the Amalekites.

Then one day Saul did something terrible: he failed to carry out properly enough an order from God. who had commanded through Samuel thus in clear terms:

"I will punish Amalek for what he did to Israel, how he ambushed him on the way when he came up from Egypt. Now go and attack Amalek, and utterly destroy all that they have, and do not spare them. But kill both man and woman, infant and nursing child, ox and sheep, camel and donkey."[4]

Saul, quite rightly, filtered out the non-Amalekites, as Hitler did with Christians in a Jewish colony, and killed everybody and everything that was despicable and worthless – such as ordinary people, their wives and sisters and mothers, their children, infants, foetus in the womb and most cattle. Quite disobediently, though, he spared king Agag, who pleaded for mercy. He also failed selectively to destroy the best of the sheep, the *oxen* and the fatlings, the lambs and all that was good.

God who had a drone's eye-view from the sky was shocked at Saul's despicable discretion in sparing lives. It made Him self-conscious that His omniscience was failing. He had made a mistake in choosing Saul as the king who was not an indiscriminate-enough killer. The trace of kindness Saul showed, albeit selective, was an abomination to God.

When questioned about this act of disobedience, Saul lied that he had spared the best among the sheep, *oxen, fatlings and lambs* for sacrifice to God because burnt offerings and peace

---

[4] 1 Samuel 15 1-3. NKJV

(piece) offerings were dear to God who loved the aroma of charred flesh.

Samuel, reflecting the anger of God at what He presumed to be Saul's rebellion, asked:

"Has the Lord as great delight in burnt offerings and sacrifices, as in obeying the voice of the LORD? Behold, to obey is better than sacrifice, and to heed than the fat of rams."[5]

Not trusting Saul, Samuel personally summoned for Agag, the rescued king and told him, *"As your sword has made women childless, so shall your mother be childless among women."*[6]

He gave Agag no chance to argue that it was not he who started the battle in the first place. In any case, his mother had no way to feel childless; she was already killed in *the man, woman, child, infant…*routine.

Thus, Samuel the prophet, judge and God's executioner rolled into one, hacked the repenting, cowering and unarmed king Agag to pieces then and there. This pleased God who had once commanded, in a spirit of good humor: *"Thou shalt not kill."*

Now, given the fraternity prevailing in the favored race of God, His favorite Prophet Samuel became afraid of Saul, who, God or no God, stayed put to his throne.

God told Samuel to take a heifer for sacrifice to Jesse, the Bethlehemite. The old prophet was received with suspicion, despite his age, but was accepted when it was found that he was once again looking for king material. Many from the village were marched before him, but God whispered *No, not this hombre,* in Samuel's ears. There was just one left, the youngest son of shepherd Jesse, a ruddy-eyed and handsome teenager, David. God

---

[5] 1 Samuel 15:22 NKJV
[6] 1 Samuel 15:33 NKJV

saw much promise in David. The very next moment, the spirit of God abandoned the disobedient Saul and entered the young man. Apparently, Saul cared a hoot.

God ordered that Saul be immediately dethroned and David, the new favorite, be placed on the throne. However, Paul stayed put.

Soon after Samuel elected David to be the next monarch, the teenaged shepherd boy, son of Jesse, landed up in Saul's palace, playing a lyre. He brought with him a tender goat, a loaf of bread and a skin of wine as gifts – things that would please any king. Saul was so pleased with the gifts and the physique of the young man that he made David his bodyguard, who would also play the harp to lift his Godforsaken spirits.

Israelites (circumcised) and Philistines (uncircumcised) were at loggerheads as ever before. A champion Philistine, taller than Sultan Kosen of Hollywood fame, and much better-built than Kevin Levrone of modern times, attired in chain-and-plate mail, bronze-protected limbs, wearing a helmet and holding aloft a heavy sword, came forward from the side of the Philistines and threw a challenge.

"Why do you come out and array yourselves for battle? Am I not a Philistine, and are you not servants of Saul? Choose one of your men and have him come up against me. If he is able to fight me and kill me, then we will be your servants. But if I prevail against him and kill him, then you shall be our servants and labour for us"[7].

If you did not take up a challenge, you lost the battle as well as your tribe's honour. That was the unwritten law.

Nobody among the Israelites dared to fight this tall giant who could, if he were in the twentieth century, easily have pounded

---

[7] 1 Samuel 17: 8-10 Berean Study Bible

Cassius Clay and Sonny Liston together while crushing Floyd Patterson in the hollow of his palms.

David found out the predicament of Israelites and their King Saul, even of God, and offered to go and fight the champion killer. Impressed by his boast of past adventures with lions and bears, or because he had no alternative, Saul fitted David with armored coats and other paraphernalia – but no sword – and sent him to fight the older, much larger and fiercer version of Mike Tyson.

Instead of a sword, David, a mere teenager that he was, carried only a catapult and a bag of stones. The moment he sighted Goliath the hunk at a safe distance, he loaded the catapult with a sharp stone and fired. It struck Goliath on his head, and he fell dead without much ado. After making sure that the giant was dead, David boldly walked up to the body of the dead man, picked up his sword that was lying in the loosened grip of his right hand and cut off his head. As proof of his feat, he took the head with him, but left the sword behind.

Philistines fled finding that their champion was dead. The brave and circumcised Israelites chased them and hacked them from behind with great courage. Carcasses lay sprawled all the way to the entrance of Gath and the gates of Ekron. Such enormous bloodletting filled pleasure in God's heart, and He loved David even more.

David presented the Philistine's head to King Saul. If Saul was impressed, he didn't show it. Saul's son Jonathan was impressed so much that he hero-worshiped David the way Indians worship film actors and the Beetles for a time worshiped an Indian yogi. Jonathan presented his own ceremonial wear and fineries to David as a sign of his admiration.

As jealous as God Himself, Saul sent David to many conquests hoping that the upstart who might one day claim his throne would get killed. David returned victorious with much plunder in accordance with God's Commandments six[8] and eight[9]. Saul had no option but to promote David to a higher rank in his army.

That was when trouble struck.

David returned after another massacre of Philistines, escorted by a retinue of dancing women who clapped hands and kept repeating the refrain that should gladden any Judeo-Christian-Islamic heart:

> *Saul has slain his thousands,*
> *And David his tens of thousands."*[10]

To be publicly reviled that he was a lesser killer was an insult no God or man of Israel – from Moses to Moshe Dayan – would tolerate. Saul, who did not know that God had theoretically unseated him, was now paranoid that David would surely grab his throne. He had to find a surer way to get rid of David.

Saul sent David away with only a brigade of thousand men to several battles in the hope that he would get killed in one of them. Because God was always with the better killer, David returned alive and victorious, bringing with him much plunder.

If I couldn't beat him, I could treat him, schemed Saul. He offered his older daughter Merab to David in marriage. David, being cleverer than Saul had fathomed, declined the plain-looking Merab. He was too lowly born to marry a princess, he reasoned to the king. Actually, his eyes were on Michal, the beautiful younger one who reciprocated his love. Soon they were married.

Jonathan tried hard to convince his father that David had no ambition to dislodge him from his throne. For a while Saul

---

[8] Thou shalt not kill

[9] Thou shalt not steal

[10] 1 Samuel 18:7 NIV

appeared convinced. However, God's holy mischief prevailed. He sent His Spirit to change Saul's mind as He did with the Pharaoh of Egypt before the Exodus. Having failed in his promise to put David on the throne, God's alternative move was to put a bad spirit in Saul and set him up against David. God did not have to try hard.

Saul continued to try to kill David while pretending to entertain him. Once he tried to back-stab David with his spear, but missed. He sent men to kill him in his daughter Michal's bed, but David had got forewarning and had run away. Michal fooled the assassins by arranging the bed with pillows and covering it with a sheet as though David was asleep. Saul heard that David had joined Samuel and had been prophesying at Naioth at distant Ramah. He went to kill David there but instead, presumably hypnotized by the wily God, doffed his royal clothes, put on *ephod* – a priestly armor which every priest had to wear presumably for protection against God's wrath – and started prophesying. Such were the powers of God.

However, Saul's determination to kill David did not let up. With little help from God, but with a lot of it by his own cunning, David escaped every time.

The Philistines, the tribe of Goliath whose killing you'd remember, were a stubborn lot. For some reason, God had not asked David, though that was his wont, to annihilate Philistines – *man, woman, children*…. you know the routine – all the way to suckling lambs and foetus in the womb. Hence, Philistines always re-grouped, and became a formidable force. This time they attacked the town of Keilah. God told David to go to Keilah and defend the town which David did, carrying off their livestock, but letting the women and children be so as to keep the story moving.

Saul pursued David to Keilah, but God had warned David that Saul would catch and kill him but He could do nothing about it. As always, God proved Himself wrong and incompetent.

David, who beat the Philistines but feared Saul, ran from place to place, with Saul on hot pursuit. A priest of God with the ephod was with David, so Saul never caught up. In the meanwhile, words came that Philistines had attacked Saul's base. Saul gave up the chase while David found a safe place.

Dealing with the Philistines took no time for Saul because there was no command from God who was sulking. Thus, the matter was settled quickly by another carnage and Saul returned to deal with David. While Saul went for a royal poop in a cave all alone, David crept from behind, held his nose with one hand and cut off a piece from Saul's robe with the other.

David was probably not sure that God had denounced Saul, or maybe, knowing God as well as he did, he didn't feel reassured enough. Despite all the chasing Saul had done, David remained devoted to the king who gave his first break in life. So, he went up to Saul and showed the piece of robe.

"Killing a king from behind while he poops is the easiest thing to do," said David : "But Lord, your servant did not do it. Because I'm still devoted to you."

Sault felt ashamed and made a speech of his own, at the end of which David grabbed Saul's balls under his thighs (for that was the custom, established by Patriarch Abraham)[11] and swore what Saul wanted him to swear – that he would bring no harm to his family of his descendants. Having obtained that oath from David, Saul went his way while David went another way. David's covenant was as good as God's – there was always a way around it.

God neither chided nor cursed David for giving such a promise and for the sacrilege of holding the balls of His foe. Saul, as we know, had not yet vacated the throne although His Omnipotence had commanded his dethroning. Imagine the shame. However, God knew that when the time came, He'd find a way to destroy Saul's

---

[11] See explanation in https://www.gotquestions.org/hand-under-thigh.html

race without David raising his hands on them and thereby keeping his oath. God, as you by now must know, was a very clever God.

While camping in a place safely away from Saul, David sent his men to a rich landlord called Nabal to get free provisions. Nabal, whose name meant fool – just as God's name was Jealous – was filthy rich. He had never heard of Samuel, nor of a Jesse and his son David. Even if he had, he was too stingy to part with his grains or money. Thus, Nabal the fool refused to give any provision – free or on credit to David and his men.

David was no man's fool. Instead of attacking Nabal's household and destroying *by the sword man, woman...* (you have by now surely learnt the routine), David sent a message to Nabal's wife who went running to him with far more provisions than David had imagined. She prostrated at David's feet and promised to do whatever he desired of her with an emphasis on *whatever*.

Having got the message right, David waited, placing his trust in God the Jealous. Though married to Michal who once saved his life, and Ahinoam of Jezreel whom he married along the way, David now desired his lovely new accomplice Abigail of Carmel, the wife of Nabal the Fool. To speed up the process God Himself, being God Almighty, struck Nabal dead after the landlord had had too much to drink at a party of the Filthy Rich and was convalescing in bed for ten days. When the statutory mourning was done, Abigail rushed to David and offered him the promised *whatever*. David received the offering in bed and married her. David a third time, Abigail the second time.

The evil spirit of God never abandoned Saul, so he pursued David again with a large army. David stole Saul's water jug and spear while he (Saul) was fast asleep in his royal tent. When he discovered what David had done, and yet had not killed him in his sleep, Saul said he felt ashamed. He blessed David and went back to warm his throne.

David went his own yet aimless way and settled down in Philistine territory; frequently marauding the neighbors – Geshurites, the Girzites and the Amalekites. Wherever he and his army raided, being a true man of God, he plundered all that they had in cattle, donkeys and camels, leaving no man, woman or baby alive. God, who had commanded that thou shalt not covet thy neighbour's property, nor his wife, nor slave and so on, loved the way David went about his killings and loved him even more for not just coveting, but plundering all the neighbors' property, wives and slaves.

Achish, a Philistine chief with a decapitated Dagon for his god, nevertheless granted asylum and a town for David to live in and plunder from. One day Achish decided to attack Israel and asked David to be his bodyguard, which neither shocked nor infuriated God – or, for that matter, David. There is no record that David was upset at having to guard in battle the opponent of his own tribe. When Saul learnt that Philistines were going to attack Israel, he went to a medium to communicate with the dead Samuel. Even the ghost of Samuel had no kind words for him, for God's anger towards him was still aflame.

Other Philistine chiefs objected to David being with their army while going to raid Israel. They didn't trust him. So, David was sent back; but when he reached Zicklag, his town, he found that all the women – including David's two wives had been taken captive and carried away. Because the raiders were not of the same Jealous God, the attackers had not killed anyone nor raped the women. David went after the raiding party, and with the help of a turncoat Egyptian who had been part of the raiders, found them at a place where they were drinking, eating and generally having fun. David recaptured all the women, and killed all the raiders – except a few young men who got away on camelbacks. He got so much plunder that he shared it with all the tribes in whose places his men had roamed.

The Philistines, the sworn enemy of Israel and God, beat Saul's army, wounded Saul and killed his sons – Jonathan (the ardent fan of David) and his two brothers. Saul committed suicide, which God presumably celebrated in high heavens. The victorious Philistines cut off Saul's head and presented his armour to their idols. The once humiliated, dismembered and decapitated (by the God of Israelites) Dagon, the god of Philistines, appeared rejuvenated. The bodies of Saul and his sons were strung up on the walls. Some faithful Israelites found the bodies and gave them an honourable funeral.

To win David's favour, a young man brought Saul's crown and arm-band to David. He said he had seen Saul leaning on his spear; when Saul saw him, he begged him to kill him, which he did. Knowing Saul's enmity with David, the man expected to be rewarded. Instead David, who mourned the death of his erstwhile master, had the man killed. Whether it was for the pleasure of killing or out of devotion for Saul, or merely for the love of writing poetry, David wrote:

> *"Daughters of Israel, weep for Saul,*
> *who clothed you in scarlet and finery,*
> *who adorned your garments with ornaments of gold.*
> *How the mighty have fallen in the thick of battle!"*

And, of his bosom friend Jonathan, David sang:

> *"Jonathan lies slain on your heights.*
> *I grieve for you, Jonathan, my brother.*
> *You were delightful to me;*
> *your love to me was extraordinary,*
> *surpassing the love of women.*[12]

---

[12] 2 Samuel 1:24-26 Berean Study Bible

If God felt humiliated at this praise of Saul by David, it is not on record. It was also not clear what David meant by *"Your love for me was wonderful, more wonderful than that of women."* Whatever he might have meant, God did not give the same treatment to Ziklag, the city where David resided, as he gave to Sodom and Gomorrah. If you do not know what happened to Sodom, God burnt it down utterly, for he hated man loving man (and, as a corollary, woman loving woman – so say Pastors from the US South.).

David then went to Hebron, the town in Judah, with his wives and men. There the people of Judah made him their king. The feud between Saul's house and David's house lasted a long time, causing much bloodshed but making David progressively stronger. Finally, the house of Saul split; The son of Saul, Ish-Bosheth, accused his commander Abner of sleeping with Saul's concubine. This was reason enough for Abner to go over to David's side, but one of David's men, Joab, killed Abner by deceit. David cursed not Joab, but, true to God's style, his future generations with leprosy. Today if you find anyone in Israel with leprosy, you'd know that he is a descendent of Joab.

Now Rekab and Baanah, two smart alecks, killed king Ish-Bosheth, son of Late Saul and now the king from Saul's house, and took the dead man's head to David. David, overwhelmed with loyalty to the memory of Saul, killed them both. Their hands and feet were cut off and the limbless bodies were hung up near Hebron's public pool as a happy sight for God and His favorite people of Israel. If you thought torture before and after death began with medieval Europe, or that it was re-invented in Afghanistan and Guantanamo Bay, now you know the historic truth. To be fair, there is no Biblical record of the victorious piddling on the defeated.

David was still young, a vibrant thirty. The people of Israel requested David to become their king, not only of Hebron, but of the entire Saul kingdom. Saul, Jonathan and Ish-Bosheth conveniently disposed of, David signed a covenant with people and became their king. After so many years of bloodshed and turmoil, doubts and setbacks, murders and plunder, Almighty God's ambition to dislodge Saul (who was dead but no thanks to God) and to make David the king came true.

When they heard that King David was marching to conquer their Jerusalem, the Jebusites scoffed: "Even the lame and the blind can ward off David." Their confidence was short-lived; David defeated them, and as was his wont and to God's liking, utterly destroyed them, and established his city there. Neighbourhood kings sent envoys and gifts to David, thereby sparing themselves the usual divine treatment of death and plunder.

Having earned himself some rest, David collected several more wives and concubines while God watched with pride and patronage. David was the man of His own heart. Several children were born to David – too many to name.

David, we know, was in possession of the ephod, which made him a priest and a prophet. All that he now needed to fulfil his divine role was the Ark of God. The sacred Ark contained good tidings for mankind – the two original granite tablets[13] engraved with the latest version of Ten Commandments, a pot of *manna* – a sample collection of sweet seeds that the Israelites used to pick for their food while wandering in wilderness for 40 years after exit Egypt – and the rod of the first priest Aaron, brother of Moses. These sacred articles were packed inside a box made of acacia wood, and covered with gold lid; its four corners fitted with gold

---

[13] *Not the true original – which Moses broke in anger as soon as he came down the mountain, but the second one, which the patient and all-forgiving God painstakingly engraved once again with a slightly modified version of the Ten Commandments.*

rings. Two images of winged cherubs stood guard on the lid of the box, and in between was engraved the name of God Jealous. You put rods through rings (never to be removed) and carry around the Ark like a palanquin. The whole affair was meant to bring good tidings to the people of Israel and curse upon its enemies. There was one caveat – anyone, not exempting an Israelite, who looked at it would surely die. You could hold the carrying-poles, but touch the Ark or look at it at your own peril.

Now a well-intentioned man named Uzzah, who was among those who were guiding the ox cart, held on to the Ark when the cart stumbled on a loose threshing floor. God couldn't care that Uzzah was trying to protect the Ark, but was furious that he, a common man, held it and possibly looked at it. God personally struck him down beside the Ark. Though it contained the laws for mankind as decreed by God; anyone who took a look at those laws in original would be struck down by God. For a moment David felt anger welling up against God; and he named the place *Perez Uzzah* in honour of the man. If God felt slighted by that act of David, He chose not to show it.

This episode frightened David. Lest he too be tempted to look at the divine junk, he diverted the Ark to the house of Obed-Edom, a Gittite who lived in Gath, a city in the Philistines. During the three months the Ark was in his house, Obed-Edom flourished. When he heard of it, David immediately called for the dangerous gift from God and put it away safely in a tent and in celebration danced half-naked. Michal, David's first wife who was Saul's daughter, chided and made fun of David for what he had done.

"I will become even more undignified than this, and I will be humiliated in my own eyes," retorted David. "But by these slave girls you spoke of, I will be held in honor[14]."

---

[14] *2 Samuel 6:22 NIV*

We are not certain whether the slave girls liked what they saw. Neither David nor Michal knew how, three millennia later, Michael Angelo, the great artist-sculptor of the Renaissance, would resurrect young David in all his splendid non-attire for viewing by all mankind – big, handsome, muscular and perfectly nude with uncircumcised genitals of a child's proportions.

During the excitement and jubilation, David felt bad that while he lived in a palatial house with his many wives and even more concubines, that God, who continued to live in a movable tent was getting a raw deal. God knew what David meant with this new worry of his and summoned him through Nathan, the prophet. He pointed out that his helping the Israelites was out of love for them, not expecting anything in return (as long as they served him meat by way of burnt offerings and fellowship offerings of cut-up meat). He said:

When your days are fulfilled and you rest with your fathers, I will set up your seed after you, who will come from your body, and I will establish his kingdom. He shall build a house for My name, and I will establish the throne of his kingdom forever.[15]

David concluded the meeting with God (through Nathan, the prophet), oozing gratitude and worshipped at God's altar (in the tent) to thank Him[16].

With the Ark of God's covenant in his tent but safely out of sight, David attacked, massacred and plundered all the tribes in the Middle East. He destroyed thousands of chariots, ten-thousands of charioteers and killed hundred-thousands of foot soldiers, plundered all the gold and silver and bronze, and to God's great delight, dedicated it all to Him. David played cat-and-mouse

---

[15] 2 Samuel 7:12-13 NKJV

[16] God's *forever* was short-lived; the massive temple that David's son Solomon built lasted less than four hundred years; it was destroyed by Babylonians, the lot that was cursed by God. Today two mosques stand where that promised temple stood. David should have known how slippery were God's promises.

games with Moabites (descendants of Lot, the dear nephew of dearest-to-God Israelite Abraham, through one of own his own daughters. God continued to love Lot but cursed the product of the incestuous offspring – Moab and hence despised his later generations – the Moabites).

David laid down all the Moabites in a straight line, head-to-toe, and killed each alternate one while God and other Israelites watched in glee. Like witch-burning that was to come several centuries later and of gassing of his descendants yet a few more centuries afterwards, these acts of David served as a spectacle sport for the tired people of Israel. David thus became the best of all generations after the great ancestor Abraham, which was why forty-one generations later Jesus, the Son of God, also came to be called the Son of David.

David never forgot his devotion and his promise to Saul not to harm his progeny. So, he called for a surviving grandson of Saul – Mephibosheth – who was lame in both legs, and gave him much land that originally belonged to Saul. He also let the invalid eat at his table. However, when a tribe who wanted to take revenge on what Saul had done to them, they requested David that Saul's remaining seven male descendants –– be handed over to them which David did without batting an eyelid or recalling the feel of Saul's balls. All the seven were killed and strung up in a public place. David spared the life of hobbling Mephibosheth.

Thus, while keeping his promise to Saul not to harm his descendants, David ensured that last of Saul's generations – save (for the time being) his disabled son Mephibosheth who had no feet and couldn't be of any harm – was eliminated. David was an honorable man. He gifted all the land that belonged to Saul and his family to Mephibosheth and his sons. How was the poor invalid to know that David's favors were like God's favors – shifting sands.

Then one evening in spring while walking on the terrace of his cedar palace, David noticed a woman bathing. The woman, her name Bathsheba, was wife of Uriah the Hittite, a loyal soldier in David's army. David called for the woman and bedded her without too many preliminaries. Because she just had her bath of cleansing after her period, she got pregnant. That's how it used to be in the days of the Bible – fertilization the day after menstruation.

Uriah sensed what happened and, unlike Joseph the carpenter, did not want to be called the father of an illegitimate child. He said nothing to David, but stopped making love to his wife, and slept outside his own house so that the public knew that he had nothing to do with his wife's baby bump. Peeved by this act of insubordination, David asked his general, Joab, to "Put Uriah out in front where the fighting was the fiercest, then withdraw from him so he will be struck down and die." Which Joab did, and Uriah fought and died a hero's death in a battle where many more Israeli soldiers died and the rest fled. David was pleased by the death of his rival in love and hence was not much upset by the defeat of his army.

Bathsheba, after the due mourning period, joined the harem of David and gave birth to a son. God, who had once ensured that Abigail's husband Nabal died so David could marry her, had a different rule for David's killing of Uriah, the husband of Bathsheba. The decision to kill or not to kill a husband of a woman desired by David lay with God; David taking it upon himself amounted to intransigence. God listed all that He had done for David, who was a poor shepherd to begin with and now a king with the heads of most of his neighbor kings in his kitty. Hence, thus thundered God:

"'Out of your own household I am going to bring calamity on you. Before your very eyes I will take your wives and give them to one who is close to you, and he will sleep with your wives in broad daylight. You did it in secret, but I will do this thing in broad daylight before all Israel[17]."

If you could play dirty without asking Him, He could play dirtier was the message of morality from God, loud and clear.

Nathan, the aged Prophet, had once reminded David that nobody could get dirtier than God. The public rape of David's wives as promised by God was to come in due course. For the time being, God forgave David and, in keeping with Commandment number 2 of 10[18], punished David's illegitimate son born to Bathsheba – thereby visiting the inequity of the father on the son.

"The LORD has taken away your sin. You are not going to die. But because by doing this you have shown utter contempt for the LORD, *the son born to you will die.*" Said the Lord[19] through Nathan.

The child suffered terribly for seven days – a suffering so gruesome that it is still spoken and written about. All those days David slept on the ground and ate little. Then the boy died. If God had expected that he could make David suffer more by the death of his son, He was wrong. David took the child's death philosophically. He got up, had a wash and his meal. Many a fish in the water, many sons in his harem.

In a royal family where so many wives and concubines shared bed-space and children of different wives and concubines played and squabbled, this was to happen someday. The son of David from a certain wife, Amnon, developed a desire for the daughter, Tamar, from another wife. Tamar happened to be the sister of Absalom. Pretending to be ill, Amnon called for the services of

---

[17] 2 Samuel 12:11-12 NIV

[18] "...for I the LORD your God am a jealous God, visiting the iniquity of the fathers upon the children unto the third and fourth generation of them that hate me..." Dueut.5:9, NIV

[19] 2 Samuel 12: 13-14, NIV

Tamar who was a noble virgin. Despite her stiff resistance and pleading, Amnon raped her. A distraught and shamed Tamar emerged from the room tearing her clothes and wailing. That's how Absalom learnt that his step brother violated his direct sister. Once the job was done, Amnon's love for Tamar turned into hate.

Absalom gathered all his brothers in a drunken orgy and had Amnon struck down by his henchmen. The other brothers, frightened, fled. Absalom, knowing David's rage and disregard for human lives, fled in another direction.

David mourned his dead son Amnon for a couple of years and then longed to see the living Absalom. At Joab's persuasion, he allowed Absalom to return, but pretending to be still mad at his son, David refused to see his face for another couple of years.

Now Absalom was a handsome man, the best in all David's vast empire, fit to be the king. The highlight of his physical attributes was a huge crop of hair, which he would cut every year-end and weigh the discarded hair. On an average, it weighed 200 shekels, something like two-and-a-half kilograms by modern reckoning. With all that hair and handsome looks, Absalom was an unhappy young man. There was no sign of David abdicating or dying, and he was impatient as any young crown prince of more recent times is bound to feel until he discovered that his mother was intent on living forever. Absalom went to Hebron, recruited a lot of able men into his army, grew popular with the populace and declared himself the king of Hebron, which was where a quarter century ago David had declared himself King.

When David heard the news that his son had declared himself the king, paranoia set in; faith in God flew out through the window. He fled, leaving the Ark of God in the city. "If God my Lord desires that I return, then I will return to His Ark," he said, thus teasing God to give him victory against his rebellious son. Weeping like a coward, he fled to Mount Olives, making arrangements for spies to be stationed in Absalom's house.

God was indeed tantalized, but had not forgotten the dirty trick He had reserved for David.

Now Ahithophel, the sagacious counsellor of David, in his great wisdom decided that David was a spent force. He went to the aspiring king Absalom and glorified him. To Absalom, who was badly in need of acceptance, wanted to know how he could make himself popular among the Israelites. Ahithophel gave him a sound advice.

According to the sound advice, and also in keeping with a curse by God, Absalom took all the nine concubines of David (God had said it would be the wives, but called them concubines when He dictated the Holy Book) and raped them, jointly and severally, atop a balcony without a parapet so the public could watch the real-life porn. This was a great strategy; the noble citizens of Israel drooled at the action scenes and admired the young king who raped his step mothers in a live show.

Ahithophel, a true man of God, further suggested that Absalom pursue his father, for David was by now weak and exhausted as were his men; so it was the best time to kill him. Once David was done away with, he said, all the men would follow the new king back to Israel, and his authority over the kingdom would be full and final.

That was a sound advice, but thwarted by Hushai, a man secretly sent by David to counter the harm he expected Ahithophel to do.

"This was not the time to attack David," Hushai counselled Absalom. "You're a great fighter, but David is still strong, so your men would be slaughtered. A great slaughter that would be. Wait for your time,"

If you must know the truth, God had had the revenge He had planned with David – it was now restoration time.

Not attacking David when he was weak and tired was a great folly, and Ahithophel, the man considered as knowledgeable as God, knew what would happen to Absalom and to himself after David recovered his kingdom. He went home, set his domestic things in order, writing out an elaborate last will on a cow-hide scroll and then killed himself. His death, say scholars, was a record, for it was the first political suicide in history.

Absalom began to pursue David rather late in the day – for the latter was no longer weak and tired. David collected three divisions of men under three of his able generals (one of them being Joab, the favorite). As ever a loving father, David instructed his officers that Absalom must not be killed.

Don't forget that Absalom had a huge crop of hair, which was nearly due to be cut in that year. As he went along in pursuit of his father atop his mule, the hair got caught up in the twisted branches of an oak tree. Unmindful, the mule trotted on, leaving Absalom hanging by his hair from the tree. General Joab and his bodyguards found him with his legs tottering in the air and finished him off with their javelins.

Thus, God dealt with the man who did his bidding by making his curse come true. The pillar that Absalom had erected in anticipation of his death stands in modern Israel till this day. David Ben Gurion, the latter-day descendant of his famous namesake, had the soldiers search for the Ark of Covenant as well as the pillar of Absalom in the Holy mountain of Zion, but failed. He and the searching soldiers thereby lived till reasonably old age.

David duly mourned the death of his son and wept bitterly. Like any father would, he expressed the wish that he had died in Absalom's place. He then put all his ten concubines who had been raped by Absalom in a house and made provisions for their survival. He never slept with them again; they lived widows' lives till they died. Any Rabi, Priest or Mullah will tell you that by not beheading the women, David showed his gentle nature and respect for womanhood.

Now, believing himself at peace under the merciful God, David sang songs, played on his harp and reigned happily. God, who hated anyone – even his favorite David – being happy for too long, struck again. For no apparent reason, He sentenced Israel to three successive years of drought and famine. At the end of the third year, it occurred to David to check with God what the matter was. God explained that he and his countrymen were being punished for what Saul had done – he had put Gibeonites to death.

Now Canaanites (descendants of Ham, the black son of Noah whose black descendants were cursed to live as slaves) were an anathema to God because they served other gods, not Him. God's promises were like shifting sands, but not his hatred of Canaanites. He even passed it on to his son Jesus who came many generations later. Jesus summarily called them dogs.

Gibeonites were a branch of Canaanites. God had ordered Joshua to destroy all Canaanites without exception. Joshua, the predecessor of Samuel had, during his attack on Jericho. somehow missed out Gibeonites possibly because they lived outside the resonant walls that the citizens of Jericho had built around themselves. Gibeonites later came to Joshua, pretending that they had come from afar, and trapped Joshua into signing a peace treaty with them. God honored covenants – except the ones he signed with his beloved Israelites themselves.

Saul, though a Prophet, had misjudged God's vacillating mind. He executed quite a few Gibeonites while he was alive, ruling Israel and chasing after David's life. God was probably too preoccupied, so he Kept the case pending for nearly 40 years till David's glorious rule was coming to end. When the nation under ageing David was faring well but for an occasional rebellion (by a democrat named Sheba, for instance, who was killed) famine struck. It took three years when the land had parched and Israelites were dying before David checked with God and was told that the punishment was for what Saul had done.

This was fair and square, God had punished Saul for not putting Agag to death; now He was punishing David because Saul put Gibeonites to death. The obedient David, though he had promised Saul that he would protect his descendants, handed over the last seven of male descendants of Saul (including the lame Mephibosheth whom he had taken under his wings and allowed to eat at his table) to Gibeonites who gleefully hung up the innocent men in proof of how God punishes the children of a sinner up to three or four generations. Thus did David keep his promise to Saul – the man who gave him a place in history – in the ways of God. In the meanwhile, God had the satisfaction of avenging the deceitful and polytheist Gibeonites by the death of the descendants of monotheist Saul, whom in his infinite wisdom he had chosen to unify Israelites.

Later David brought the bones of his lord and master Saul and his son Jonathan (who had saved David's skin several times and who loved him more than any woman) and had them buried honorably. For some reason, God didn't mind this.

David and his men went on plundering the never-ending populace of Philistines and lived happily, which, as usual, enraged God.

God ordered David to take a census of all Israel and Judah, which David did. His men traveled all over the country and took census. The hard work took more than nine months. Joab counted the number of men in both countries capable of handling a sword. For whatever reason, David felt guilty at what he had done and begged God for forgiveness for the crime of doing what He ordered.

The merciful Lord gave him three options: 1. Three years of

famine in his kingdom. 2. Three months of pursuit of David by his enemies. 3. Three days of plague in the land.

David, being a benevolent king who loved his people, but hated the idea of being pursued by his enemies opted for three years of famine or three days of plague for his people. The merciful Lord sent his angel of pestilence to spread plague all through the land. When seventy thousand had died, and the angel, in his killing spree, was on his way to destroy Jerusalem, David appealed to God to stop the plague-making angel's run on the land. God assented and withdrew the angel. Thereupon David built an altar for God and sacrificed many oxen which he had bought for a generous sum of fifty shekels of silver.

God had promised to plant David and his family in a secure home where they would no longer be disturbed. As is the rule with God's promises, this was not to be. The Philistines, whom God failed to annihilate men, women, children and babies in the womb and all the cattle, continued to pester David all through his life. Many of them were killed – including a man who was so powerful that he had six fingers on both his hands and feet whom David's brother killed without the least fear of his extra fingers and toes.

Nevertheless David was a happy king. When battles were not raging, he would play on his harp and sing.

As this story was going on for too long, David aged and became a feeble and crumbled and cringed shadow of himself. His faithful men decided that the best way to keep him in good spirits was to have a beautiful virgin by his side. Abishag, the most beautiful of them all and a virgin (which was important except when the King desired another man's wife) was found and placed at his service. The girl served David faithfully but, possibly due to erectile dysfunction from senility or being over-satiated, David refrained from getting her into his bed. We know the fate of his ten concubines, but not the fate of his six wives.

Adonijah, the one next in line after the usurper son Absalom, decided it was his time to take over the kingdom. Joab, the General who had till then be faithful to David joined Adonijah who had invited all but David's favorite prophet Nathan and his favorite son, Solomon. Adonijah sacrificed a huge number of cattle which obviously pleased God. Hence God did not alert David although both were on talking terms.

Nathan, in revenge, went to Bathsheba – the woman for whose sake David had got her husband killed and himself suffered the humiliation of his wives being violated by his own son. So reminded, Bathsheba took a bath and went to David to stake this claim. David said: *"I will carry out this very day exactly what I swore to you by the LORD, the God of Israel: Surely your son Solomon will reign after me, and he will sit on my throne in my place."*[20]

David had his son Solomon anointed as king by his prophet Nathan and a few other trusted men. An obedient people rejoiced and played on their pipes. The noise was so tremendous that it reached the ears of Adonijah who was holding a feast with his men.

Adonijah, weak-kneed and not much of a king material, sent word to king Solomon that he would surrender if he would be allowed to live.

"If he shows himself to be worthy, not a hair of his head will fall to the ground; but if evil is found in him, he will die," answered Solomon, who was to become famous throughout the world for his sense of justice. Adonijah returned home.

Adonijah, restless at the loss of the kingdom, went to Bathsheba, the mother of Solomon with a request: "Please, Queen

---

[20] 1 Kings 1:29 Berean Study Bible
1 Kings 1:52, NIV

Mother, have pity on me. You know that the kingship was mine, but now it has gone to Solomon. You could tell Solomon to let me marry Abishag, the Shunnamite. He will not deny you."

Bathsheba, was of course aware that still a virgin or not, Abishag was David's wife. Not averse to such exchanges herself, she conveyed Adonijah's request to Solomon.

"Mother, I will surely do your bidding," said Solomon, and had one of his men strike down Adonijah by the sword. Thus did Solomon establish his capability for sound judgment.

Before he died, David gave his last royal counsel to his successor: a hit list of several men, including Joab, who had been loyal and fought many battles for him, but had gone over to the side of Adonijah, the last rebel. Accordingly, Solomon the Just had them all put to the sword.

David finally found peace and Solomon the Great began his rule with the wisdom imparted by him, and acquiring in the process a thousand wives, thus establishing his judicious nature and judicial wisdom forever. He also built a great temple for God that was supposed to last *forever,*

David lives on through the living name of his spiritual son, Jesus Christ. Before his death he composed many songs, as merciful as God's. Like:

> *O Daughters of Babylon, doomed to destruction,*
> *Blessed is he who repays you as you have done to us.*
> **Blessed is he who seizes your infants**
> **And dashes them against the rocks.**[21]

If you didn't know, the only crime of Babylon was trying to bring unity in the whole world

---

[21] *Psalm 137:8 Berean Study Bible*

"And all married women (are forbidden) unto you save those (captives) whom your right hand possesses."

Quran, Surah 4:24; Sahil International

WHY GOOD WOMEN ARE STONED

A young woman approached the Great Messenger and confessed to him that she had committed adultery and wished to be purified. There was no written *Book* then, but she had heard her uncle recite from a stone-slab, on which he had scratched what the Messenger had dictated the latest message from God:

> *"Those who commit unlawful sexual intercourse of your women - bring against them four [witnesses] from among you. And if they testify, confine the guilty women to houses until death takes them or Allah ordains for them [another] way.*[22]

The Messenger was not certain if the woman had quoted the verse correctly or her uncle had recorded it right. Giving himself time to reflect, he asked the woman to come next day.

The woman went away happily. Of four witnesses she was not sure, but confinement to the house was no big deal; it was what she was used to anyway. Her rape did take place while she was inside her house. In a joint family, uncles, cousins and

---

[22] Surah 4:15 Sahih International

step-brothers and step-fathers used to be great lovers then, as they are today.

The Messenger thought and thought. He recalled at least three more *verses* that the Angel dictated to him when the latter came flying on his six wings, gems and pearls dripping from them like drops from a *Houri's* wine-jar in heaven. Once the great Angel had dictated:

> *But whoever is forced by severe hunger with no inclination to sin - then indeed, Allah is Forgiving and Merciful.*[23]

He rejected this command, for it was all about food. It meant you could eat a filthy swine if you were *that* hungry. What if the woman was hungry for many days and finally submitted herself to a wolf of a man? Shouldn't he ask the woman? When he racked his brain again, hoping someone would note down all those commandments that came streaming in according to need and regretting he could not write them down himself, the Messenger remembered another Verse:

> *The woman and the man guilty of adultery or fornication,- flog each of them with a hundred stripes: Let not compassion move you in their case, in a matter prescribed by Allah, if ye believe in Allah and the Last Day: and let a party of the Believers witness their punishment.*[24]

That night, while fantasizing the image of six-year-old Aisha,[25] all tantalizingly wrapped up in silk that Angel Jibril had given

---

[23] Surah 5:3 (last part) Sahih International
[24] Surah 24:2 Yusuf Ali
[25] Sahi Al-Bukhari, 5 58 235

him to present her with, and wondering how to approach her father Abu Bakr, younger than himself, to ask for the little one's hand, the Messenger decided that a hundred lashes for the woman as God commanded would be just right. Perhaps he should ask the name of the co-conspirator in the evil deed of unmarried love. Hundred lashes each for two would be more entertaining for the war-weary followers.

The woman came the next day with a news that further complicated matters. She said she was pregnant by the sin. This called for further racking of the brain or even consultation with Jibril – the Angel of six wings and dripping pearls.

The Messenger told her to return after she delivered the baby. The sin was compounded with pregnancy, which was certainly the woman's fault. The burden of it rested, along with the foetus, on the womb of the woman. The Messenger gave no further thought to the possible partner in her crime.

"Come back to me after you delivered the baby," commanded he.

During the next seven months, the Messenger was too busy to wonder if the woman would run away and escape punishment. He spent all his time in the city, judging the division of spoils of plunder among the soldiers, himself and God[26], apart from the heavy work involved in performing his masculine duties satisfactorily in bed with eleven women who knew the ropes from their previous marriages.

The woman with the baby hadn't forgotten. Ever a true believer, she went back one day to the Messenger, cradling a beautiful baby in her arms. The Messenger, ever fond of babies,

---

[26] Surah 8:1 "They ask you concerning the spoils of war? Tell them: 'The spoils of war belong to Allah and the Messenger. So fear Allah, and set things right between you, and obey Allah and His Messenger if you are true believers." -https://www. islamicstudies.info/tafheem.php?sura=8

coochy-cooed the little one and told the woman to take him back, nurse him well and return after he was weaned.

The young woman went home, pleased that the Messenger was smiling. She felt forgiven. Swinging the baby in his cradle she sang:

> *The Messenger didn't ask who dunnit,*
> *He didn't ask why I'd dunnit*
> *He's like God-the-Great, all-forgivin'*
> *There'll be no lashes and no stone-flingin',*
> *Forgiveness praised by Surahs, You'll see*
> *Will let your Ma live, and she'll be free*

Full of hope and enthusiasm, the woman returned to the Messenger two years later. The little one had had his drink of Mama's last drop of milk. He walked with her, pleased and proud to be holding his mother's hand.

The Messenger was rejoicing after the latest message that came from God and wondering how to celebrate its contents with his companions. The girl whom he had married at the (her) age of six had menstruated at nine, and he had this important duty of deflowering to do, which was one way. Blessings from God Almighty seemed to come by avalanches.

Shortly thereafter, Angel Jibril reported that God had given him explicit permission to marry his adopted son's wife.

It happened like this

A pretty woman named Zaynab, his cousin from his father's side, being the latter's sister's daughter, had grown up with him in the same house. He knew her – though not like *knew her* in the Bible – and liked her, but not in terms of adding her to his harem. For some strange reason, the thought had not occurred to him.

Zayd was a slave boy gifted to him by his first wife, now deceased. Being gracious and broad-minded, the Messenger adopted Zayd as his own son. God was very kind to Messenger, but, in his wisdom, had never given him a son. Since the boy grew up to be a fine handsome young man, the Messenger wanted his cousin Zaynab to marry Zayd, his adopted son.

Zaynab was not happy marrying a former slave. But the Messenger could not be defied; so, the marriage took place. As God was to say later, Zayd had what he wanted from her – there is no mention if Zaynab got what she wanted from him. So, for all we know, Zaynab and Zayd lived a happy life together in bed and away from it.

Then one day the Messenger had reason to want to see Zayd in a hurry. The front door of the house was open, so he walked in. Through a sheer curtain, he spied the voluptuous shape of Zaynab combing her hair after she had just had a bath, and had not dressed as yet. Well, you know what happens to virulent men at the age of fifty-three at such a vision. It happened to the famously more virulent Messenger. He urgently wanted his married young cousin in bed.

The Messenger rushed back lest he sinned by committing adultery. However, he opened his heart to a trusted companion, who passed it on to another trusted companion, and thus the chain stretched till it reached Zayd's ears.

Now Zayd was a grateful son, although adopted, and knew that angering the Messenger was the same as angering God the Greatest. He rushed back to his adopted father.

"*Abba*," he said, "you can have my wife, I'll divorce her."

That was good news, but what would the community think about the Messenger marrying his son's – even adopted son's – wife after forcing a divorce?

The then ten-year-old wife, but very wise for her age, had once half-jokingly said that whenever the Messenger has a need for one, God would send him exactly that message."

Precisely that was what happened. The Angel with pearl-dripping six wings rushed in, and passed the latest post:

> "...while you concealed within yourself that which Allah is to disclose. And you feared the people, while Allah has more right that you fear Him. So when Zayd had no longer any need for her, We married her to you in order that there not be upon the believers any discomfort concerning the wives of their adopted sons when they no longer have need of them. And ever is the command of Allah accomplished.[27]

And, Further,

> There is not to be upon the Prophet any discomfort concerning that which Allah has imposed upon him. [This is] the established way of Allah with those [prophets] who have passed on before. And ever is the command of Allah a destiny decreed.[28]

The gist of the message was: After your adopted son had *accomplished* what he wanted from you cousin, then there's nothing wrong in your marrying her. There was no way men could question God's decree.

This message was passed around like wild fire lest the foolish public blame the Messenger. Thus, with no blame on anyone, Zayd divorced Zaynab by saying *Talaq, talaq, talaq* three times. The Messenger married her with a clear conscience, performing the commandment of God by saying *Nikah* just once, and took her straight to bed.

---

[27] Surah 33:37, Sahih International
[28] Surah 33:38, Ibid.

When he was thoroughly done and happy, came a knock on the door.

The young woman who stood outside the door with a cheerful face holding the hand of a plump and handsome infant, brought recollections of a series of meeting with her. And he knew what to do.

Celebration by public entertainment. The Messenger – the last and the most important among the chosen ones – could any time modify God's message according to need and context. He proposed to exercise that unwritten privilege.

Commandment to confine the adulterators for life and the other to give them a hundred lash each was thus overruled since they lacked entertainment value. So the Messenger promptly called the nearest companion and said:

> *"Take care of this child and bring him up. Make him
> a soldier of God. No sin shall visit on him."*

While the woman waited for her pardon as per one merciful Verse or another, the Messenger got a ditch dug up deep enough to cover her up to her chest. It is not known whether she wailed aloud or whimpered *God is Great and Messenger is Greater* while she was seated comfortably in the ditch, her clothes were tied tightly around her body, her head and shoulders above ground level.

Then the Messenger ordered that she be stoned, which the believers did with great enthusiasm in a spirit of piety and celebration, all the time shouting that God was Great, the Messenger was greater.

The companions of the messenger were unanimous that God's penal code for adultery was too indulgent, so the Messenger, may God give him more messages that were less lenient, was right to issue a code of punishments like decapitation and amputation which would be even more blissful to God and man.

The woman kept wailing while a barrage of stones rained on her. *Khalid bin Walid*, one of Messenger's favorite disciples and a judge (Qazi) by profession, raised a huge rock above his head and lobbed it on the woman's head. Her head split, blood splattered on the face of the pious Qazi, for which crime he cursed her.[29]

The ever-merciful Messenger did not rebuke him, but advised him to be gentle, for she had repented. Then he got her buried, presumably satisfied that his own view prevailed.

Then he went back to the bed of his adopted son's divorced wife. While on his way, the Angel flew down, dripping gems and pearls like snowflakes in a scorched desert, and whispered in his ears:

> "......*And he has not made your adopted sons your [true] sons. That is [merely] your saying by your mouths, but Allah says the truth, and He guides to the [right] way.*"[30]

With that appropriate dictum delivered just in time, Zayd lost his wife as well as his surname which had given him the status of Messenger's son.

With that message in his hand, Zaynab joined the harem of her cousin and lived happily, being frequently entertained by the virility of the Messenger.

The descendants of the great Messenger, after several meetings and heated arguments finally agreed that the Messenger's punishment will prevail, that of God will be damned.

---

[29] *Sahih Muslim 17:4209*
[30] *Surah 33:4; Sahih International*

He (Lord Rama) is small, thin and fine and soft in three attributes - (viz. the lines on his soles, hair and the end of the membrane virile)

-Valmiki Ramayana, SundaraKanda 35:27

HOW RAMJI GOT THE BEARD

"Ten Thirty sharp," the voice from the mobile phone had cautioned. "Not a minute late".

I arrived at nine thirty at the gate of the Lion's Den, then drove around the block and under the fly-over, trying to find a parking space in the shade on the roadside. Eventually I found a place two kilometers away, behind a long line of SUVs and limousines.

When I got out, a five-foot-and-pot-bellied-as-usual policeman showed up, waving his two-foot baton known as *lathi*.

"*Chalo, chalo*," he said, waving me to get back into the car and drive away. I palmed him a twenty-rupee note.

"*Chalo*," Go away, he insisted, looking at the money with feigned disdain.

I pulled out a fifty-rupee note, without handing it to him. He grabbed and pocketed it in a flash.

"Only ten minutes," he said.

"I have an interview in *the Lion's* Den".

"Then it's all right." He picked up a handful of mud and put it atop the bonnet. "That's a sign that you're Lion's visitor. Nobody would bother you now."

It was nine-fifty. I decided to walk the two kilometers back, cursing myself for not knowing that putting a handful of mud on the bonnet would have saved me the money for a litre of petrol. As it was, I was ruined; if I could still save the car, that one litre would be worth its weight in gold.

I walked slowly, marking time, noticing that every vehicle parked in that line had a handful of mud heaped on its bonnet. I arrived at the door of the Den at 10:28.

There were benches on either side of the verandah, all occupied, save a few inches of bare wood at the far end of the bench at the left.

I rushed to the door. A short man in eighteenth century warrior's makeup, not forgetting the sword in its scabbard slung by his hip, stopped me.

"The queue," he said, pointing towards the far end.

"I have a meeting with Lion Sahib," I said: "10-30 sharp."

"I know you, Mr. Ashok Ghatiya, the *fillum* producer," he said, with the faint shade of a smile. "You see that gentleman at the head of the bench? He has a meeting at 9:30 sharp."

The fiftyish handsome man with premature wrinkles who sat at the head of the queue looked up and smiled.

"Indian standard time," he said.

"Is your Paki standard time any better?" asked the guard in historic makeup. His mustache bristled with patriotism.

"It is worse in Pakistan. No need to get angry," said Mr. Handsome with thinning hair and Caucasian face wrapped in brown skin.

"My, my, the famous Mr. Irfan Khalid of the Justice-for-Islam Party," I exclaimed, stretching my hand for a handshake.

"Do I know you?" Asked Mr. Khalid, ignoring the extended hand.

"Of course, of course. You are not supposed to know Indian *filmwalas*, are you? Not in a place like this. But, tell me, what brought a famous man with great potential from Pakistan to *the Lion's* Den?"

"The great potential," said Irfan Khalid. "To win, I need Hindu votes in Pakistan. Only the Lion *Meherban* can help me".

Meherban. The Merciful one. I badly need some of that mercy myself.

"How can Lion Sahib help you with the Hindu votes in Pakistan? I have heard that they shoot the Hindus when they come out of the polling booth after voting."

"False propaganda by Americans and Indians to defame my beloved Country managed for the time being by non-beloved people. It never happens that way. Of course, people of the losing party blame Hindus for their loss and spend some time with their wives. They never find the men after elections. Shooting, by the way, is reserved for Shia Muslims when they come out after Friday prayers. Also stoning for blasphemy reserved for Christian women."

"Good for Hindus", I said. "*Spend some time with their women.* That's a good one. But how can Lion *ji* of India help the Hindus of Pakistan? He is only the Landlord of India's Hindu hearts."

"Simple. If the Lion picks up the phone, long-distances the Hyena in Dubai and asks for protection for Hindus in Pakistan – true, Hindus have no souls, only us Muslims, Christians and those Zionists have, that's what the Book has said – but some of the Hindus have votes; and if they come to realize that their safety is assured through my good offices, they become my vote bank." Like a true politician with a future, he said it all in one breath.

"But aren't the Lion and the Hyena enemies? How can…"

Khalid didn't let me finish.

"You know nothing about politics, you're *a Chuthia*, not *Ghatiya*," he said. *Chuthia*, which sounded vulgar because the first syllable suggested female genitals, merely meant dumb.

"So, you know my name, why, you might even win a Who-wants-to-be-a-millionaire show with your general knowledge." I said, walking back to my four inches of butt-space on the bench, determined not to antagonize the Pakistani political upstart any further.

I spied Anand Swami, the man who lost 100 kilograms from his bottom and 16 kilograms from his torso in an *Ashram* that only served bitter-gourd juice for breakfast, lunch and dinner. After that fantastic diet, he looked merely obese. Actually, even before I spied him, he stood up to greet me.

"*Lift kara de, yaar,* gimme a lift, man" he said, taking a beleaguered breath and extending a hand.

"I am here for a lift myself," I said, taking his hand. It wouldn't do to offend Swami, never mind the depleting lard and a name that sounded like a Southie *Brahmin's* patented surname. A film might even run on the strength of a song from a Pakistani singer. That nomad woman – what was her name? – had proved it. Then there was another man with throaty voice who proved it even more.

"I know, I know," said Swami, who neither looked nor was a South Indian *Pattar*. "Your new film has bombed – was bombed, literally. I am sorry. I hope the Lion gives you a lift."

"Then I might give you a lift," I assured him.

As I sat on the last four-inch space of the waiting bench, a sweet and smooth fragrance engulfed me, the feel of soft flesh tickled my left butt. The plump, pale and beautiful woman sitting next to me was Qiraya Tariq, the Pakistani actress, I instantly recognized, never mind she wore a charming nine-yard *sari* and a matching blouse that showed off her flat midriff like a fourteen-inch television screen.

In those now-forgotten days, midriff made an Indian actress sexy or otherwise; the cleavage had a mere second place. Flowing saris and bare-backed *cholis* gave the midriffs the job of titillating the front-benchers whose passionate howls marked the success of a movie. As a producer, the very best among them till my last film, I could tell an actress just by looking at her midriff.

"Mr. Ghatiya, the producer!" she exclaimed, surprise and pleasure oozing from all the pores of her body that I could see. "You produce great movies!"

That exclamation did not seem to arouse interest in anybody in the sitting line ahead. Successful Indian men did not show interest in Hindi movies; they only watched them in private. They went to multiplex theatres to watch Hollywood movies, which most of them didn't understand, but would wait for the next man to laugh at jokes so they could laugh too. These were men of great importance in the trades that they plied, not youngsters who swooned over the men and women who swept film-studio floors.

I had heard that as a rule, lone women were not allowed to sit in the line outside the Den, and most women who came in were led to the kitchen by the guard in fancy-dress.

"Bharatiya Naris (Ladies of India) should behave and be treated like queens," was a well-known quote from the Lion. "They rule over men's hearts when they toil in the kitchen".

"How did that made-up soldier from the graveyard allow you to sit here?", I queried of Ms. Tariq.

"I'm not alone. I've come with *Anand,* you know," she said, nudging Swami with an elbow. One rumor was that Swami lost 116 kilos by running from a crowd that pelted stones when he sang an English remix of the famous Bollywood song *Chholi-ke-pichhe-kya-hai,* which meant "What is behind the blouse".

"Why are you wearing a nine-yarder like a local nanny? Aren't you supposed to be in *bikini?"* I asked Qiraya.

"Lion would only be pleased with a genuine nine-yarder sari. Bikini is only for Hindi films. You see, when the trailers of my movies are released, with me in the role of a housewife lolling about in Monaco in bikini, some jobless lawyer or another busybody is sure to file a suit to ban the film. He would say that it is an insult to Indian womanhood. Indian women don't even own a bikini, he would argue. We put out the film promos with my bikini-in-Monaco photos a year ahead of the shooting to make sure that the jobless lawyer or some other busybody gets to work and files a suit to ban the film right away. By the time the judge decides to see the movie, we are ready. He watches it, drools, and permits the release. The caseless lawyer or the jobless busybody is happy seeing his name in print and mug on the TV for a whole year, and stands a chance to get some or other party's ticket for the next elections. We are happy with the free publicity. Producer collects his cost in three days and a lot of profit till the next Thursday."

Being a producer, albeit now a failed one, I knew the importance of Friday – the crucial day when a movie was released. By next Thursday, whether successful or otherwise, it was buried or sold as television rights. Even pirates buried their remaining DVDs of the previous movie in the darkness of next Thursday before paying for a front-bench ticket to walk in to a multiplex with a mobile phone to shoot a video of the new movie straight off the screen.

I mulled over it. That must be how Bhim Chopstick, that fat financer sitting fourth in line, made all his money. Perhaps he has a couple of busybody lawyers on payroll to sue for the banning of his own films.

"Don't tell anyone I told you this," cautioned Qiraya. "Chopstick won't *chodo* me for revealing the trade secret".

Chodo had many meanings, depending on how one pronounced the second syllable, *do*. If the word rhymed with *cho-dough,* it meant *let it/him/her be.* If it sounded like *cho-though,* it was an invitation to rape, I let that pass, skipping the chance to ask her which *chodo* she meant.

"Tell me, don't you get into trouble with your Pakistani countrymen for your bikini shows?"

"Never. In Pakistan, only a woman who complains of rape gets stoned. She can't get four male witnesses to vouch for the rape; the rapist won't confess. So, who is the only known person guilty of fornication? The woman. She gets stoned, and the spirit of Shariah is fulfilled. The Mullahs cry hoarse about the haram in Indian movies, but cover their faces when they go to a shady theatre to watch them and salivate from the front seat. I wouldn't cry rape even if you raped me," she chuckled. Swami glowered. I feared an erection was on its way.

Irfan Khalid came out, smiling from ear to ear. He stopped and whispered to me:

"The Lion long-distanced a call and made the Hyena speak to me directly. You are now speaking to the future President of Pakistan – with Hindu votes! One day, you'll see, I will be *Sadr-e-Mumlikat-e Pakistan-e-Hind* - President of Pakistan and India. He drooled at the very thought, and then at Qiraya and rushed out.

The guard with the graveyard makeup and sword walked up to me on tip-toes.

"Come with me. Quietly. You got priority," he whispered in my ears.

"I am not a chief minister or something," I cautioned.

"The Lion once made a *Madrasi* woman chief minister cook his lunch in the kitchen. But you're coming with me straight to the Den. Lucky you. Let the business *murgas* who are waiting keep waiting." *Murga* meant a chicken getting dressed for dinner.

I was afraid his hoarse whisper was audible among the waiting population of tycoons on the bench, including two foreigners in business suits. A third white man with shaven head half-smeared in crimson vermilion and wearing Hare-Krishna *dhoti* had just walked in.

As he led me to the door, there were murmurs of protest. Made-up man gave them a collective cold stare, and the murmur subsided. Bhim Chopstick, the film financer, looked as though he was filling up like a balloon. Suddenly he raised one buttock and broke wind. Qiraya Tariq giggled like a little girl while the business tycoons held their breath and their dignity.

If I ever get a chance to produce another spiritual movie, I would give Qiraya the role of – who? – may be Draupadi, the innocent and chaste woman with five husbands. Nice name too, I tarried at the door, musing, "**Chaste Woman With Five Husbands**". Incredibly mystic and in English. That name could easily beat *Seven Murders, Excuse* foolishly titled in Hindi, and, though written by the great Ruskin Bond, flopped. Indian movies have to have English titles. "**Chaste woman…..**", the name would be, **CWWFH** for short, if I get to make another movie, so help me Lion.

The made-up guard opened the door quietly into a dimly lit but heavily festooned hall, and I walked on the plush carpet towards the frail skeletal shape on a reclining chair. But for his newly grown white beard and scant hair with patches of remaining black dye, you could see little of a face. The newspaper he owned, '**Take It With Salt**', and wrote or dictated every column, described his eyes as fierce, fiery and penetrating. I barely saw anything beyond the sockets.

"Come, come," the skeleton croaked, "You are privileged to shake my hand".

The Lion stretched his left paw to me.

His right paw held the hand of a young teenager with thin limbs innocent of muscles.

I took the bony fingers, cold and lifeless.

"I don't get up to shake hands with anybody. My enemies –
what do you say in Punjabi? *Mathru-chod* – Mother fuckers – say
that it's because if I got up, I would break in two. Hah, *hah, hah.*
Do Lions break in two?"

The laughter sounded hollow, but I chortled for the sake of
my future.

"Moreover, people – even Michael Jackson – what a polite
boy – didn't expect to shake hands with me. He touched my
feet. These Americans have great culture. But I don't like Indian
women wearing skirts and – what do you call it? – jeans. Our
women are *devis* – goddesses – you know".

Of course I knew. Goddesses not fit to wear jeans, but good
enough to be kicked and beaten when one was in a drunken
mood.

I bent down to touch the lion's feet. What Michael Jackson
could do, Ashok Ghatiya could do better. Prostrating at old and
withered feet is part of my culture.

"Sit down," he said, pointing to a stool in front of him. "You
are lucky. That's the stool where Michael sat, not to mention
Show-Stop-Khan who keeps coming and apologizing, for God
Knows what."

"Grandpa, every visitor sits on that stool," intercepted the
non-muscular wonder.

"See, see, always argumentative. My grandson Sunny Lion.
Just like me. I call him Toad-*phod* Lion cub. Since family loves
English names, he's called Shatter-Lion. How many hospitals have
you burnt, Shatter?"

"Three."

Though a regular Punjabi producer of Hindi films who
gave interviews only in un-punctuated English and titled my
horror movies in regular English, I knew that *toad-phod* meant
smash-and-break.

"And how many football courts have you dug up?"

"Four".

"How many houses have you set on fire, and how many buses did you break?

"Grandpa, how could I count them all?"

"Just like me. Angry, argumentative, shatter-skilled. Next-in-line Lion of the Pride. Twenty years from now – after I die, if I die."

"But what about his father – your son? Shouldn't he be leading the pride after – if – you die?"

"Ah, let's stop this talk about sons and nephews and daughters-in-law. I have no plans to die yet. Forget my affairs and tell me your problem."

I wasn't ready yet to get down to my problem. More buttering up was needed. So, I looked around and said: "I see that all the Shiva-Lingams have come back to their original places. Last time I came to pay respects with my ex-wife and to offer our condolences, you had thrown out all of them."

"Very observant, very observant like a producer-director – isn't that what you are? – should be. Yes, there was something I wanted the Lingam to do for me, which it failed to do. So, I threw out every semblance of a Lingam except my own. Now that those things don't matter either way, I have let God and his Lingams come back and take their places. Now tell me your problem."

"You see, Lion-*ji*, this new movie of mine that has cost me everything I had – even the carpets and the fridge in the house....."

"Cut out the sentiments. Why did you name it **Ravan's Story**, Eh? Are you a kaloo Ravan-worshipping South Indian?"

He referred to all South Indians – black, white or indifferent – as *kaloos,* the black ones.

"I'm Punjabi, Pure Son of Punjab. White without makeup. And a great devotee of the Lion *ji*. You see, all movies in the industry with names that began with Ra and ended in *won* did *roaring* business in the box office lately. That name became a fetish in the trade. **Rawan, Ra-one, Raw van**, anything with **Ra**. Like K some years ago. My writer suggested that name. You know, Lion-*ji*, I am really into spiritual movies. Fierce ghosts, toothy Draculas, horse-riding Jinns, long-nosed and nosey witches, skull-faced Satans and white-saried singing ghosts come alive on screen in my movies. Children can't get sleep for days and their mothers teach them *Hanuman-Chalisa* which finally eases them to sleep. A million children learnt *Forty Odes to Hanuman* from their mothers solely because of my movies. Purely spiritual. Till this time, they were lapped up even *in* Pakistan – because the Mullahs had said it was against their Shar…shar..whatever *law,* I make the pirated versions of my own movies for them, which sell like *Shalijani Gosht.* There used to be a lot of money in it. Till last week." I sighed a long sigh.

"Nobody had objected to any of that. Even my little *Shatter* likes your movies. Particularly those ones with skull-faces and sexy women in white saris singing sweet Lata songs and roaming in the dark. He led the breaking and shattering of your Ravan's Story because….."his voice was beginning to strain and shudder – "You put a beard on Bhagwan[31] Ram! Such insult to Hinduism, such humiliation to the purest of divine souls ever known to man! Such insult to me, the Landlord of Hindu hearts! To put a beard on his handsome face, look at the audacity!"

The tinny sound of a series of cough polluted the air for a couple of minutes. He hadn't finished.

"Moreover, the hero himself – no, not Ram*ji,* but the one who acted the role of Ram*ji* in your movie – Karan Arvind – came to me a week ago. He complained that with so much hair plastered all over his face, nobody would even recognize him as the actor

---

[31] *Bhagwan* – an adjective for a divine being. Also a noun when used alone.

who played Ram. How would the public worship him and touch his feet and give him gifts and money if they didn't even know that he was the Ram in the movie? Didn't you know that the actor was one of my boys in his heart of hearts? A beard on Ram, imagine!"

I noticed that he was stroking his own thin beard while saying it. Which made sense.

"My writer coaxed me to put that beard on Ram*ji*'s face," I pleaded. Imitating the writer's Bihari-accented Hindi lisp, I continued: "He said, 'Ram lived in the forest for fourteen years. He took Laxman and Sita with him, but not a barber. Wasn't he a real man? Don't real men have facial hair? Do you expect a proud *Kshatriya* – warrior class – prince to stoop so low as to shave himself? Even assuming Sita could shave *him,* since a woman can stoop to any depth or rise to any height (only if she were taller ha-ha-ha) to serve her husband, who is her God, she wasn't with him part of those fourteen years. To imagine that Ram and Laxman shaved each other would be sacrilegious. Were the divine brothers hairless eunuchs? No. So Ram and Laxman had to have beards. That's how the *Behn-chod*[32] convinced me.*"

The old man scratched his head. Thought came to him hard though speech came easy.

"Do *Puranas*, our scriptures, speak of a Ram with *beard*?". He addressed that question to the shadow behind him.

"Don't the epics describe the beards of Valmiki-*ji*, Vasisht-*ji* and Viswamitra-*ji*?" I countered, peeping into the shadow with some trepidation.

The Lion kept scratching his head. A female voice in the shadow spoke up.

"But they were sages. Sages wore beards."

---

[32] *Behn chod* - One who rapes his sister.

"Narada was a sage. Why don't they show him with a beard? Sai Baba had no beard."

"Our gods do not grow *beard*. Not Brahma, not Vishnu, not Shiva."

"Brahma sports a beard in many movies. Ram was an Avatar of God, in human form on our beard-growing earth and not hairless *Vaikunth*, the heaven. Like *Parashuramji* and, some say, Sri-Sri Hari-Om-*ji*, they have beards. Even you, Lion-ji, who is no less an *avatar* of god to us humble Hindus, wear a beard ".

"Don't argue with her...er...me," croaked the Lion, trying to put some power into his voice. "Rama had no beard. Period. You remove the beard, and your movie will get an audience of millions of my subjects. It's not my concern how many million Pakistanis watch the pirated videos of your bearded Ram."

"How can I remove the beard of Ram from every frame? Please, please help me."

"Don't argue with me. Only my *Shatter* is allowed that privilege." His voice was getting faint. Cough and spittle clouded the air.

The young man, Shatter-Lion, beamed with pride, but said nothing.

"I am ruined. I thought you'd save this old devotee, who touches your feet before and after launching a film, even the feet of your photos, but you abandon me. I have decided to forget the movie and become a *coolie*."

Coolies were the thin, frail men who carried big headloads of burden for a pittance.

"*Join* the Lion's *pride*," said young Shatter-Lion, addressing me for the first time. "Unemployed Hindus around here join the Pride. We don't give them jobs, but only a *danda* – stick – to each. We train them to break and smash properties and dig sports grounds, whereby they get respect and money by way of donations to the lingam. If you prove good enough, we might even give you a gun and the license to kill. You could then live like the wealthy producer you used to be. Even some Muslims try to join *us,* but we don't let them in. So, they join the Hyena's Cackle. The Hyena is very grateful to Grandpa for helping to swell the Cackle. He offered to send a trainer to teach us making bombs. Grandpa declined. Who needs bombs when we have the police?"

The youngster was on the dot. One wouldn't need bombs if one had the police to do the damage. I felt the time had come for playing my trump.

"Lion-*ji*, I have decided. I have nothing left but a mere one million in my last bank account. What would a *coolie* do with a million? My wife has eloped with the script-writer who got me into this mess after wangling everything but this million from me. I leave this last cheque for a million rupees as *donation* for your party – sorry, Pride. Do what you will. I wish you a long life."

The voice in the shade emerged in the form of a five-yard sari, grabbed the bill and faded back into the shade.

I was not sure whether it was my wishing him long life or the cheque that lit up a light-emitting diode which shone through the transparent skin of his scalp. He tried to sit up, pushing down hard on the arms of the chair, but gave up, probably for fear that he would break in two at the middle. His elbows creaked.

Perhaps the Lion sensed that the cheque would bounce if the movie didn't run. He was not known for great thinking, but was clever in counting his money and coining slogans.

"I got it. You are right. There was no way Ram could have had a clean-shaven face through the fourteen – or was it thirteen – whatever – years of jungle sojourn. Look at me. I didn't shave for a month and I have this beard. Ghatiya is right, Ram had a beard at least those fourteen or thirteen – whatever– years in the forest".

"And Laxman," I said

"Who cares about Laxman, that South Indian upstart who thinks he can bat better than my boys in cricket?"

"Not *that* Laxman, the Madrasi cricketer. He means Ram's brother Laxman," intoned the sari that had disappeared into the shade with my dud bill.

"All right, if he's Ram-*ji*'s brother let him also keep his beard. Right from NOW."

The emphasis worsened his cough. His birdcage-sized chest reverberated like the beating of a tribal drum.

Shatter-Lion turned towards his grandfather.

"Shall I tell the Pride to stop beating up the ushers in multiplexes and burning down smaller theatres? That windshields of public buses and private cars should be spared? That chosen shops should not be looted and *Babua*[33] legs need not be broken? That the Pride should announce to the Hindus that Ram had a beard, his brother Laxman had a beard and that the Ghatiya movie must be seen by all – or else – and all that?"

"Yes, yes," the Lion coughed and coughed. "You know, Ghatiya – cough, cough – we never burn down multiplexes. They are owned by my poor rich admirers. My boys only beat up ushers because those bloody *Babuas* can't pay up for *Linga-puja*. Muslim ushers are worse, they won't pay up even if they can. It doesn't matter what's the provocation, we target the right people and right things. *Babuas*, *Bhayyas*[34], all the helpless ones. Ever since that *Kaloo Nayagan*[35] interfered, we decided to spare the *Madrasis*. Moreover, they have franchised my pride down South. We touch Muslims if we have a big enough mob and they don't; otherwise we let them be. We don't spare public buses, private cars, ambulances and hospitals – anything that is helpless.

---

[33] A nickname for the immigrants from a different state.
[34] *Nickname for job-seekers from yet another state.*
[35] *Nayagan is Tamil word for a leader of men*

Burning hospitals are great fun, my Shatter-Smasher grandson tells me. You could watch *langdas* – people with fractured legs – those on drips, crying babies, dying oldies, – no, don't look at me, I am not dying – trying to run, falling down, and running again."

His thin shoulders shook as he chuckled at the very thought.

"Pregnant women deliver. Those who aren't pregnant – well, my boys in the Police have a solution even for *that*. Nobody should play with *the Lion's* Pride and our sentiments. If they do, the usual helpless ones will pay for it. I will let Ram-Laxman keep the beard."

I touched the Lion's withering paws with oozing gratitude, saluted the Shatter-Smasher of the times who surely had a future, and turned to go.

Lion gestured me to stop and get closer to him. Then he whispered, "you know we do not deal in cheques and bank drafts, only cash that brings no tax burden with it. We will keep your cheque as security in case the distributors kill you in the next couple of days. A day after Ravan's Story is released, you will come back with cash, a full million, all in *Gandhis*. If you don't, you know what could happen."

Gandhis, in the common language of Lion, the Landlord of Hindu hearts, Hyena, the Muslim Emperor-in-exile in Dubai, and all wheeler-dealers of black money in the market, was code for five-hundred-rupee notes, the largest denomination of currency those days.

I nodded, bowed and touched the sticking bones of his knees with my forehead and walked out.

Qiraya Tariq and Anand Swami, hand in hand, were being marched in.

"Seeking blessings for a movie you are planning together?"

"No", said the Brahmin-sounding Pakistani cheerfully.

"Seeking his blessing for our marriage together. Otherwise

the wedding hall would be stoned and I would lose half of the remaining hundred kilos".

"Good for you," I whispered. "Last time I had come here, I had come with my wife to seek blessing for our marriage together. Yesterday she ran away with the Bihari writer."

"Good for you, too," said Swami with a wink." Many a fish in the water"

I didn't pause to see Qiraya's reaction.

"......*And then all the peoples of the earth will mourn when they see the Son of Man coming on the clouds of heaven, with power and great glory.......... Truly I tell you, this generation will certainly not pass away until all these things have happened.*"

Matthew: 24:30, 34 NIV

HOW SUPREME COURT PLAYED SPOIL-SPORT

I sensed that the man sitting by my side at Hong Kong airport had been eyeing me for some time. Probably in his forties, he wore a crumbled grey suit without tie on a lanky frame. His face was rather oriental but with large bulging eyes; skin not light enough to be Chinese and not pink enough to be thought white.

Perhaps I stared back for a moment; he seemed pleased with it and nudged closer. Then he noticed the passport I was holding up above my handbag as a sign for recognition by the Chinese driver who was to pick me up.

"Can I take a look?" he asked, pointing at the passport.

Bloody hell, I thought, somebody from the Customs or immigration. But I had nothing to fear. My visa was in perfect order. I was carrying nothing but some old clothes and a toothbrush. Yet I panicked a little.

I handed him the passport.

He flicked the pages like a professional card player flicks cards. He paused for just a moment at the first page, turned back the cover and returned it.

"Indian," he said.

"Yes".

"Krishan Sharma, Hindu."

"Good detective work".

He ignored the sarcasm. I was beginning to guess what the guy was up to.

"How many gods do you pray to, Mr. Sharma?"

This was getting even more interesting. I no longer wished that the driver would land up any time too soon.

"Depends," I said, pretending to be in thought. "May be a hundred, may be ten thousand".

"Wrong, Mr. Sharma. Sixteen thousand and eight. Krishna, Buddha, Lingam…Some male, some female."

I patted his thigh. "Amazing. You hit the nail on the head."

"Got to. I was a Hindu like you before."

Of course. Nearly cream-skinned like a Chinese and freckled-but-not-pink-enough-to-be-white skin showed it. And his knowledge of Hindu Gods. Krishna, Buddha, Lingam!

"You do look a Hindu too," I answered, suppressing a chuckle that threatened to well up beyond my throat.

He nodded uncertainly.

"Then I saw a wonderful light."

I looked up at the airport illumination.

"I know. I am noticing the lights myself. Incredible."

"Not this light. This is nothing. I mean the true light. Light of the Living God."

"Lucky you. Seeing the lights of sixteen thousand and eight living gods. Krishna, Buddha, Lingam.".

"There is only one Living God. The true God. The God who created you and me, Mr. Sharma. I notice your sarcasm. But I should tell you this: This is no time to laugh and make fun of somebody who hopes to save you."

He paused as if to shatter a breaking news.

"He is coming, Mr. Sharma, He is coming as sure as you and I are sitting here."

"By which flight is She coming?"

"Not she, He. Your goddesses are fake, as are your gods. Believe me, incarnations of devil, wearing skulls around their heavy hips and blood dripping from their tongues. The Real God is kind and merciful except to the rebellious and the unbelieving. He wants to save you. He will forgive you for worshipping sixteen thousand fake gods and goddesses and take you into his loving fold,"

He appeared to be getting agitated.

"Believe me, Mr. Sharma, this is the time for you to accept Him. He mounted the cross to save you. Don't you see the signs? War in every Muslim world, war between Hindus and Muslims, war between men and women, poverty, famine, new – new unheard-of diseases, earthquakes, calamities."

"And world wars fought mostly by Christians, then terror-war between Protestants and Catholics, Reformists saying that the Pope is anti-Christ," I interjected.

"World wars are over, a long time ago, Mr. Sharma. Talk about the present. Every occurrence that is happening now is prophesied here".

"I know. A Christian man with the name of Joseph hiding his own teenaged daughter in the basement of his house and impregnating her four or five times in 24 years. A young pious guy walking into a church and shooting black worshipers. Young Christians converting to Islam and rushing to Syria so they could take part in the killing. Another Christian collecting automatic guns and mowing down 558 humans within ten minutes. Not to speak of George Bush taking a direct instruction from God and destroying a cherished ancient city as if it were the cursed Babylon of the Bible…signs are everywhere."

"Irrelevant arguments, Mr. Sharma. Most irrelevant. A Christian name does not make you a Christian. You got to be a born-again Christian, like I am and you have the chance to be now and save yourself."

He tapped a bag by his side that I hadn't noticed before.

"All the fourteen signs announced in this book have come to pass".

"That's interesting. Show me the sign about the civil war in Syria, and how it is going to end. Does it say Assad would resign or would he end up getting lynched?"

"Mr. Sharma, you should believe. This is no time to joke and ridicule, as the gentiles and the Pharisees did two thousand years ago. I have solid proof. Two Peter, Chapter one, nineteen to twenty-one. The time is here. He mounted the cross two thousand years ago to save you today. He is coming back."

"In Hong Kong?"

"Don't be silly. In Jerusalem. He will rule the world from there. The whole world would be his kingdom. Those who placed their trust in him would be saved. Those who didn't," he looked up, joining his hands as if praying for mercy. His shoulders shook at the very thought.

"Thank you for your concern. I am truly touched. You haven't told me your name."

"John. John Chang. It was He who brought me here to meet you."

"Then He or She would know that I haven't got much time, Mr. Chang. The driver would be here any minute. He charges me by the minute from the moment he spots me."

"When the time comes you will forget about money and regret your folly. I will cut this short. I am not here to give you a long sermon. You look intelligent, you won't need a sermon. I will just tell you this one thing...."

Then he dropped the bombshell:

"God wants a relationship with you."

"Don't you think I am a bit old for any woman – even a god – to want a relationship with me?"

"God is not a Hindu devil-goddess, but He is God. He. The living God."

"So, he is a man?"

"God is God, not a mere man. He made man in his image."

"which means that since man looks like him, He looks like man, simple logic. Has things that I, a man, have?"

"Man was created in the image of God, not the other way around."

"Isn't that the same thing? To my mind, Mr. Chang, since man – you and I – are made in the image of God, God resembles the mean average of you and me, and is equipped like you and me."

"That's a silly way to put it".

"And this living God, who is equipped like a man, not a she-devil woman, because he created man in his own image, wants a relationship with me".

"Yes. From this very moment. He sent me here to help you."

A stocky young Chinese was walking towards us. He noticed the passport in my hand and stopped. "Mr. Sharma?"

I nodded, got up and extended my hand towards John Chang, the Hindu who saw the light and found that God is coming to Jerusalem to rule the world and wanted to have a relationship with me.

"I am sorry, Mr. Chang. I have nothing against such relationships, but I happened to be heterosexual. I would have thought twice before refusing your offer of relationship to your God, even though you say he is male, who would be the King of the world. Who would refuse bedding with a king? Sadly, the Supreme Court of my Country has banned such relationships."

My extended hand was not taken. When it remained limp for nearly a minute, I withdrew it and walked with Nelson Lang, the driver.

SWEET BALLS FOR A MAN-GOD

This is a true story. It is not nice to tell true stories about dead men, I know. With gods and godmen, it is different. They do not die even when they appear dead to mere materialists. Sathya Sai Baba's devotees tell me that he'd never die. He just changed an aged and worn earthly body, promising to don a new one to appear as *Prem Baba* – the name would mean Love-Father.

However, it was usually easy to find a genuine Baba, real god-incarnation. Such a *Baba* would have a few white devotees in tow. Presence of a couple of whites attested to a godman's bona fides. Sathya Saibaba had several white people – old and young – moving around with him, clanging their cymbals and singing his hymns:

> *When we think of you as One, you're many;*
> *When we feel you're Many we realize You're One.*
> *Oh, how would this ignorant and vain us know*
> *Your glory, our Mom and Dad in one, Sathya Saibaba*

*Thu*s they sang the glories of the short-statured, bulb-nosed and fizzy-haired man-god.

Sergeant Jeevan Reddy was the leader of the team of NCOs specially selected for installing sophisticated and newly acquired radar equipment in various military units. His friend, Sergeant Narender Verma, led the wireless team, entrusted with the work of introducing ultra-high frequency communication between aircraft and ground controls. Both lived in married quarters next to each other.

Reddy was an ardent Sathya Sai Baba devotee, as most Hindus from his home State tended to be in those days. The Supreme God in human incarnation being from their own province gave them some kind of reflected glory. The *Baba* only spoke in Telugu – a unilingual god, as most gods tend to be – Krishna liked his prayers in Sanskrit, Allah in Arabic, and Jesus could be best supplicated in Latin, a language he probably did not know existed as he roamed the scorching Arabian deserts sermonizing in Aramaic.

Sorry, I am digressing.

Lots of preparations were required before a team set off to make an installation in a distant military station – checking parts of heavy radar antenna and their complex motors, dish-antennae, controls and display systems. They had to be packed and listed for assembling upon arrival at site, and ensuring that nothing was missing. Then there would be a briefing by the Operational officer who had never been to a site, not to mention a talk on security by the absent-minded adjutant, you name it.

Sergeant Jeevan Reddy conducted a *pooja* – homage or sacrifice – in his house the night before the date of departure. He and his wife prayed in front of an enlarged photograph of a smiling Sathya Sai Baba in blessing posture, his right hand raised, palm facing the worshipper and dispensing grace. Reddy and his wife would pray for his safe travel and also – so Reddy claimed – for the safety of all the team members including that of the grouchy officer who was supposed to be commanding them, but did nothing in practice.

The worship involved garlanding the photograph, placing flowers and a small silver plate with God's favorite special *laddoos* for the palate pleasure of the *Baba*. After the worship, the Reddy's would go to bed in a state of blissful trance – that is what Reddy once told me. A bronze oil lamp would be kept burning on low flame all through the night in front of the divine photograph. Like all Gods, Sathya Saibaba loved to have an oil lamp kept burning in the room while He went to sleep.

Next morning, Reddy's wife would have her ablution and ritual bath before she went to prostrate before the divine photograph. She was not surprised to find a *laddoo* – sometimes a couple of *laddoos* – left half-eaten. She would praise the kindness of the God for not eating the whole *laddoos*, but always leaving some *Prasad* – the divine leftover – for His ardent devotees. She would mouth a very small piece from the half-eaten part of one *laddoo* and give another small bit to Reddy who would by then be ready to depart.

Sergeant Reddy was a considerate man, and knew that the safety of the team, and hence himself, depended on the blessings of the *Baba*. Young Mrs. Reddy shared that feeling. So, the remaining part-eaten *laddoos* were wrapped in an oil paper and carried to the office with great care and devotion.

Reddy would break off a bit of the *laddoo* – not forgetting to show that the bit came from the half-eaten part – and present it, along with a smart salute to the grouchy officer whose frown would momentarily change to one of subtly expressed gratitude and piety. Then tiny bits of the remaining '*prasad*' (divine pleasure, if you had forgotten) would be distributed among the lesser – and far less grouchy – Other Ranks, most of whom accepted it with both palms cupped in reverence, and placed it with shut eyes in their mouths.

Corporal Sharif, a Muslim, was initially reluctant to accept this bit of pleasure from a Hindu man-god. When Reddy explained how parts of the sweet balls disappeared in the night after the only door and windows of the prayer room were closed and he and his wife had gone to sleep, Sharif asked:

"Did you ever try to peep through the gap in the doors to see your *Baba* emerging from the photo and eating it?"

'I did look," said Reddy. "I won't tell a lie. Maybe I am a sinner from my last birth. I could never see *Baba*. My wife saw him like a fleeting shadow through the key-hole. That was the only time she looked, she got so frightened and was laid up for three days."

Thus convinced, Sharif did accept the bit of the divine pleasure and kept it carefully wrapped up with him for giving it to his wife who had had miscarriages twice before. Reddy assured him that Baba would certainly bless him, that He did not discriminate between religions, and, in fact, He was the reincarnation of Shirdi *Sai Baba,* who was believed to be a Muslim. Sharif did not know, or did not care, with the prospect of a calamity of another miscarriage in his mind, that his religion did not take kindly to the idea of reincarnation.

On the eve of their departure for a joint radar and wireless installation in a distant and somewhat risky North-Eastern part of the Country, Reddy's neighbor and fellow-Sergeant Narender Verma along with his wife joined the prayer session. Verma carried a packet with him in to the prayer room, which Reddy thought was a gift – an offering – for the Baba. Just as he expected, Verma placed the packet, unwrapped, between *Baba* and himself as he sat facing the sacred photograph. *Baba* loved to accept the humblest of gifts from poor devotees and to give away Rolex watches and gold rings to his filthy-rich devotees and even richer politicians.

Bhajans – hymns – that were Baba's favorites, and then hymns in praise of Baba himself were sung In Telugu and Hindi. Young Mrs. Verma, only two-years married and sadly deprived of a child yet, joined in by singing some of the Hindi Bhajans at *Aarti,* when a brightly lit oil lamp with a long S-shaped handle was circled seven times in front of Baba's much-garlanded portrait. Everyone present sang a *Baba*-modified parody of a regular *aarti* hymn usually sung in temples during mass worship.

It appeared to Mrs. Verma that the *Baba* beamed even brighter when she took the *aarti* lamp and circled it with her own hands, earnestly whispering the prayer words under her breath. When the entire ritual was done, and the four worshipers had picked up pinches of ash from a small bowl and touched it to their foreheads, all except Verma stood up.

"Get up, Verma, we need to start early", said Reddy.

"Get up, *Raja*, you need to sleep early to get up early", said Mrs. Verma. Young North Indian brides addressed their newly-bought (with a hefty dowry) husbands *Raja*, meaning Prince. After children were born, the Prince was demoted to Billoo's Daddy, assuming that the child was pet-named Billoo.

"I will sit here and seek Baba's blessings, I have taken a vow," said a stoic and calm Verma.

Reddy said, "Pal, that would be dangerous. My wife had only seen a fleeting shadow through a slit in the door, and she had fever for the next three days."

"You cannot force a *darshan* – vision – of *Baba* by yourself," he explained. "If *Baba* wished to give you a *vision*, He would appear before you wherever you might be. There are hundreds of instances, when *Baba* appeared before soldiers in Ladakh and Aksai Chin, why, even in Delhi. I have heard that Baba gave *darshan* to a wounded soldier on Pakistan's border and healed him while He was also seen at the same time at his Whitefield *Ashram* in Bangalore."

"You can close the door," insisted Verma. "Unless you mind my staying in your prayer room for a night".

Of course, said Reddy, how could he stop his best friend and neighbor from staying in his house if he had taken a vow to pray all night?

"We will have to close the door, though," said Mrs. Reddy. "I am a God-fearing woman. I had seen a fleeting shadow and was frightened to near-death. Maybe God did not like my peeping like a doubting atheist."

Verma ignored the accusation in her words.

"Close the door and bolt it from outside, if you have to," said Verma.

Reddy leaned forward and whispered: "How would you do the – you know, su-su?"

"I have done it, and I don't get up in the night," said a straight-faced Verma.

Mrs. Verma nodded, bearing witness to her husband's claim of not needing to piddle at night.

When her pleadings were of no avail, Mrs. Verma went home alone, whispering why in hell her parents gave her away to such an adamant man. Then she consoled herself that he could be praying for a son or a commissioned rank, or both.

Reddy's retired for the night, switching off the electric light in the prayer room, leaving a single bronze lamp flickering in the dark. They apologized for leaving him alone, but felt sure in their minds that some untold calamity would befall Verma. The small flame on the lamp projected a black, bouncing shadow of Verma on the wall behind him like an ominous sign of something terrible to happen. In bed, they jointly prayed that the *Baba* wouldn't think that they had anything to do with the stupid North-Indian's impious temerity.

"He's going to get nothing out of this vow," Reddy assured his wife. "Except Baba's anger."

They liked Verma, but that he could get a commission in the

military while Reddy rotted in the ranks was unthinkable. With that solace, they held each other and went to sleep.

Half hour later, when all was quiet but for a muffled and rhythmic snore from the Reddys' bedroom, Verma switched on the light and opened his pack. It was an instant Polaroid camera.

At five-thirty next morning, a reluctant and terrified, but duty-bound and religiously sanitized Mrs. Reddy opened the door of the prayer room to find Verma seated as before, dozing. He heard her, woke up with an apologetic start, picked up the packet, and stood up. Mrs. Reddy was surprised and somewhat annoyed – you don't take back an offering that was given to *Baba*, the one and only Supreme God.

"Did you see *Baba*?" asked the lady with a shudder.

"Yes," said Verma.

His nonchalance disturbed her. Two *laddoos* were partly eaten.

"Only a fleeting shadow, of course," said Mrs. Reddy.

"No, in his full image, and very clearly" answered Verma,

Too excited to ask more questions that came up in her mind, Mrs. Reddy rushed to announce the miracle to her husband while Verma strolled off to his quarters.

Jeevan Reddy wondered how it was that Baba gave *darshan* to a not-so-pious Punjabi but not to him, a humble devotee from God's own *native place*. For a moment he thought that Verma could be lying. If he was, who nibbled the *laddoos*?

After getting himself ready for the long journey and hazardous work in far-away and rebellious North-East, Reddy knocked at Verma's door to ask what exactly he had found.

Mrs. Verma said her husband had left early, saying he had much work to do before setting off for the distant place.

Reddy reached the office, full of pride, excitement and curiosity, with a packet of the *Prasad*, the divinity of which he now had a witness to vouch for.

After observing the protocol of first saluting and offering the *Prasad* to the grouchy officer, he sought out Verma,

"Did you really, really see Baba?" he asked, just as his wife had before. He bristled with excitement. Verma nodded

"How did he look? In his saffron clothes and full-blown fizzy hair?"

"In his birthday suit," said Verma.

Reddy stood frozen in disbelief. For a millisecond, the vision of his Lord's pubic hair and his dangling divinity flitted past his mind. To his chagrin, the profane image stayed put in his mind for a few seconds.

Verma showed Reddy a photograph of two rats munching on the *laddoos*.

"This was your Baba who bit your *laddoos*," he whispered. Verma later told me that he had no intention to embarrass Reddy by showing the photos to others.

Reddy stood staring, full of disbelief and rage, feeling deceived by a close friend. Then he broke into a broad smile.

"Oh Baba, my Holy Baba, truly Sathya Sai Baba, what a miracle! Even when you found this prying man sitting in your sacred temple with his polluted camera, you did not reject my *laddoos*. You came in the form of rats!"

He joined his hands and bowed his head before an imaginary figure of his god in the disguise of rats.

Reddy's strange gesture and loud exclamation got noticed; men of all ranks gathered around and had a good look at the Polaroid photo. Some hissed in disgust, others made strange noises in their respective languages.

To Reddy's bewilderment, nobody accepted the miraculous *prasad* since then.

Nobody, except the grouchy officer.

"He who desires offspring should offer to Soma a brown beast, and to Agni one with a black neck; Soma is the depositor of seed, Agni the producer of offspring; verily Soma deposits seed for him, Agni produces offspring; he obtains offspring."

Yajur Veda, Kanda 2:1.2.6

THE GREAT HORSE SACRIFICE

East of the river Sindhu, South of the snow-clad mountains where gods resided, all the way to the long, meandering mud-valley towards the East where River-goddess Ganges flowed, were the vast plains named *Aryavarta*. In its green-and-gold meadows cows grazed and with them thrived Aryans, the sacred, light-skinned people who called themselves *devas* or demigods.

Indra, the thunderbolt-wielding king of all gods, assisted by *Agni*, the fire-god, *Marut* the wind-god, *Aditya* the Sun-god and quite a few others helped Aryans destroy the fine brick houses, open squares and public baths of the indigenous black people whom they called *Rakshasas* or demons and to appropriate all their wealth they considered valuable – cattle and gold.

The relation between the gods thus described and the Aryan godmen in the plains was one of give-and-take. Aryans sent up burnt offerings which were a sweet aroma to any god anywhere; freshly butchered piece offerings gave them visual pleasure. Humans could only consume meat if they had been first offered to gods in sacrifice. In return, gods, headed by Indra but overseen by their Supreme Godhead Vishnu, sent down blessings, prosperity and sons when in need. You could achieve any wish by making the right sacrifice – material, human or animal to the right god, chanting the right incantation or *mantra*, and observing the appropriate procedure.

Situated in the midst of those sacred and now purified plains of Aryavarta, were some five-hundred-odd city-kingdoms, their belligerent *Rajas* fighting among each other after getting rid of the *Rakshasas*. Among them, by the fertile banks of the Sarayu river, which was a tributary to the sacred Ganges, was the kingdom *Ayodhya*. The name meant the Unassailable – the land against which none could wage war. The king who ruled that powerful kingdom was so brave and prosperous that they called him *Dasha Ratha* – Ten Chariots – either to mean that he owned ten chariots (just as not long ago a great Indian sage who was for some time worshipped by the Beatles was called 99-Rolls-Royces) or simply to describe his power and strength with a befitting name. In this story, since *Dasha-ratha* is an unfamiliar phrase for most readers, I will only refer to the great king as Ten-Chariots.

Valmiki, the poet-historian who wrote this hoary history in the form of a ballad, states in passing that Ten-Chariotss reigned for 60,000 Years. Three-hundred-fifty crowned wives – of whom only three were considered significant – lived with him, as did numerous concubines who provided him daily variety all through a calendar year. Hopefully, the wives and concubines shared his longevity. We only know that the three significant wives outlived him for a few years.

Chief Priest Vasishta, ably assisted by a lesser Priest Vamadeva, advised the king on spiritual as well as many mundane matters. Seven other wise ministers did the executive work, and an army of several thousand able-bodied men protected the kingdom. The ministers were so noble and fair-minded that they never persecuted Brahmins or *Kshatriyas* to fill the royal coffers. Persecution and taxation were reserved for *Vyshyas* of the trader caste who toiled in the soil and herded the cattle. *Shudras*, who were born to slavery were to pay the most taxes on account of their bad *karma* in past lives. This was a fair arrangement, agreeable to all Aryan men, gods and Godhead.

Under such benign dispensation, the population of over a million subjects led happy lives in their respective roles and castes (also described as *varnas* or colours) as determined by their past *karmas*. Following the example of their lord the king, they never told a lie, never had to steal and never needed to visit a *Vaidya* or the medicine-man. They did nothing that would even remotely hurt a Brahmin. In accordance with the great Aryan tradition, the women obeyed their husbands without question, never looked at anyone other than their singular husband with many wives, washed their clothes, cleaned their chamber pots and cooked food of which they gratefully ate the left-over and lay in abject submission during some auspicious and many passionate nights, thereby presenting their husbands with many sons.

Sons counted in this life by carrying on the trades of their fathers when they lived, and ensuring, through prescribed rituals, that they were well fed and allowed to lead an undisturbed existence in the nether-world after they passed on.

Daughters had no such hallowed role, and because they were a nuisance in the house, making demands that they be fed the same food as their brothers and be allowed to play with their toys, the loving parents waited for them to attain the marriageable age of six to ten. Usually, after announcing the proposal for marriage, the patriarch of the bride's family devised a sport for selecting the best males of their class. The winner from among the contesting suitors of any age – ten, twenty, thirty of seventy – took the child away to join his harem. Girls of royal lineage joined the harem of a king, those of lesser status were collected by noblemen or, if lucky, became concubines of the king or a person of the royal household or one among the nobility.

The women, who were captured along with their menfolk who lost a battle had no such luck. They were bundled out to the victors' houses as slaves. Such slaves were considered excellent gifts, and part of a dowry, particularly if they had been queens or princesses before being captured.

> *Today a reigning queen,*
> *Tomorrow a pitiful slave*

was a popular adage.

Gods looked down from snow-capped mountain-tops with admiration for all such glorious Aryan traditions. They particularly admired King Ten-Chariots of Ayodhya with a tinge of envy.

Thus did King Ten-Chariots rule the unassailable Ayodhya, reigning famously, amassing wealth and earning fame and divine pleasure. When not engaged in the job of ruling the subjects and dispensing justice, he hunted in the lush forests for stags, wild boar and mongoose for the royal cooking pot, not to mention elephants for their ivory (the best among them for the cavalry) and tigers and lions for their hides and heads. Venerable sages blessed the king when he presented them with a freshly tanned tiger-skin to sit on. Meditation felt better sanctified when a sage had his bottom grazing the furry hide of a dead tiger.

Trained on ear-shot hunting technique, Ten-Chariots only needed to hear the breathing of a deer, soft mooing of a blue-bull or the gurgle of an elephant drinking water from the river beyond the trees and out of sight, to aim and shoot to kill.

This special skill once got him into deep trouble. He shot an arrow in the direction of one of those gurgles – believing it was an elephant drinking water, but actually was an adolescent

Brahmin, named Shraavana, dipping a pitcher into the river to fetch water for his pious parents. The noble king sought out the dead boy's blind parents and confessed with profuse apologies the unfortunate killing of their boy by mistake. The devastated mother cursed the king, saying:

"Today, we shall die from the sorrow by the death of our son at your cruel hands. A day will come when you die in grief for the separation of your own son."

The king knew that even a female Brahmin's curse never went in vain. Before he could plead for some kind of a redemption from the curse, both the parents breathed their last.

The curse hit Ten-Chariots with a double-whammy. One, some day he would die grieving the departure of his son. Two, he had no sons. Thereupon realization dawned that age was catching up with him and that of his three queens who mattered of whom two were nearing menopause.

Another worry cropped up when he recounted his misfortune to his spiritual consultant Sage Vasishta. The latter said, "Oh king, I don't need to remind you that as a noble descendant of the *Ishvaku* dynasty which descended directly from the Sun-God, you are obliged to conduct the sacred colonial raid sanctified as *Ashwa-Medha*, the Horse Sacrifice, thereby capturing and vassalizing all the kings in the world. If you did not colonize the known world, you would find no place among the gods in heaven after you leave your body on this earth."

Ten-Chariots was aware that conquering and colonizing the known world was a noble deed, if correctly, procedurally and successfully brought to a close. Now that the Royal Guru had rubbed it in, Ten-Chariots had to get to work on the profound protocol right away.

Thus, on a magnificent day when the right constellation was on ascendance and the Ominous *Shani* (Saturn) was on its downward course, King Ten-Chariot set in motion the Horse Sacrifice that would last a whole year.

Hundreds of Brahmins who hung about the palace for alms and free meals but were knowledgeable in the Vedas, particularly in *Yajur* Veda that described the preference in flesh of each deity, instantly recited appropriate verses when a reference was needed. Sage Vasishta and his able assistant Vamadeva were quite adept at the procedure. For handling the finer details of such an important sacrifice, the most renowned specialist of the sacred ritual, Sage Rishyasringa was brought in from the deepest caves in the highest mountains after much persuasion accompanied by a royal promise of alluring rewards.

The most resplendent horse, imported from distant Khamboja Kingdom (later to be named Kampuchea and further vulgarized as Cambodia by white barbarians), one that was never ridden by anyone but the King himself on the most ceremonial of all occasions, was duly brought out, and bridled with golden halters and silk-cushioned saddle, gold-thread frills, caparisoned with gem-embedded golden ornaments from head to its hind legs. As incantations to the deities recited by the sages and by the Brahmin mendicants rose in decibels, cymbals were clanged and drums thundered, the King lovingly patted the horse on its head and ruffled its glistening mane. Then, with his face towards the sky in solemn prayer to the gods watching and waving from above the clouds, he finally gave a gentle push to its smooth rounded back. Sensing that it was a signal for it to move, the stallion trotted smartly on the red-carpeted royal path while the cheering crowd moved aside to give way.

An infantry of ten thousand foot-soldiers, a cavalry of five hundred battle-ready horses and a squadron of two hundred fierce elephants, each of them led by Warlord-caste (*Kshatriya*) officers who were commanded by the *Up-Senapati*, Vice chief of the military staff, ceremonially paraded behind the noble horse while a bronze band (since brass was not invented yet) played marshal music and marched behind. The Vice-chief who was in command held the reins of the horse, not mounting it, but marched alongside. A low-ranking soldier held up a red umbrella with gold spines and golden frills all around its hem protected the horse from sun and rain. Another lesser man fanned it with a fan fashioned from lions' hair. Once out of the city limits, the horse would be allowed to freely roam as far and as wide as it pleased, always protected, escorted, and fanned, but never left out of sight.

If any foolish king or his men of another city-kingdom dared to stop the horse or to seize it, there would follow a fierce battle, which, of course would be won by Ten-Chariots' men. The resisting army would be made to surrender and the rebellious king and his minions riddled with arrows. The booty of tons of gold, million bushels of grains and thousands of busty maidens would be carried homeward by couriers in captured palanquins and bullock carts.

Victory was assured because Ten-Chariots had the backing of all the gods who had reason to be grateful. In his entire long life the King had lost only one battle, which was a long time before the Horse Sacrifice had begun. Ten-Chariots had gone to help the gods who were engaged in a battle with magic-demons. The gods were beaten comprehensively. When Ten-Chariots intervened in gods' favour, the cowardly gods beat a hasty retreat under cover of the King's army. However, it turned out that the strong, well-exercised muscles and fierce weapons of the King Ten-Chariots and his men were no match to the demons' magical skills with their swords, spiked maces and arrows. In the end, Ten-Chariots was badly cut up and forced to make a hasty retreat while his men ran helter-skelter. Many were pinned to ground with magical spears and let to die in agony.

Fortunately for Ten-Chariots, Queen Kaikeyi, the most beautiful and amorous among all his wives and concubines, was accompanying him as cheerleader and chariot-driver. Unruffled by the bloodshed around her, like a true female of the *Kshatriya* warlord-caste, Kaikeyi picked him up, placed him gently in the chariot, and drove away, showing the middle finger at the chasing demons. Back in the safety of the palace, Ten-Chariots recovered soon enough. That episode of incredible bravery and sacrifice on the part of the queen overwhelmed the King. He promised her two precious boons any time she asked for it. The tragedy that awaited the fulfilment of this promise was too tragic and far too long for description in this story, whose sole intent was to show why gods in the sky were obliged to King Ten-Chariots

Back to the Horse Sacrifice.

As per the rules of the game, the kings who did not resist the sacred horse but surrendered would be recognized as noble vassals and treated as Princelings, but granted the right to call themselves *Rajas* – minor kings – only within their own land. Booties, which would be renamed tributes, would be voluntarily given away to the victor from the Vassal Raja's treasury and grain store. The best, youngest and the shapeliest of the maidens from his harem would accompany the material tributes. Annual taxes would be collected by such princelings from the crops of the *Vyshya* traders and the money earned by Shudra low-castes, and a chunk of it would be transferred as Goods and Services Tax to the coloniser who conducted the horse-sacrifice and who would henceforth be called *Bhupati*, Lord of the Earth, to be renamed King-Emperor several millennia later.

The horse would roam for exactly a year and, partly steered by men and the other part by the watchful gods above, it would return to the palace from where the long and eventful but victorious long march had set out on the same auspicious day and time a year before.

That was always the way with the horse-sacrifice *dharma*[36], and so it was with the Sacrifice by King Ten-chariots who was grateful that the gods above were careful to ensure that the horse never strayed into the West-Coast land where the magic-demons, his only powerful nemesis, lived and which was struck off the world map.

For receiving the horse and the parade of its military escorts trailed by carriages with tons and tons of booties of gold and silver and hundreds if not thousands of captive maidens, the palace was readied with festoons and fireworks. Lovely young maidens were brought out in their best waist-costumes of the time, their young and firm breasts bouncing gently as they walked, like those of the latter-day dancing *Moulin Rouge* beauties of far-away *Paris-nagaram* in the white barbarian land. Adorned with garlands, waist-belts, bangles and tiara of pure gold, these young ladies with kohl-lined eyes as large as lotus petals arrayed in line on both sides of the royal road to palace, holding out oil lamps to receive the victorious horse-led procession.

Even as this joyous pageant was on its way accompanied by beating of drums and blowing of conch-shells, the king and his three primary wives pondered over their private grief. There simply were no heirs to carry on the great tradition of the *Ishvaku* race that originated with the Sun-god. Many an ignorant atheist – there were many in the garb of pious Brahmins skulking in the crowd – did whisper that it was only natural that the king had no sons from his regular queens when he was a spent force after servicing 347 other queens and an uncounted number of concubines all through the nights of the year. Spies who mixed

---

[36] *Dharma* in Sanskrit means virtuous action or responsibility, mistakenly translated as religion by the intruders from the West

with the crowds reported any atheist who was found whispering such blasphemy. Such seditionists were promptly caught and burnt alive by the King's Brahmin entourage with the power of their *Vedic* chants[37]. This was the treatment for all times due to any atheist in a god-fearing and virtuous kingdom. Atheists were known as *Char-vakas* meaning *Four-words;* by the time they reached the fifth word of their blasphemy, they were done away with[38].

As the Horse Sacrifice was in progress, a great idea hit King Ten-chariots like a bolt from the blue. He proposed a *Putra-kameshti* meaning Son-Wish-Ritual to immediately follow the Horse Sacrifice. He received full consent from his eminently laudable Chief Priest Vasishta and other seven ministers who were well-versed in all the Vedas as well as Manu's Code of justice, that he could conduct, immediately with the conclusion of the horse sacrifice, but under the same marquee, and before decorations and festoons were pulled down, a second sacrifice – the Son-Wish-Ritual.

A gate-pass to heavens was assured to all colonizers and his generations to follow if the deities were fed with horse-fat and all other prescribed animal flesh and fat in the Horse Sacrifice. By sneaking in a second sacrifice without once again having to invite all the five hundred kings and their retinues, warlords (*Kshatriyas*), traders (*Vyshyas*) and the servant class (the despicable[39] but unavoidable *shudras*) from the Aryan plains, and having to gift thousands of cows and millions of gold coins to sages and

---

[37] Burning alive Charvaka, an atheist in the garb of a Brahmin sage by real Brahmins by the power of their incantations is mentioned in Mahabharata, the other great epic.

[38] A clever one to escape death by fire; yet cause further mischief was Jabali, the rationalist.

[39] Manu, the ancient sacred law-giver had ordained that a Shudra must be named with a contemptible first name soon after he/she is born.(Manu Smriti 2:31

Brahmins, only once and not twice, he could fulfil his need to please the gods while fulfilling his desire for a son or sons to inherit his kingdom. That was a great plan indeed.

The conclusion of the Horse Sacrifice had to be as diligent and precise as the victory-filled march of the valiant horse and its escorts through a whole year, covering the entire earth that mattered. The king called for his first wife, Kausalya, the officially reigning queen, to conduct the climax. Kaikeyi,. the second and the normally favourite queen, and Sumitra, the youngest of the three significant queens, along with lesser queens and concubines were allowed to watch from the balcony, which was where the royal ladies, even queens except the participating one, belonged. Their alternative places of belonging were their private chambers that admitted only the masculine King when in passion, and neutered guards who were clinically deprived of passion.

The victorious stallion, who recognized its exalted status obtained through the long ceremonious journey where he was the cynosure of all eyes, and had sensed that its very presence had sent out tremors into the heart of many a heroic king and his minions, marched with a befitting regal air, bearing up with the long-winded classical music played by the bronze band and thunderous noise of its drums. As it came sauntering in, the king received the horse with much joyous aplomb. After reciting a few Vedic chants dictated by the great sage Rishyasringa himself, the king handed the reins and the horse to Queen Kausalya who had been thoroughly instructed on her role.

Skilled carpenters had carved and erected, full-stretched-arms apart 21 posts, each 21-cubit in height, gold-plated and wrapped in silk for the sacrifice. Three hundred animals – four-legged, slithering and aquatic, records Poet Valmiki –were brought in and, as per the preference of each deity for whom a sacrifice was due as prescribed in the Vedas, fifteen of the animals were tied to each of the twenty posts[40]. The last post was reserved for the ritual horse. The arithmetic of the arrangement was perfect.

The sacrifice was carried out in systematic and procedural sequence, more efficiently than in the royal butcher house. Sacred mantras from *Black Yaju Veda* rose loud in the air along with smoke, smothering the sound and sight of bays and wales of protest and cries of fear from the animals tied to their respective posts. The incantations, calling out each god went out to the heavens loud and clear while animals were beheaded according to their sanctity and seniority. Soma, the intoxicating juice of the holy plant that was the proud ancestor to humble marijuana of present times, was offered to the gods and sages, particularly to god-king Indra, the grandest connoisseur of Soma wine. The sight of blood and sounds of dying agony of so many animals gladdened the hearts of Indra and lesser gods in the sky above and of the sacred sages, Brahmins and lesser beings on earth below.

The ritual horse himself, tied to the 21st post, stood unmoved by the heart-wrenching wails of other animals. His heart had hardened watching the many killings along the way during his year-long journey; he was always with the killers, not with the victims. He stood proud and indifferent; if the skin of his fore shoulders occasionally seemed to shudder, that was to shake of a fly, not from fear. He was the victorious part of the royalty, not a mere horse.

Finally it was the turn of queen Kausalya to perform her assigned role. She walked up to the 21st post, and with great jubilation[41], circumambulated the till-then stoic – and no doubt curious – stallion seven times. Then, as becoming a lady of the

---

[40] Valmiki Ramayana, Balakanda 14:30 to 14:32 mentions three hundred animals – of land, air and aquatic - plus the ritual horse for sacrifice.
[41] In Sanskrit, *paramaya Muda*

warrior caste, she, with precision and even greater joy[42], stabbed the horse three times on its previously marked-out vitals. Her warrior-class action, even though feminine, was swift and effective; the horse neighed in incredulous surprise with the first stab, but cried in agony the second and third time. Then its legs shook violently, and became still. As is prescribed in the great scriptures, the dead horse was then carried reverentially to a bedecked royal bedroom.

Queen Kausalya knew her next duty was to bear with the humiliation that was the lot of any woman of her proud status. She was not to participate in any of the further sacrificial rites. Instead, she accompanied the dead horse without a demur. Protocol demanded that the senior-most queen sleep with the sacrificial horse. So she curled up with the bleeding corpse of the dead horse all through the night[43]. Evidently the king had no qualms about his wife sleeping with a dead horse. In the morning, the queen got up, her clothes still in place but smeared with blood and traces of horse-dung; her hair unruffled. Some say she watched the dead horse's living soul make a vertical take-off towards the heavens.

The rituals went on for three days. During nights the five-hundred-odd royal invitees regaled themselves in the ways that kings do and spent their nights with loaned-out maidens, scholars debated, drama troupes performed ancient sacred legends, horsemen raced, wrestlers wrestled to the death of one or both, swordsmen gored each other to enhance the visual spectacle. There were stages on which many dramas were staged and *deva-dasis* (holy whores) danced as choreographed by the great King Bharata, the most famous ancestor of Ten-Chariots. While at

---

[42] *Valmiki Ramayana, Balakanda 14:33. Some apologetic scholars say that the horse was already dead before the gentle queen stabbed it. Poet Valmiki is unapologetic on that score.*
[43] Ibid, 14:34

it, the *deva-dasis* chose the most promising clients for the night. To more elite private audiences, well-known musicians sang strumming on their one-string guitars while some blew conch-shells to mark time.

Hours before sunrise the *Hotars* and *Ritwicks* – priests trained in sacrificial rites had their ablutions by the river. Then with loud incantations they poured gallons and gallons of pre-boiled butter in the fire that blazed within brick frames of prescribed dimensions. The Fire-god, *Agni*, was requested, in the divine language of Sanskrit which alone he knew, to take his fill and pass on the oblations that were addressed to Indra, the royal god, then the gods of wind, of water, twelve different-but-same sun gods and *Yama* the god of death. The twin gods Ashwins were pleaded to dispense cure to those who were injured in the races and the few weaklings who fainted in the melee. The international god, Mitra, was not forgotten when oblations were posted through the Fire-god who alone was visible by his burning presence.

After the day-long oblation to gods by the priests, elegantly dressed and ornamented waiters served heaps of food for all kings, sages and humans according to their caste distinctions. After each sumptuous meal, the satisfied Brahmins addressed the King thus:

"Oh, descendent of Raghu, we are fully satisfied with the meal."

This gladdened the heart of Ten-Chariots no end.

Towards the end of the sacred ritual and the feasts, three of the officiating priests were praised by the king, his ministers and the Brahmins for the perfect Vedic precision with which the Horse Sacrifice was conducted. In deep appreciation, suitable rewards[44] were proposed for those three worthies. Their names were announced in proper sequence, and were respectively handed

---

[44] Ibid, 14:35

over the following gifts by the hand of the king himself as he graced a special podium erected for the purpose.

- Chief Officiating Priest *Hotaa* was gifted with a crowned queen – One from the other remaining 347 after excluding his three significant queens.
- Vice-chief Officiating Priest *Adhwaryu* was awarded a neglected wife of the King – An uncrowned queen whom the king had not bedded for years in living memory.
- Young *Udgaataa*, the apprentice priest, received one of King's concubines – presumably the youngest and the most alluring among the three.

The gifts, needless to say, much pleased the priests who had been forced into celibacy all through the long preparatory period of the great sacrifice. The crowned queen, neglected wife and the concubine who were thus bartered away as free gifts were not asked their consent. There was no need. Asking women before giving them to men in marriage or as a reward was not in the Aryan tradition then, nor was it for ages to come till this day.

After the sex-award ceremony, as it is prescribed in the golden palm leaves of the scripture, the noble horse whose body had the pride of sleeping with the queen and whose soul had reached heaven, was cut into 16 pieces. These were offered to Indra with a pitcher filled with Soma juice and then to the fire-god at the special altar prepared in the name of the King by sixteen Brahmins on his behalf. They with due reverence chanted the *mantras* which the King parroted after them while pouring melted butter, reverentially recalling the name of each god and muttering *Om-Swaha* – Oh god, this is for you, and then offering layers of *omentum* and fat to the respective gods.

That completed, it was time for *Putra-kameshti* – the Son-Desire Ritual. Incantations for this sacred protocol was prescribed in the *Atharva Veda* – the lowliest of the four Vedas, whose magical remedies, which had dangerous side-effects for the uninitiated and were not prescribed for ordinary Brahmins. *Rishyasringa,* whose name meant the noblest and the most scholarly among the sages and who was invited with much persuasion and promise, was entrusted with this difficult and rather hazardous form of sacrifice. Even before he began to chant the prescribed verses and to offer boiled butter to Fire-god, the wise sage who, like many modern Sadhus and Gurus, knew the sacred protocol to make childless women conceive, made a prophetic announcement that King's three wives would deliver four valiant sons. Ten-Chariots was immensely pleased, and the sage began to read out the verses from the first chapter of the Veda of Magic-remedies so as to make his prophesy come true.

To watch this *Maha yagna* – intense sacrificial rites - being performed, Sages, Brahmins, Kshatriyas of the warlord caste, Vyshyas of the trader caste and Shudras with their contemptible names were assembled in their respective places by the thousands. Gods and demigods, belching from the lards of animals that they had imbibed and feeling dizzy from Soma juice, gathered in the clouds on wobbly legs. When among them they sighted Brahma, the Creator of all beings who was himself created by Vishnu the Supreme Godhead, the gods and demigods surrounded him.

"Oh, Great Brahma*ji,* your Divinity," they cried almost in unison, "You had done us great injustice when, impressed by Demon Ravana's deep meditation in your name and by *tapas* – (near-suicidal gymnastics to raise temperature in the preferred deity's abode to uncomfortable levels), you had granted a boon to the fearsome demon that no god or demon could kill him, whatever his misdeeds. Armed with that all-powerful boon, he had been attacking our godly regions, tormenting our very king, Indra, whose thunderbolt-sword has proved totally ineffective."

The wise and wizened God of Creation smiled a soft smile of sympathy. Fondling his long snow-white beard with his age-shrivelled hand, he said:

"No reason for you to whimper and cry like bangle-wearing goddesses. That idiot Ravana, – never mind that he's my ardent devotee – had left a loophole in the boon he asked for, and which I granted. In his arrogance, he asked that neither gods nor demons must be able to destroy him. He left out human – the most cunning of the lot – because he believed humans were puny, powerless underlings. The trick is to find a brave and strong – not to ignore cunning – human to kill that trusting devotee of mine."

Not to waste time, for the Son-Desire-ritual was nearing its end on the earth below, Brahma sent an urgent request by divine telepathy to Vishnu, the Supreme Godhead who usually rested on his serpentine bed, hoisting his head on his right hand folded at the elbow. On receiving the telepathic text, the omniscient and omnipotent Godhead immediately stood up, brushed himself, mounted Garuda, the massive bird with divine powers, which flew at lightning speed as directed. Sooner than a priest could chant *swa-ha,* Vishnu appeared on the scene with a flash of light as if by a camera-trick in an old Hindi movie.

"I have divined your need," said Vishnu whose permanent smile verged on a smirk aimed at the foolish gods, humans and demons. "I will soon incarnate on earth as four sons of the King of Ten-Chariots whom I spy whining and labouring on that patch of earth down below at the *Atharva-Veda* ritual for sons. In due course, I will find a reason – such as abducting the incarnation of my dear wife Lakshmi in the *avatar* of Sita, Rama's earthly wife – to kill your devotee Ravana, his brothers and sons, chief of his army and all those dear to him, but spare his two-timing younger brother, Vibhishana. Two-timing, as you all know, is a virtue in my Book of Morals. You will recollect that I two-timed and destroyed a noble demon-king named Bali for being too virtuous and for spreading socialism in his empire. I will soon select the demi-gods whom I shall incarnate in the land South of the Vindhyas as darker-skinned man-monkeys, well-versed in Sanskrit and the art of warfare, but nonetheless monkeys, to help me."

Since Vishnu never faltered on his words, gods, demi-gods and Brahma himself were immensely pleased. Their musicians, namely Gandharvas, played on their flutes and sang songs in praise of the Supreme Godhead. Apsaras, the beautiful – though not necessarily virgin – *yakshis*[45] danced in gay as well as hetero-abandon. The sonorous rhythm of the dance and music in the firmament above reached the ears of those assembled below as a sweet, divine hum.

On the parch of earth below, in the Invincible Ayodhya, high-priest Rishyasringa's incantations kept rising in speed and decibels. When they reached their cadenza, a radiant human figure – his hair smooth, shiny and fizzy like the mane of the Lion King, his face as brilliant as a thousand suns, emerged from the sacrificial fire. Cupped by his bejewelled hands the divine Being held a bowl of sweet-porridge. Its sweet fragrance reached out and enthralled all those present.

Presenting the bowl to the pleasantly surprised king, the divine being intoned in his enchanting like baritone: "Good tidings to you, Oh King. Give this to your three wives. They will have four sons."

Then, just as in a movie, the Being with King Lion's mane atop a brilliant divine face vanished in a flash.

---

[45] Beautiful witches who qualify neither as goddesses nor as demonesses. Many of them lead happy lives dancing and singing; some entice men to their parlour atop palm trees disguised as mansions, and, not unlike the praying mantis, eat them at the end of a roaring love-making session.

King Ten-Chariots was, needless to say, overjoyed. He was valiant, strong and of imposing stature, but slow on simple arithmetic. So he called his three significant wives to partake of the sacred porridge, but divided the bowlful into only two halves. After presenting a half portion to queen Kausalya for her brave act of killing a powerful royal stallion with three stabs and then sleeping with its carcass, the noble king realized that there was only one portion left, but two wives to feed. So he cut the half-bowl of porridge into two quarters and gave one to Kaikeyi, his favourite, though only second in rank. Not wanting to equate his third wife, young Sumitra, with her two seniors, he cut the quarter-cake into two one-eighth sections and gave her one. Noticing the look of dissatisfaction on Sumitra's face, and gratefully receiving a that's-OK wink from dear Kaikeyi, he gifted the last one-eighth too to Sumitra.

On the pristine silvery bank of the Sarayu river where beach-sand glistened like tiny bits of diamond, the last meal was served. Sages were offered pedestals to sit on, Brahmins were seated on gold-bordered bamboo mats, Kshatriyas on tiger-skins, Vyshyas on straw-mats and Shudras on bare ground[46]. The wholesome meal won much praise for its taste and nutritional value. At the end of the distinctive community meal and after the Brahmins had walked away to wash their hands, many pious Shudras rolled their bare bodies on the banana-leaf plates left behind by Brahmins with some bits of food and pieces of chewed-out

---

[46] "Gently place food in front of low-castes, dogs, grave-diggers and the sick that must suffer for their past karma. - Manu Smriti, 3.92

deer-bones left on them[47]. It was well known that such abject self-humiliation by Shudras would bring them a higher post (say, from cobbler to washer man) and relative prosperity in this life, apart from the assured chance of a better birth – as a Vaishya if not that of a Warlord or even a Brahmin - after death.

Finally, since the sages said they had little value for wealth, the king joyfully gifted much of his land to Brahmins, who said they had no use for lands because their holy caste was neither expected to till, sow or reap, only earn their keep from lesser castes. However, they accepted all the gold – trillions of coins - and tonnes of jewellery for their wives; thousands of cows for milk to oblate to their gods.

Then all the visitors, more than a million if you could count them, were given gifts in gilded red packets. They dispersed on wobbly legs on account of the Soma with which they washed down so much delicious, sacred food. Poets among them made instant songs in praise of King Ten-Chariots; Astrologers divined (imprecisely as usual) how handsome the princes and how beautiful the princesses would be when they would take birth. Only a few ungrateful Vyshyas muttered that the Ritwiks[48] who made the offerings to gods through fire should have left some fat on the flesh of the middle region, which would have made the food even more delicious and nourishing. Wiser beings walked away from the grumblers, lest a royal spy report their names as well to add spice to their reports.

---

[47] *Though modern-day Brahmins (other than those from the North-East) no longer eat meat as a rule, the practice of lower castes rolling over Brahmins' left-over food on plantain leaves continues in some parts of India*
See https://www.hindustantimes.com/india-news/centre-asks-sc-to-ban-inhuman-practice-of-dalits-rolling-on-brahmins-leftovers/story-yqwz6gd8H6ZN5myvu6CSkJ.html
[48] *Meat after being offered to gods in a sacrificial rite can be eaten by all castes-Manu Smriti 5.27 -5.30*

The King's ministers and *Senapati* – Chief of Military Staff – went back to their respective roles. Rishyasringa went back to the Himalayas with the satisfaction of a job well achieved and with unaccountable gifts of gold, jewels and tiger skins. The King himself had a large swig at *Soma* mixed with a concoction specially prepared by royal *Vaid*[49] and named by him as *Viagram* and departed for the chambers of Queen Kaikeyi.

Later that night in her love-chamber the queen whispered in the King's ears :"Go easy, I already have a baby bump." The King was so ecstatic that he never stopped to wonder what his role was in making the bump.

The river-bank lay strewn with half-eaten meals, entrails of sacrificed animals and chewed-out bones. Crows and vultures, some of whom were the re-born ancestors and manes, had the best of their meals. Some occasionally hopped up and pecked at each other fighting for a bone with some flesh on it.

Yet non-chalantly did River Sarayu meander on, its water filled with blood, animal entrails and human excreta mixed with flowers and prayer-beads all the way to join the sacred River Ganges which, with matching indifference, gurgled along, hurrying to the sea to get rid of is rotting burden of human bodies and cattle carcasses.

---

[49] Medicine man

With the spreading of vice, O Krishna, the women of nobility become immoral; and from the immorality of women, O Vrishni, mixing of castes (colours) occurs.

-Bhagavad Gita 1:41
Translation by author

THE PURPOSE OF A PRAYER

At five in the morning, this music, almost ethereal, comes wafting in through the window. The rustling leaves of the trees just outside the window makes it difficult for me to make out the words or even the language. I recognize the sweet voice, though. Anuradha Podwal, the one famous for Hindu hymns called *bhajans*.

"Gayathri," my wife answers the unasked question as she turns side in bed. *"Sweetie plays that CD every morning."*

Sweetie is the pet Punjabi name of the grumpy and rather pretentious Mrs. Rahul Malhotra who lives on the 14th floor, 12 floors above our unpretentious flat.

Of course. I should have known. *Gayathri*, the four-line verse in an ancient dialect that originated in *Rig Veda* and joyously traversed the other two *Vedas*, and then through every Hindu scripture to this current generation. I had tried to find the meaning of the mysterious lines that sounded pretty close to Sanskrit, but not the same, by looking up on the internet. I tried six sites, and got six different meanings. A bearded and saffron-uniformed *Baba* I met in the dentist's waiting room gave me a 7th meaning. My painful mouth prevented me from laughing out aloud,

Ram Sundar, a senior division clerk in the local government office who used to moonlight in my small-scale die-making workshop for a little extra money but pretended that he did it only for the experience, had once advised me that if I chanted the sacred Gayathri *mantra* 100,000 times, all my financial woes would be removed, I'd be able to disburse salaries on time, my business as well as my health would improve and my family would be prosperous and happy ever after.

"I am through my 89,000th chant," he had told me that day: "4 or 5 days to go. I will conclude it with a worship in my quarters on Tuesday. Within a few months, if not weeks, I will be an officer."

Less than a week later, on a hot and sultry Wednesday, I rushed to the Government Hospital when I received a message that Ram Sundar had a scooter accident. I found him, possibly sedated, in silent tears while his wife was howling. The doctor had decided that his left leg and three fingers of his left hand would need to be amputated. His wife, through tears mixed with prayers to her God, lied to me that the accident happened when her husband was on his way to my workshop. Ram Sundar, a passably honest guy even before he started chanting the Gayathri, winked at me through the lingering sedation. My workshop was closed on Tuesdays. For the sake of security and ease of patrolling, the government had allocated a different holiday for each zone in our town.

With a bit of mischief in my mind, but with no pleasure in recounting it, I reminded my wife of that tragic accident of Ram Sundar and its unlucky connection with the holy *mantra*. I added, having taken into a statistical probability, that Ram Sundar must have concluded his 100,000th Gayathri recitation on the fateful Sunday or the latest on Monday. He had bought the scooter just a few days before the accident with a loan from the government. With one of his legs gone, and if the superiors could be convinced that he was traveling on duty, he would be retired with a small disability pension. Otherwise he would be jobless with zilch to show for all his years of hard work and no way to pay back the loan. Sadly there was no way I could give a job to a one-legged and seven-fingered man to handle heavy steel blocks on my heavy-duty lathe machines.

"You have a twisted mind," retorted my wife. "Suggesting that the Holy chant caused the accident and the misfortune that follows."

"I never meant that," I said: "Only that chanting the *Gayathri* did not save him. He might as well have chanted *'Abracadabra, I see through your slip and padded bra.'*"

"I hope the children learn to be more decent in their language and respectful to our religion – *my* religion," she said. "Why don't you see that if it wasn't for his chanting the sacred mantra, he could be dead and his wife would be a widow?"

A prayer, she argued, could be expected to soften a blow but not entirely stop it. Sundar could well have lost both his legs and both hands if it was not for the power of the *Gayathri mantra*

My wife had always been a pious woman. Till a godman named *Sathya Sai Baba* (the name meant *True Mother and Father*, hinting that all other *Sai Babas, mothers and fathers* were frauds) died twelve years before the date of his death he had prophesied, she would go with a horde of other pious women from our town to the *Ashram* of the holy charlatan. There she peeled potatoes and obeyed haughty white women who were probably retained with a monthly payment. She swept the floor – a menial job for which, back home, she employed servants. Such activities would teach one humility and respect for manual labour, she explained rather sheepishly, recounting the experience. My asking her why she didn't teach herself the value of humility and respect for manual labour by doing those things at home made her accuse me of ingrained misogynistic nature and masculine chauvinism.

She had collected compact disks titled **A thousand Names**

of Vishnu who resided, lying on his side propped up by his right hand in the lap of a thousand-hooded snake in the middle of an ocean filled with milk. His busty and beautiful wife, Lakshmi, sat massaging his legs as though He suffered from arthritis or sciatica. Other compact disks she had purchased from India played the **Thousand Names of Lakshmi** who came out of the milky Ocean when it was churned as a joint venture between the smaller gods and the demons. First emerged from the heaving milky surface of the ocean a white elephant, *Airavata*, whom the chief of demi-gods, Indra, caught and stealthily took away. Next emerged Lakshmi, the most beautiful woman of wealth, whom Vishnu, the referee, married without giving either contenders a chance. Finally showed up a cauldron of *Amrit*, the nectar of immortality, which Vishnu helped the demigods snatch and run away. Thus, we know that Vishnu, the dark-skinned but fair-minded Super God is the best; next are the gods who earned immortality through treachery; and last, the demons, who were the losers ended up as the worst. Naturally, scriptures, like history, have been buttering the winners' side of the bread ever since

In the treasure-house of my wife's piety were also Forty Odes to monkey-god Hanuman, homage to elephant-headed and pot-bellied Ganesh and several dozens of other hymns, followed by a rhythmic and sweet-sounding chorus called *Aarti* – homage to Lord Shiva, the three-eyed God whose dance would end in the annihilation of the universe. Musically reminding the elephant-head that he was pot-bellied, had a broken tusk and a mouse for his chariot evidently pleased him. All Gods and Goddesses loved the toadying of their moon-like faces and doe eyes; of the exquisite beauty of their gem-studded golden jewellery, of the weapons that their multiple arms held in readiness to fight the demons. The hymns included the names of the relations of the gods – their spouses, parents or children, and also the names of the losers - the forest-dwelling indigenous demons whom they killed.

She would play those disks all morning, lip-syncing some. To some others, she would sit enthralled, persuading the temporarily gullible grandchildren to sit with her and close their eyes.

The first hymn she played was always,

Wake up, Govinda, wake up
Wake up, you who has on his flag
Garuda, the king of eagles
Wake up, you husband of Kamala,
Bring glad tidings for the three worlds

I'd remind her that this wakeup call to God was composed in India, which was five hours behind the largely God-forsaken and hence orderly (after decimating most of the disorderly but relatively peaceful indigenous people) and the reasonably prosperous country where we lived. At five thirty in our morning, it was just past midnight in India, our Motherland, and where Govinda possibly preferred to sleep in the arms of his amorous wife.

God is everywhere, she'd tell me. I'd smile and remind her that there is a new time-zone every half-hour if not less across the globe, and the poor *Vishnu* (Govinda is one of the thousand names of Him) would be woken up every half hour – ten times – between us and back home that morning if there was at least one person of piety chanting the wakeup call in each time zone. Assuming there was at least one pious person in each time-zone of the world, Govinda would get at least forty-eight wakeup calls a day. Since all clocks and time-pieces in the same time zone are not synchronized, God would continue to get too many more wakeup calls than a dozen hard-working cardiologists.

"For your information, God never sleeps."

"Then why on earth are you waking Him up?"

"I am waking up myself with that prayer. I'm praying that good tidings come to the three worlds. God does not answer prayers for your own good. But when you ask good things for others, He answers you."

I am amused. "I had heard a Christian preacher yell the same thing to a street-side crowd. Your prayer to bring good tidings to the three worlds was composed at least a couple of hundred years ago, and the world – at least in terms of peace and good tidings – have only gotten worse."

Readying myself for a long verbal dual, I took a long breath.

"There was not a single year, a single day when children did not die in fire or by drowning, women were not raped and killed, men did not fight to please their bosses or had not killed each other in the hope that they would reach the heaven for brave-hearts. In Bengal millions of Hindus and Muslims died in famine, in Germany Jews were killed by starvation and gassing. In Siberia, Orthodox Christians died with overwork. When war was raging across the globe, Christian Churchill made millions of Hindu Bengalis starve to death, while anxiously waiting for the news of Gandhi's death. When Hitler was gassing Jews, Churchill's predecessor Chamberlain was hobnobbing with the former and hailing the treaty of mutual permission to annex the rest of the world. Stalin starved a million Ukrainians, Mao allowed a few thousand – some say millions – to starve and to die in his own country. In the supposedly peaceful transition of power, Hindus and Muslims massacred each other, their wives and their children. A year later, officers of the newly established Israel forced the exodus of thousands of Palestinian Muslims resulting in a bloodshed reminiscent of Biblical times. In Korea and Vietnam, Christians killed Buddhists and atheists. George Bush had a call from his God to attack Iraq against the wise counsel of the United Nations, but God won and see what was the result,"

I had to pause again to catch my breath. Pretending to ignore the flush on her face, I continued: "In Philippines, a Catholic president has instructed his police to kill anyone and everyone suspected of selling, buying, possessing or taking any powder suspected to be narcotic substance. Police use that law to kill anyone who filed a complaint against their misdeeds, or someone whom they didn't like. In America, anyone – that is everyone – who has a gun is killing anyone – a whole crowd if need be – in churches, ball rooms, malls and banquet halls. Islamic State, in the name of God…"

My wife closes her ears with both hands. Her frown creases all the way to her hairline. She shuts her eyes, praying for patience. Then the wisdom that she had received from the scores of discourses by *Swamis, Babas and godmen* while she was in India, and had been receiving them from their television performances these days, comes pouring out.

"You do not see the truth," she tells me. "If millions of prayers by people like me go up and yet there is human suffering, imagine how terrible the suffering would be if no one prayed at all."

There was no way I could challenge her to try out that theory.

'The night when Shiva and Uma play with each other, that is Shivaratri (Shiva's Night)

-Malayalam folk song.

THE GHOST WHO SIGHED

As I recall my most vivid image of her, Grandmother must have been around seventy-five. She was bent like an inverted L, wrinkled and light-skinned with deep crow-feet on her cheeks under fading grey-green eyes. Yet she was sprightly and active, humorous and generous to a fault. No beggar was sent away without a coin or a palmful of rice, no untouchable *kurava* and his wife who came to our house to sit at a distance in the front yard with their crude one-string instruments to sing the many glories of gods, went away without a little money or food.

Yet Grandma was as much a casteist as Arjuna and Lord Krishna of her sacred *Gita*. Not even the head of our share-croppers, the noble Kannan, or his wife coal-black and beautiful Karumbi[50] was allowed to get too close to a member of the family.

Caste mattered. Grandmother also believed there was something lowly about the things that had anything to do with the people she called *Maplas* – people who were not Hindus. Christians and Muslims were neither considered low-castes nor were they untouchable, but they ate the flesh of the sacred cow. The British – all white people were considered British and addressed *Sayip* – were greeted with respect, but not received in

---

[50] *The name meant black (implying beautiful) girl.*

one's house if one could help it. They were secretly rumoured to be more unclean than the lowest *Pariahs* because they wiped, not washed, their bottom. The word *Sayip*, reserved for the white man, though a localized form of Hindi *Sahib*, was spoken with an element of contempt.

When one day Brother Pedro, the heavily tanned and freckled Italian *Sayip* from my missionary School came home to 'teach the true religion' and to gift her a gilded copy of a vernacular Bible, Grandma received him with appropriate courtesy, dragged out a reclining chair on the veranda and offered him pre-boiled ginger-water in copper-tumbler to drink and betel nuts and powdered tobacco wrapped in manicured betel leaves to chew. Both were declined, I noticed, with a tinge of disdain.

She listened to him with all the politeness that was becoming of a light-skinned brown woman while talking to a heavily tanned white man. The fiendish shadow of the British rule darkened every Indian thought.

The white man's air of condescension borne by Brother Pedro and the brown woman's politeness on Grandmother's visage evaporated when Pedro suggested that it was foolish of Grandma to worship a black goddess adorned with dozens of human hands hung around her waist and a garland of skulls adorning her neck while blood dripped from her tongue. Such a morbid and ghoulish image, said Pedro in practiced vernacular, was of the devil, not of a goddess. There was no goddess, only one God, he said, and that God alone was worth worshipping.

Grandma bristled and barely managed to control her temper.

"Devil, the *Chekuthan*, was that half-naked god of yours who was hung up good and proper from a tree trunk, nailed on his hands and legs and bleeding all over. Who would meet such a terrible fate unless he was the devil himself? I would rather worship the goddess with the hands of such devils hanging around her waist and their skulls around her neck than worship a god who was nailed up."

I noticed that Brother Pedro's mouth twitched as he tried to peel a fake smile but failed.

Grandma's body still shook in anger when Pedro stood up.

"You are agitated, the devil has possessed you. Maybe you'll see sense some other time," said Pedro before he picked up the gilded Bible that was meant to be Grandmother's gift and walked away.

When Brother Pedro went past the gate and disappeared around the corner, Grandma mixed fresh cow-dung in water and washed the chair where he had sat, and the entire veranda and the steps where he had walked.

"I didn't mean to insult *Christu*[51]," she whispered half to herself and the other half to me while wiping the cow-dung paste off the stone-tiled floor. "But that *sayip* made me do it. C*hristu* was a good man. Maybe a god himself. Who knows the mysteries of the divine? You must never say bad things about other people's gods."

I had no intention to insult any God or gods, for my examination was coming close. But I liked the way Grandma deflated Pedro who was our teacher in physical training classes. Besides, he coached me in football. I hated the way he would feel for and twitch my little tool from outside my shorts and knead my nipples under the football-singlet when no one was looking. I knew what all that meant, because a distant relation, *Mani-Chechi* was a better trainer in that game.

Thus, I grew up under the care of my doting Grandmother while my parents lived in far-away government quarters with my elder brother. When Mother was pregnant a third time, she came home, delivered the baby whom Grandmother midwifed.

---

[51] Malayalam for Christ.

A month later she went back with the baby to live in the far-away place in the hills. The following few nights I woke up feeling that I heard the shrill cry of the baby, but soon forgot the cry and the milky odour that the little one radiated around her.

I remained with Grandmother. She loved me dearly, fed me well and told me godly stories after the evening prayer while frogs croaked in the back yard and stars twinkled in the sky like a scattering of tiny oil-lamps. I don't recall missing the rest of the family – even the baby after those few days – although I looked forward to the days when Father would come home. He brought new clothes and sweets and tales of my big brother's mischiefs and how the little one had begun to crawl and sit up.

Once a year Grandmother would leave me in the house and go for the *Shivaratri* fair that celebrated Lord Shiva's amorous night with his wife Parvati. The first trip of hers I could recall was when I was five – the year I joined school. The pleasant evening chill in January was nearly gone; the roar of the sea two miles away had flattened to a low note and the frogs became silent since the winter rains had given way to nights swarmed by mosquitoes.

A couple of days before the trip, Grandma invited a buxom spinster in her late twenties or early thirties, to stay with us for my protection. I never learnt her real name; she told me to call her *Mani Chechi* – literally, Bell-Sister. To get me used to being alone with a stranger in our midst, Grandma would sleep in the next room. Being of the right caste, though not really a true relation, *Chechi* was allowed to cook, serve and eat dinner in the caste-sanitized kitchen. In return, she was to tell me stories at night and sleep on a mat spread on the floor beside my bed so as to dispel my fear of the dark. As it turned out, it was a more-than-fair arrangement.

On the evening before *Shivaratri*, Grandmother would prepare to leave, entrusting me to the care of *Mani Chechi*. When the shadows had begun to lengthen and the faint golden beams of the setting sun climbed to the top of the coconut fronds way high and the ground below faded into twilight, Grandma would set off with a cloth bag filled with sacrificial flowers, coconuts and beads tied to her arched back and a walking stick in her hand. The *Chechi* would serve me dinner without insisting, unlike Grandmother would, that I say loud evening prayers in praise of Lord Rama. That was some relief.

Soon the oil lamps were put out; I would lie on a sheet spread over a thick cotton bed on the antique bedstead with thick, carved legs. The *Chechi* would spread her mat dutifully beside the cot. She was no good at story-telling; her voice was a monotone, not expressive like Grandma's. After the oil lamp was snuffed out, she would make up for her poor vocal skills. Her fingers would sneak in through the hem of my shorts and gently peel my foreskin, and then deftly close it to start all over. I don't recall if it hurt the first time or I was shocked or traumatized. Perhaps, at five, I thought it was a way of tickling me, and I liked it. Yet, I knew that this was something I was not supposed to talk about.

I didn't miss my Grandmother then, so I never complained. On occasions, while the fondling hastened, I would give a start, overcome by an abrupt feeling of exhaustion. At other times, the *Chechi's* hand would slacken; the fat and fleshy fingers would fall off leaving me disappointed. Some of those nights when Grandma was away, she would climb on to my cot and press my knee to her bushy mount and let me fondle her ample bosom. I would sleep with a faint guilty feeling those nights; but would look forward to her fingers reaching out to me the next.

Grandmother would walk some seven miles – distance was counted in miles those days – to the sands of the Aluva River, which had by then receded to spread out a large sandy beach. The appearance of the beach in February, only to disappear under swirling waters when rains came in June, was believed to be a miracle from Lord Shiva.

Shivaratri meant Shiva's night - the time when the Lord and his wife Parvathi spent their time making love while their devotees fasted and sat guard outside chanting their glories. Loudspeakers blared out tinny music picked up from shaky gramophone records, said Grandmother, so the night was far noisier than before. the mosquitoes and clanging of bells deafened her ears. She did join the loud *Shiva-Shivo-Shiva* chants which did not seem to interfere in the divine couple's passionate activities inside. From the graphic details she spelt out later, I could imagine the many radial paths, brightened by kerosene-fueled contraptions called *petromaxes* hung out by better-off hawkers. that converged on the small temple.

Grandmother said the temple itself glowed with hundreds of oil lamps that formed several parallel golden chains all around its white, oily walls. That, with the clanging bells accompanied by loud chants could fill piety into the heart of even a hard-core atheist. Hawkers added joy to the glitter with their wares – mostly food and toys. Arabian dates packed loose in open jute bags had the pride of place; then there were baskets of puffed rice, flattened rice, sweet and grainy *halwa*, prayer books and toys, colourful paper fans that turned in the wind. There were rubber snakes that would crawl on the ground when thrown, she said, gesturing how they crawled. On wooden shelves stood little gods with spring-loaded heads that rocked sideways atop stiff necks like classic dancers if you shook them or when the wind blew. Women tried on and haggled for glass bangles. Grandma looked forlorn when she said she had no use for bangles after grandfather died.

Long before daybreak, basic human needs of tens of thousands of men and women jostling for place on the strip of a river-bed would start demanding priority on the river that had retreated shallow for the season. Most of the pious, forgetting the hygiene that their religion demanded, would start doing their morning affairs in the sacred water or its banks downstream, but Grandmother would have none of it. She would begin her trek back home after the temple bells were rung to signify the opening of the door of the divine couple after they had had their pleasures for the night and Grandma had said her final prayers. It was perhaps an hour past midnight; very dark and it would be dark through most of her sleepy and exhausted walk back home, burdened by the packs of dates, sweets and toys meant for me and for my siblings who would visit when the bigger one's school would close a month later.

Only a couple of miles from home, Grandmother had to pass through a dirt path that wound its way through a maze of tall, thorny bamboos in *vedi-murra*. The name meant Shooting Screen although there was no screen nor a wall in sight. Where the bamboos ended was a clearing on which stood a banyan tree that loomed frighteningly tall and wide; its knurled and hairy roots hung down from the branches looking like menacing brown spirits.

A little distance from the tree stood a broken-down platform of grey planks of rotting wood. Till a few years ago in the days of the *Maharajah*, Grandma had heard from those in the know, convicts were hanged atop that platform from a wooden beam. Perhaps the place came to be called Firing Screen when some of the convicts were made to stand against a wall and were shot with muzzle-loading guns. A policeman filled the gun's long barrel with gun-powder from the muzzle-end, packed it tight with a rod and stood at the ready. When the Maharajahs' officer raised a finger to signal go, he pointed the barrel at the trembling and pleading victim and fired. The man died, but his wails of pleading echoed through the trees night after night, Only the worst among the godless unbelievers argued that what was being heard were the mating calls of flying-foxes, not wails of the scoundrels who were done away with at the ghoulish Firing Screen.

Even in daytime men were afraid to cross the Firing Screen. In the dark no one dared go that way. Ghosts of those who were strung up and those who were shot lived in the banyan tree and mauled those who after sunset passed by the clearing. They made loud shrieks, it was rumoured, and laughed aloud or cried pitifully. Some eye-witnesses claimed that they had seen white clothes dart about in the dark on top of the broken-down platform. Some claimed to have heard chilling howls and curses coming from the place at midnight. In daytime, their souls rested inside hundreds of flying foxes – huge bats – that hung upside down on every branch.

For Grandmother, the alternative path through a village of the low-castes was ethnically taboo, too far and round-about. In early February, the chill of the tropical winter had nearly departed, yet fog descended in the early hours of the morning when crickets screeched their shrill vibratos, multiplying the eeriness. Grandmother said when she emerged from the limits of the hanging place, she wasn't sure whether her few remaining teeth chattered from fright or from cold.

A couple of miles from the Firing Screen was a Muslim village. A white mosque with its polished brass dome and spire loomed large in the faint glow of the horizon signaling the appearance of dawn less than an hour later. Between the mosque and the muddy footpath was a waist-high thicket of shrubbery beyond which was the grave yard where white tomb stones stood up like ghosts in the twilight. The rumor was that all through the night a *jinn* on a huge white horse roamed the area protecting the mosque and the graves. He cut with a heavy sword anyone who wandered about the mosque after the fifth and the last prayer was said and the devotees had safely gone home. Never a thief was heard to have strayed into the Muslim village after midnight for fear of the *jinn*.

She often hoped that her return walk would time with the call for the morning prayer when many Muslims in white clothes and caps would make a beeline to the mosque. She had no watch, so such precision timing rarely happened. Grandmother tried not to look at the dark bush, the white grave stones, or the domed mosque with its shiny brass spire. Yet she couldn't help making a furtive glance, which made her blood freeze for a moment.

Grandmother didn't tell me of these escapades; I overheard her reeling them out to the *Chechi* who went to the veranda to help her unload the packages of gifts she brought for me and the rest of the family that was to arrive later. Grandma always had a separate packet for the *Chechi* to take to home when she left a few days later.

When the major part of the night's events was discussed, I kept my ears screwed if the woman would spill the beans on our nightly mischief. She never did. I had always believed that I was somehow the major conspirator in the minor orgy. As years passed, I actually became one. I once went down on to her mat and tried to mount her the way Hamza, a worldly-wise classmate, told me how men did it to their wives. *Chechi* tried to help me, but I failed. She held me tight, sinking my face in her soft cleavage. To sooth my failure, she stroked me till a dry orgasm ran up my spine to my head and put me to sleep. When I woke up in the morning, I was on the cot, and *Chechi* was curled up, her clothes in place, on her mat below.

I was around eleven when *Mani Chechi* found a husband and that put an end to her annual visit. That year Grandmother arranged for a low-caste woman to sleep outside my room. On the night when Grandma was gone to the sacred river bank, I lay in bed, hoping that the woman outside would come in some time and wank me to sleep the way *Chechi* did. She didn't, so I stroked myself, fantasizing how her new husband would be mounting the woman who used to be mine. I felt overcome with jealousy, but also relieved that we were never discovered.

Grandmother came home exhausted, nearly faint, next morning. She did not allow the woman to help her unload the burden from her back. Casteism, she had learnt from the Bhagavad Gita she used to read every day, was important. If castes were abolished, women would become immoral, high blood would be adulterated, families would be ruined. A Low-caste could not be allowed to touch the dates and puffed rice that was in her back-packed cloth bag. How many people of what-all castes and casteless *Maplas* would have handled those bare dates while being transported from Arabia to the premises of her temple could not bother her. Now they were in her high-caste hands.

So, I was called to help.

I was wide awake in bed, still hard from the night's fantasy, and a bladder ready to burst. I rushed out and piddled under the coconut tree that wore a part of its roots over ground like a pleated skirt. I remained embarrassingly hard and felt wet in my knickers. Yet I walked up to her, hoping that the morning shadows would hide the wet circle in front of my shorts.

"You piddled in your knickers, go take a bath," Grandmother ordered. I watched her twist her body and unload the stuff from her back on the high veranda without help. Then she heaved herself up and lay down on the veranda floor, sighing a long sigh of exhaustion. The woman moved to help her.

"Don't touch me. Did you touch my grandson? I hope not. These youngsters have no sense of caste. You can go; come back later and collect a measure of paddy for your services," said Grandmother to the woman who had disappointed me at night.

The woman walked away, evidently feeling humiliated and

spitting to show her feeling. Many men and some women of her class attended the secret study-classes held by the local Communist Party in some house or another. They learnt, to their surprise, that they were equal to any other castes and must resist any assault or insult. However, the higher castes wielded the land that they share-cropped, and the government of the Maharajah under CP Ramaswamy had given a free hand to the police to deal with Communists any way they liked. So real resistance was subdued; study-class teachers were forced to stay underground in daylight.

Grandmother, though sensitive and kind-hearted, believed the Manu's sacred law that low-caste Untouchables were so created for their *karma*; so they should know their place. She never forgave the Regent Queen, the young king, or his *Dewan* – Prime Minister – for proclaiming a few years before I was born that low castes could be allowed into the temple premises. Gods, she once told me during story-time, will not forgive the Regent Queen or the young *Maharajah* who had gone to England to study thereby sullying the purity of his caste and had returned after learning the demonic ways of the brutish Whites. A good king though he was, he would still be made to pay a penalty in the next world for the desecration of temples with the footprints of Untouchables. Our traditions have meanings, she had admonished me: those traditions must be respected and heeded.

After a trip outside, grandmother would never enter the interiors of the house without finishing her morning routine and a bath in the pond behind the house. This time she acted different.

"Help me get up, I want to lie down. I will sleep on your cot", she said when I reported after changing my clothes. She let me lead her to my bed.

I feared that Grandmother would detect the peculiar smell of my self-indulgence that yielded nothing. She didn't. I sat beside her, crying. What if she died? She was breathing hard and her body was warm. Was she dying because I jerked last night?

> *"Hand-wanking is good fun and exercise for your arms*
> *But will damage your eyes and kill your soul."*

Was a limerick that secretly circulated among the boys of my school. Some kids believed it; others laughed at it but never revealed their personal choice between strong arms and healthy soul.

A couple of starving hours later, Grandmother sat up.

"Did you think I was dying?" she asked, laughing.

I hugged her, still crying. "Don't go to *Shivaratri* again," I said.

"We'll see about that a year from now," she said. "No *dosas*[52] today. I will make some rice gruel and boiled yam in curd for you," she said. "First, my morning things, and you yours".

From a basket suspended from a low-hanging rafter of our long, thatched roof I picked a pinch of charred paddy-husk for brushing my teeth. To clean my tongue, I tore off and split along its length the spine from a leaf of the coconut frond that hung low behind the house. Still brushing my teeth with the coal-black husk, I doffed my knickers and jumped into the pond in the midst of water lilies. Frightened, a thin water-snake slithered hastily ashore and vanished. When Grandmother came down to the pond to bathe, I was already out of water and rubbing myself.

"*Ammamma*, do you believe in ghosts?" I asked her just as she was swiping away water-lily leaves from a half-circle that she had cleared and lowering herself in the water.

"Why do you ask that," she asked. "You surely think I'm

---

[52] A delicious flat, soft and thin bread made from rice-and-lentil batter fermented overnight.

dying". Then she laughed, showing her one front tooth stained with pan-leaf chew and lengthened by retreating gum. I recalled she had a lovely row of teeth when I was younger; she lost most of them by chewing betel nuts wrapped in strips of dry tobacco leaves.

"No, of course not. I was all alone last night in the room. The woman you asked to sleep outside to guard me snored so loudly. Every time the shadow of a swaying palm-frond registered on the wall, I thought I saw a ghost."

"I had taught you the Hanuman-*mantra*. You should chant the *mantra* before you sleep, and keep your eyes closed."

Of course, I knew the *mantra*. I could recite it with ease:

> *Oh, Hanuman of Alattoor Shrine*
> *Don't let me see terrible dreams.*
> *If I have a frightening nightmare,*
> *Wake me with your tail lest I fear*

I didn't argue that the *mantra* was not much help for one who was already awake and doing the wrong thing with himself. Doing the wrong thing kept my mind off ghosts just for a few minutes,

When we sat down, facing each other, with crossed legs on low flat stools and began to eat gruel and curried yam, Grandmother opened up.

"Every time I walk by that shooting-screen and then the Muslim graveyard, I expect to see a ghost. I had been walking for fifteen years in *Shivaratri* nights by that way before the morning twilight all alone ever since your grandfather died. He was not afraid of anything. But, tell you the truth, I am."

"Did you ever see a ghost – even a passing shadow of one?"

"No, never. For forty years, he walked ahead of me, same path, same time, and never looked this side or that. I walked behind him, reassured that if I so much as whimpered, he would be by my side, handling any ghost with his bare hands. Before he died, he told me never to stop going to Aluva *Shivaratri*. Shiva took care of the dead; the best way to keep the departed happy was to make them offerings by the river-bank on Shiva's Night. I go there, say a prayer and make an offering of a coconut, rice ball and *Tulsi*[53]-leaves to the deity to protect your Grandfather's soul, then for the souls of my ancestors. There are times when I feel that he walks behind me, not ahead. Once when he came to me in my dream, I teased him. Men are supposed to walk in front of their wives, not watch their behinds."

She giggled with a tinge of sadness. She must have loved Grandfather dearly.

"Why am I telling you such things? You are just a little boy," she said.

A little boy? Only last night I did what older people do. If I was older, I could have married *Mani Chechi* and did it right and proper every night.

"I am not a little boy," I said. "I am eleven, soon to be twelve. When you came in this morning, you looked like you had seen a ghost".

"Ah, that. It was faint light already, and I did see something in the graveyard by the Muslim *Palli*[54]. I saw a movement, and a bald head showing above the shrubs. The head was whispering something, and it drove a sharp chill up my spine. I ran, and while running, I realized it was the voice of Kutty Muhammad, the *Mapla* who deals in coconuts for us and buys our paddy – you know him, the old man who lost his wife last year. I had heard that Kutty Mohammed visited his wife's grave every morning and gossiped with her ghost. So, I took courage, walked back and

---

[53] A small holy plant that Hindus hold sacred. Belongs to the basil family.
[54] A Christian or Muslim place of worship.

got to this side of the bush behind the old *Mapla's* bald head and screwed up my ears. Would you believe it, he was sweetly asking his dead wife's permission to take a new wife!"

Grandmother's wrinkled shoulders shook; her laughter sounded like hiccups, yet full of mischievous merriment. The folds of her throat danced up and down.

"Then what happened?"

"You wouldn't believe this. It was either an owl or a bat, I am not sure. It happened so fast. The thing gave a shrill cry and darted over the *Mapla's* bare head. Maybe its wing slapped him, I'm not sure, Kutty Muhammad shot up in fear and stared in the direction that the bat – or was it an owl – flew. By now it was lighter; I could see him clearly; he was shaking. First, I thought he was shaking with fear. No, he was angry. Guess what he said?"

"What?"

"He glowered at the grave. Then shaking his hands at it, he screamed: "You *haram* – ill-begotten bitch' (no, I mustn't say those words to you, but that's what he said). Then he said, 'I get your message, but you like it or not, I'm going to marry sweet young Nilofer, your lucky niece. You lie here and burn with jealousy till Judgment Day and may Allah send you to hell!' Then he spat, grabbed the towel he had over his shoulder, slapped the grave stone with it and walked away."

Grandmother didn't laugh this time. She heaved a long sigh.

There was an eerie chill in the air when she finished her story.

"That was funny, wasn't it?" I said, wondering why Grandmother looked sad at the end of the story.

"No, but that's what I thought first. Then something happened." Grandmother looked away when she said that.

"What happened?"

"I heard the grave heave a sigh, a very long, clear, sad sigh."

"Come on, Grandma, you imagined it. Stones don't heave

sighs. Maybe it was the wind. What did the dead woman care whether the bald orangutan married again or not?"

"I don't think she cared that the old *Mapla* was going to marry again. It was the abuse that must have hurt her. No woman, dead or alive, likes to be abused."

She was looking away at nowhere; her faded green eyes looked glazed. Seemed to me there was a ghost of a memory in those eyes.

I didn't dare ask if Grandfather, who died long before I was born, ever abused her and if she still nursed the hurt.

"An eye for an eye will make the whole world blind."

MK Gandhi

A SAM D'CRUZ TERROR STORY

Sam D'Cruz was a friend and neighbor. He lived by, among other things, arranging fake degrees for youngsters who were trying to go abroad for a job. Having been in and out of jail in his youth, he also moonlighted as a police informer. A good man in the eyes of his God, yet to atone for any unintended sin he could be committing during the course of his work and for squealing on his fellow-thugs, D'Cruz sent Rupees five thousand to a Pentecostal church in his home town every month.

The point is: Sam D'Cruz knew which terrorists were building bombs, which ones from the other camp had bought automatic machine guns from weapon smugglers, and how many policemen and officers were involved in each smuggling operation of weapons or drugs. D'Cruz held enough anecdotes in his cerebral kitty that he could have written the script for a never-ending television serial in Hindi or in the local vernacular which produced a lot many action thrillers. Instead, he used the anecdotes to regale us in our private club of Rum-and-cola buddies. Among the many true stories about police cases he told us was this one about a bear masquerading as monkey – or was it a monkey masquerading as bear – I couldn't yet decide while recording this story almost *ad verbatim*.

Mangat Ram Sharma, son of Late Lala Tangat Ram, President of the local PETA – *People for Ethical Treatment of Animals* – went scouting in a reserved forest outside the City of Gandhipur. Before he could pull the trigger of his double-barrel at a spotted cheetal deer, a notorious bear caught him from behind and hugged him to death.

The body bore the tell-tale marks of a bear-attack, so pressure fell on the police to find the bear. The Chief Minister, whose election was financed by the victim of the bear-hug, who was also to finance his next election, called the Home Minister, and the Home Minister roared at the Inspector General, Inspector General at the Deputy Inspector General who in turn warned, cutting proper channel, the local Police Sub-Inspector that if he did not find the bear in the next 24 hours, he would be transferred to some town where there were no bootleggers and whores or, for that matter, elephant-tusk poachers.

The Sub inspector (SI for short), who had wangled the posting to Gandhipur police Station at great personal cost of half a million rupees and lived a happy and prosperous life at the expense of forest poachers who smuggled out rare birds and elephant tusks, was greatly upset. Occasionally when a *Thakur* (of the landlord-caste) beat up an untouchable *Dalit* to death or raped his wife or some similar unremarkable event occurred, Sub Inspector Rattan Lal made a fortune by not recording the complaint from the victims or their relations. So, naturally, he did not want to be posted out at any cost. He ordered his constables to go get the notorious bear – and after an afterthought – *any damned bear*. The thunder in his voice shook the roof of the police station.

The policemen combed through the forest all the way to the international boundary. When they found no bears, they chased monkeys – the larger ones with black fur. Some langurs who bared their teeth at the policemen scratched and bit a few others. They were shot and wounded, but quickly hopped away into hiding. None could be caught.

One of the monkeys, a lion-tailed macaque affectionately known as Kiki in the harem of his father, learnt what the two-legged apes were looking for. He knew the killer bear who once hugged and mauled his mother, so had a raw bone to pick. He made bold to land up at the police station to report that he knew the bear, and where he (the bear) could be found. He was promptly arrested.

"This is the one, for sure," said the *Senior Police Constable*, so ranked for his vast experience.

Can't find the culprit, catch the one on the pulpit was a favorite adage among the police.

"But he is not a bear," moaned the SI, who woefully lacked Senior Police Constable Kuldip Singh's seventeen-year experience in the same rank and the same posting, during which time he had managed to build a mansion in the nearby village and to bag a wine-shop contract for his son in the city. Kuldip Singh made three times the earning of SI Rattan Pal who had to bargain with prostitutes, pimps, dacoits and killer *zamindars*[55] for his monthly receipts. For Kuldip policing was a hobby, for his boss Rattan Pal, it was his main lifeline on which hung all other sources of income.

"Now, now, Sir, we will make him one", said the *SPC* with a suggestive twinkle in his eyes. The SI respected the old bandicoot's thirty-five years of experience, seventeen years as a senior con, in the force.

"Then *do the needful*," ordered the Inspector whose eyes too bore a reflected twinkle.

Every police station keeps a constable with great agility and

---

[55] Prosperous land owners who held court in villages and small towns.

ability to roll live human bodies under his boots, stretching the victim's balls till they looked like ribbons, folding his stronger arm and pounding the victim on his back with the elbow-bone and punching him in the solar-plexus. Such a person in Gandhipur Police Station was Kamlesh Trivedi, a pure Brahmin who always bore, defying police regulation, a blood-red vermilion-dot on his forehead and a thin tuft of long hair at the back of his short-cropped scalp. Trivedi's specialty was driving pins under the victim's nails and rolling a heavy pestle over his body till bones cracked – the last technique he learnt while on a deputation to Kerala Police down South. Nobody believed his boast that he was trained in a distant *Amrikyan* place called *Gantu-namo Bay*.

So, the same Constable was called for doing, as they say in India, the *needful*.

At lights out, Trivedi started working on extracting confession from the monkey, Kiki Macaque, that he was the killer bear. The exercise went on through the night. Nearby houses – Police Stations are housed in rented places in or near housing colonies for citizens' safety – familiar to the screams and wails that rose from the police station every night, closed their shutters, wondering why this time the screams and wails were somewhat shriller than human screams. They didn't dare investigate.

Next morning, the monkey Kiki Macaque and Constable Kamlapati Trivedi emerged from the *pooch-thatch* (interrogation) room – both disheveled, woefully exhausted, and smeared in simian blood.

Any event in the state was invariably a cause for a mob riot. Outside the police station, crowds had assembled wanting to tear apart the killer of Mangat Ram. They shook the barricades planted outside the walls to forestall such a mob attack. Hundreds of hired workers were brought from the city in Corporation buses which stopped outside the gate and disgorged protesters holding up ruling-party flags written with the slogan

Blood for Blood, Life for Life,
We'll Kill the Bear and rape his wife.

The air was celebratory like the occasion of *Durga Pooja* when several colorful idols, some huge and some tiny, of the beautiful and plastic-bejeweled mother goddess astride a ferocious lion were drowned in the local lake. They demanded that the police hand over the killer bear so they could drown him in the same lake or hug him to death the way he dealt with beloved Mangat Ram-*ji*.

When that demand was rejected outright, the leader of the procession looked for any police jeep to burn. None could be found because with wisdom borne out of long experience, the only jeep, three motor cycles and five bicycles had been hidden away the previous night. Exasperated and deeply disappointed, the leader instructed his followers to burn any jeep, car and public bus within a radius of four kilometers.

The drivers of the two buses that brought the rioters to the scene tried to turn around and speed away, but were caught and beaten up. As an afterthought, it was decided to spare them and the buses so the leader and his hirelings could be transported back home later in the evening. Only their windshields were smashed. No fun in demonstration without destruction.

Soon black smoke and flames rose up from several winding and narrow streets, a few explosions of bursting of fuel tanks resounded in the air. One small car, a newly made Maruti-Suzuki, shot up high into air, hovered for a few moments like a flying saucer as the excited town watched. It fell like a crane-load of cement blocks. Men clapped their hands in joy. The leading sloganeer came up with a new verse:

Bear, you will go to hang,
Mangat Ram-ji will live for long.

Kamlesh Trivedi, as soon as he recovered from the exhaustion of rolling, kicking, nail-pulling and punching the monkey all through the night, realized that he needed an urgent bath before his morning worship of Lord Ram followed by a recital of forty odes to placate monkey-god Hanuman. The odes were more important because the monkey whom he rolled and banged and whose nails he pulled out was of the same species as of Hanuman-*ji*. He also had to mend a few scratches and a bite he got from the macaque who was not aware of the law that preventing a policeman from discharging his duty was a serious crime. The crowd outside had thickened; there was no question of his being able to go home for a bath or for the bandages.

The monkey, though of Lord Hanuman's tribe, was in no shape for a bath. He sat licking his own blood and mourning under his breath.

At 9 AM sharp, the Sub-Inspector of Police (SI) Rattan Pal, the highest officer in the vicinity, and the one entrusted with the arduous job, entered from the backdoor to avoid being mauled by the crowd out in the front. Promptly, as if on cue, the telephone rang.

SI Rattan Pal picked up the phone.

"Shamsher here," growled the voice from the other end. "Did the bear confess?"

That was DIG Shamsher Singh IPS[56], Deputy Inspector General of Police.

Rattan Pal suddenly felt piddly, but tightened his belly to avoid an embarrassing overflow. He called out to Trivedi who promptly put his head out through the door of a one-tap bathroom of the

---

[56] *Indian Police Service, the topmost all-India executive cadre*

rented two-bedroom house which housed the police station. A few months before, the owner of the house tried to get the place vacated through judicial channel. His other house, a one-room tenement was promptly found to be hiding two kilograms of Cocaine. Thereafter, the man withdrew his case and gave no further trouble; the policemen stayed put, sleeping on a bed that the poor man had bought with the arrears of his pension, and enjoying a bath in the single bathroom after a strenuous day guarding a politician or rolling an ordinary man.

Rattan Pal turned around and asked aloud: "*Pandit-ji*, did the bear confess?"

Though a lowly constable, Trivedi deserved to be addressed *Pandit-ji* because he was a twice-born Brahmin. Once born from his mother's womb, then born again to a superior status when he was adorned with a looped sacred thread and taught a secret *mantra* of Gayatri and was initiated into the study of *Vedas*. The ceremony assured him a place in heaven and a higher status among ordinary men on earth, especially Shudra-castes who could wear no such thread. Trivedi wore the thread around his torso like a cross-belt that reached out from his left shoulder to his right hip.

Trivedi had just answered the nature's call, so to answer his boss's call, he only showed his hairy torso and head through the gap when he opened the door just a little. He was almost nude, only hiding his bare essentials with a strip of wet loin-cloth which failed to hide his abundant pubic hair. One end of his sacred thread was tucked over his left ear to avoid the other end touching his crotch and thereby losing its sanctity.

"Saa'b, the Sister-fucker keeps lying he is a monkey, that his name is Kiki and that he had only come to report a bear-sighting."

Sensing the inspector's frown in disapproval of his nudity, Trivedi closed the door till only his head was visible. It showed his short antenna of a few strands of knotted hair behind his cropped head. The antenna was meant to speed a Brahmin's communication with gods above when he chanted the sacred *mantras*.

Rattan Pal ignored the fact that Constable Trivedi did not wish him *Jai-Ramji ki* (Victory to Ram) which also reminded him that he hadn't wished the DIG either. Too late now; but he hoped that Shamsher Singh did not notice the lapse.

"Could you not make the sister-fucker confess that he is a bear?" He screamed into Trivedi's face that stood out between the door and its frame as if it was a decapitated head.

"*Saa'bji,* I swear on Lord Ram, I broke every bone in his body. He is out there in the *pooch-thatch* room, his bones jutting out, his body bleeding all over, his balls flattened into a plastic footrule. Yet the mother-fucker lies that he is a monkey – some kind of a Maa-kak."

Every police station, however small, had a torture room, named the *pooch-thatch* (interrogation) room with its stock of coarse leather belts, knuckle dusters, pestles, nails, pliers, hammers, pounders, the works except a wooden cross and a quartering wheel whose secret mechanism the old British masters never revealed to their Indian subjects. When not in use, those valuable tools were hidden away in a secret corner of the *pooch-thatch* room.

Deputy Inspector General of Police Shamsher Singh had overheard the entire conversation. Sweat glistened on his forehead, the incompetence of his abject subordinates induced an urgent need to rush to toilet. But this was not the time for such niceties. He knew that the Home Minister was listening in on the other line; there will soon be calls from the Chief Minister himself. Killing of the President of PETA, out on a secret hunting trip, was no simple rape-and-murder case that could gather dust among a mountain of files cast away on rusting slotted-angle shelves. Mangat Ram was the highest contributor to the ruling party during elections.

All that he ever wanted in return was the continued presidentship of the state's branch of the PETA (which gave him a free run on the forests), weekly full-page government advertisements to his daily *Din-Rat Samachar* (Day-night News), chairmanship of the state board of cricket with a chance to go to the Board of Cricket Control India and thence to the International Cricket Council and a seat in the State planning commission. Known as a truly great soul and benefactor of the poor. Mangat Ram's wife had threatened, amidst long wails, that she would expose the government and its misdeeds if her husband's killer was not caught and hanged in the next seven days.

To make matters even worse, there was an article in the opposition's mouthpiece newspaper implying that Mangat Ram was eyeing the Chief Minister's chair and that the government had deliberately released a man-eating bear during Mangat Ram's inspection visit for ensuring the preservation of rare birds in the forest. It was due to Mangat Ram-*ji*'s strenuous efforts and frequent visits, said the op-ed, that cheetals were no longer endangered, that elephants held on to their tusks, the Adjutant Stork (sacred *Garuda*) and Brahmin Shelduck were being sighted again. Though nobody had ever heard of a man-eating bear, the article created a storm among conspiracy theorists and opinionated busy-body circles that circulated in way-side tea shops. The CM had every reason to worry, and hence to be furious. Those tea-shop gossips held the key to electoral victory.

"Sir," pleaded SI Rattan Pal to the DIG. "The Pandit I got here for the job, pardon me, is a *chuthiya*; the killer has not confessed, but is now nearly dead."

Chuthiya had a sexual connotation, but normally was included among the relatively decent profanities. It was taken to mean imbecile, ignoring the first syllable, which meant female genital.

It was not too bad a word that you could not use while speaking to such a big superior

Shamsher Singh grunted a grunt that oozed sarcasm. Unmindful, Rattan Pal continued:

"There is a huge crowd outside roaring for the blood of police more than that of the monkey – I mean bear. There is no water in the fire hydrant or else we could drench the mob to cool tempers. All the tear gas we had was used up on the *Eid* procession that threw stones at a way-side Ganpati temple and the Ganpati threw back soda bottles. The affair ended in the death of three Mussalmans and two Hindus. If we don't make the monkey – I mean bear – confess and he is taken to court, there will be a repetition of the killings – this time between Thakurs and *Dalits*. You need to send the reserve police, five tankers of water and lots of tear gas. Or the police station will burn down and we will die inside. By the way, Sir, why not we throw the bear at the mob and let them tear it apart?"

"Idiot," roared the DIG. "Won't they all realize that what you caught is not a bear? They will tear you apart instead, not the monkey, not the *dalits*."

Dalits was a recently introduced dignified name for the traditionally undignified low castes, the same way as black people became African-Americans in the US.

Rattan Pal's mouth gaped open in the sudden realization. He ordered a constable to drag the monkey deeper inside the secret room, and keep him in the shade, far away from any prying public eyes. Howls of agony rose from inside the *interrogation* room as the monkey was dragged.

"You people are bloody useless brothers-in-law," said Shamsher Singh.

Rattan Pal was shocked and felt deeply humiliated. The word *Sala*, meaning brother-in-law, was an expletive worse than being called sister-fucker. *Sala* is the brother of one's wife; hence the word implied "I will screw your sister."

"Who is the *chuthiya* hitman of yours?" Asked DIG Shamsher Singh

SI Rattan Pal, still nursing the hurt of being called *Sala*, said: "Trivedi, Sir. Constable Trivedi."

"A fucking Pandit for a hitman in a police station! Oh God, next there will be a Brahmin hangman, and I won't be surprised. This *Sala* Pandit could be a Chaturvedi for all I care. Totally useless. Bloody *chuthiya*. Can't get a confession out of a monkey even."

The name Trivedi meant a Brahmin *Pandit* who mastered three Vedas, Chaturvedi was one up, for he was supposed to know four Vedas. Shamsher Singh, being a high-caste Hindu, knew the caste hierarchy in the religion. Perhaps it was dinned in at his IPS training.

Shamsher Singh was painfully aware that the Home minister was still holding on to the other line, and listening in. He could hear the hard breathing. He paused to raise expectations on the part of the Home Minister. Then, after the pregnant pause, he exploded:

"You guys are useless. Buck-wash. I'll use my *Ram Bann* and get the monkey – I mean bear – to confess!"

He ground his teeth, hoping that the Home Minister will not notice his slip-up in mentioning monkey – the word was by now a state secret.

Ram-Bann was an arrow with which Lord Ram, the incarnation of Supreme God Vishnu, killed 14,000 forest dwellers in one night to please sages who wanted a free run on sacrificing wild deer to please Indra the god who wielded lightning for his weapon, the wind god, fire god, twin gods and several other gods. As on earth, mass killing raised much excitement in the heavens.

Gods were praised for their weaponry and tagged with the names of their victims – male, female or animal. Since the killing of 14,000 with a single arrow, *Ram-Bann*, Ram's arrow, was used to mean something deadly and beyond compare.

SI Rattan Pal waited. He felt a snigger coming up from his throat, but didn't dare jump the gun and challenge what the DIG's *Ram-Bann* was.

"I'm right now asking the DSP of Bhagwanpur to send Saligram Mandal to your police station. He will teach the monkey to confess and not flinch about admitting that he's the killer bear."

SI Rattan Pal Khatri felt knocked out. He had heard of Senior Police Constable Saligram Mandal. Who hadn't? The most notorious – or famous depending on who was asking – among the policemen of District Bhagwanpur, if not of the entire State.

He could not help thinking of the public ridicule that would bring him and how other inspectors in the Police Club would needle him for his surrender to the SI Raghunath of Bhagwanpur, a mere *Kurmi*, way below his own Kshatriya caste – the warrior class from Mahabharat times. They would laugh in his high-caste face that the hitman trained by him couldn't get a confession from a mere monkey, something that a low-caste Kurmi could.

Till a couple of years ago, it was well-known, that the district of Bhagwanpur and its surroundings were in the grip of a horde of criminal gangs. Nearly every train that passed by was stopped and looted, bus passengers were unloaded, their baggage snatched, those who resisted were stabbed or shot with country-made pistols. They pulled aside better-looking girls as if they knew the law of Moses[57], and gang-raped them in public view. When trains and

---

[57] Law of Moses : *".So now, kill all the boys, as well as every woman who has had relations with a man, but spare for yourselves every girl who has never had relations with a man." Numbers 31:17-18 Berean Study Bible.*

buses refused to run in protest, they attacked houses; beat up the men and took away the younger women.

The bigger fish among the thugs were difficult to net, and those who were caught were soon released by orders from the politicians in power. So, most of those who were caught were *Bangotras* – a nomadic tribe with no land, no money and no job, declared a criminal tribe by the British a hundred years before and prevailing as such in police records.

The general consensus in the police department was that the law was an ass and the judges could not be trusted. If a few – guilty or not – were shot or seriously wounded, then the others would be too frightened to go in to loot and rape. The best technique in that line was called *encounter*. Catch a few crooks – some of them hard nuts, others expendable *Dalits*[58] – and shoot them dead. While at it, a marksman would shoot and scrape the skin off one of the junior policemen among them to prove that the dead had shot the first rounds when they were encountered; the police acted in self-defense. The constable thus injured got an award and a small cash prize for his bravery half of which he was made to share with the guy who shot him for taking care not to kill him.

A list of the known, suspected and unknown criminals was soon drawn up. Names of Thakurs, members of the *Zamindar Sena* (army of landlords) and pick of hired killers in the employ of political bigwigs were struck off by the Superintendent before it was sent to the Inspector General for scrutiny and then to the Home Minister for final approval.

It was not the protests by the press or criticism of a few

---

[58] Humans derided and discarded from the mainstream community as low-caste, generally engaged in sweaty jobs such as shoe-making, pottery or scavenging, presumed to pollute a higher caste by mere touch, hence also described as *achhyut* or untouchables.

self-styled do-gooders that put an end to *encounter* killing. Government decided that expenditure on the police department was shooting through the roof. There was the perpetual cry for better salaries; senior officers kept asking for beefing up the manpower to justify their promotions. An even greater matter of concern was the mounting cost of bullets.

"No more encounter except under direct orders from the CM," was an order circulated secretly among the higher-ups. The worker-class ranks up to Head Constables couldn't understand why they were being given fewer live targets ticked off as Maoists for target practice; those in the inspector ranks had an inkling, those above Superintendent-level privately cursed the legislators who had money for raising their own salaries and pension, but none for bullets, and none at all for giving the police officers a raise.

In the meanwhile, the rise in crime rate overshot the inflation rate. Every police station in the state was given a free hand to find their own solutions to stem the rate in their area, but without encounter-killing.

Sub Inspector Raghunath Kumar Kurmi of Bhagwanpur police station hit upon the technique of meting out exemplary punishment without encounter. With his invention he hoped to earn a hurried promotion to Assistant Police Inspector and a President's Police Medal.

Once the inspiration struck him, he used his constables to collect empty eye-drop vials from the government hospital. Not even the doctors dared ask why so many empty vials from the hospital's garbage dump were being picked up by uniformed policemen. Another couple of constables were sent to secure for free a few bottles of Sulphuric acid from the automobile shop nearby, which they did by twirling their mustaches and pretending to look for criminals hiding inside their shop.

When the accessories were collected, SI Kurmi explained the plan of action which impressed most of all ranks below him. The head constable said the plan was even better than any encounter-killing he had witnessed. Only one young man, Constable Madhusudan Jha, a rookie just out of police training school where they taught great principles of policing and psychological techniques of investigation said it was a terrible idea. He felt a nausea coming up. His name meant Madhu-killer, Lord Vishnu the greatest killer of them all, but the namesake proved to be too soft a sissy, a spineless *hijra* (eunuch). Madhu-killer's revulsion towards the great plan enraged Kurmi; he was told to go home and look after his ailing mother and get back only after she was completely cured. Shocked to hear that his mother was ill, and intrigued that his relations sent the message of her illness to the inspector and not to himself, which was cause for concern, Madhu-killer rushed to catch a bus to his distant village.

It was Saligram Mandal, then a low-level Constable who suggested bicycle spokes. A number of spokes was cannibalized from the confiscated bicycles disintegrating in the station's junkyard. To the surprise of other constables, Saligram, who became the *de facto* leader of the operation despite his humble rank, chose only rusted spokes along with their fat metal caps.

The empty eye-drop vials were filled with battery-grade Sulphuric acid. When an ageing constable's hand shook while filling the vials and acid spilled burning the knots of his knurled fingers, someone suggested the use of a rubber glove, which was promptly and forcefully procured from an electrician's workshop. SI Kurmi suggested sharpening both ends of the spokes. Saligram said that wasn't necessary, that the metal caps of the spokes created more space for easy flow

"You are not going to take them for a walk in the park," said Saligram. Kurmi conceded the point.

SI Kurmi, being tenth-class pass and BA-fail, technically inclined, suggested that they first try the technique on an easy target – a human prototype. Prisoner No. 17, Daulatram, whose name meant Rich-God, forty-seven years of age in the books, but already bent down, of unsteady gait on spindly legs, not much matter between his ears under a scalp topped with white dandelion-hair, and did not know what he was in prison for, was chosen for the prototype.

"Daulat, do you know why you get caught so often?" asked SI Kurmi.

"*Kismet*," said the Rich-God. Bad luck. "I haven't hurt an ant."

"That's the problem. Your eye-sight is bad, very bad. We will repair your eyes with *Ganga-jal*, the sacred water of Ganges."

Since then battery-grade Sulphuric acid came to be known as *Ganga-jal*, water of the sacred river Ganges or *Ma-Ganga*

Old Rich-God suspected something was up, but to avoid a pounding with elbows on his painful back, he obediently lay down on the bare *charpoy* of bamboo frame and bamboo legs, woven with rough coir strings for bed. For reasons Rich-God couldn't quite fathom, four policemen pinned him down hard on the coir strings. Saligram was quick; wearing the rubber glove on his working right hand, he drove the bicycle spoke hard and straight into the pupil of Rich-God's right eye, gouging the cornea, shattering the lens inside. Even before the horror and the pain shot through the victim's wearied nerves, Saligram pulled out the spoke, whose blunt capped end came off with some jelly-like stuff and blood. It happened with clinical precision, just like so many millennia ago, 12-year old Lord Ram's arrow removed the nose and a breast of a woman named Tadaka. But for the blood and the sticking jelly that marred the beauty of the perfect hole, Saligram had made a precise opening. Rich-God howled like a pig in a village slaughter house; his back arched upward;

his legs flayed, his manacled arms stiffened. SI Kurmi passed a vial of battery acid which Saligram squeezed into the hole he made. Rich-God tried hard to flay his legs while howling like the proverbial pig in the butcher shop.

Without further delay, Saligram went for the left eye while the policemen pressed Rich-God harder to keep him immobile. After a shill cry, Rich-God fainted. He fell through the broken coir strings on the floor and emptied an incredible volume of urine around himself.

Operation successful, Saligram, now in virtual command, called for the next patient. SI Kurmi felt irritated by the air of authority that the mere Constable had begun to assume, but couldn't help admiring the surgical precision of the man. So, he personally called for Prisoner No. 1 whom he called patient No. 2. Since the coir strings were in tatters, and for hygienic reasons, it was decided that the next Operation *Ganga-jal* will be done on another part of the floor.

By eight-o'-clock in the evening, eight patients were operated with the capped ends of the rusted bicycle spokes. While those who underwent the surgery squirmed, rolled in their urine (three on their poop) on the floor and howled in pain through the night, new ones were picked out early next morning. Several concerned citizens – among them community leaders, teachers and students who skipped their classes – dropped in to see what the *tamasha* – performance – was all about.

SI Kurmi stood on the edge of the veranda and addressed the crowd. He had learnt the format and technique of public speaking from the many ministers behind whom he had stood as bodyguard when they addressed similar restless crowds.

"Brothers and sisters," he began although there were no women present in the crowd yet.

"We, who worship *Bharat-Mata* (Mother India) and the

Father of the Nation, have been silently suffering when thugs and crooks, *Bangotras* and other mother-fucking low-castes have been committing dacoity in our houses, in buses and trains and dishonouring our mothers and sisters. You had been blaming us humble *kotwals*[59], doing our duty and trying to stem the crimes peacefully with only *lathis* (batons) for our weapon. The bandits are better equipped, they have the latest guns. Dacoity, thuggery and rape are rising day by day. This should no longer be allowed to go on."

He paused to catch his breath and to let the applause die down. Then he raised his voice and dropped the bombshell:

Law is blind, so the criminals would have to be blinded.

The applause this time was deafening. Some shouted *Bharat-Mata Ki jai*! (victory to Mother India). Though Mother India was not at war, the rest of the audience echoed the slogan with much gusto. Such shouting was mandatory; a modern-day sage had warned the world that he would behead any Indian who refused to shout Victory to Mother India whether or not the Mother was at war.

One young man who wore jeans and T-shirt and held a roll of newspaper in his hand asked:

"How do you know all those blinded are really criminals? Are they sentenced by a court to be blinded?"

A fat man in translucent *dhoti* and Gandhi-cap on his head tapped the nape of the young man's head.

"*Abe, goray*, do you think the police are all *chuthiyas*? Are you teaching them the law?"

Gora meant white man, a pretender to civilization and hence the word served as an insult to any self-respecting brown man.

The young man, finding no support, pursed his lips and walked away.

---

[59] Hindi for policemen. Probably originated from Constables in English.

"*Gandu*," (Assole), spat the fat man in Gandhi-cap.

Eleven *patients* - four sentenced criminals and seven under-trials - were blinded that day. Mandal had picked up speed.

Eighteen, and counting.

The young man who asked the impertinent question and was dismissed as an *assole* determinedly cycled to the police superintendent's office twelve kilometres away and reported what he believed to be a terrible atrocity against human rights going on in Bhagwanpur police station. He offered to give a complaint in writing. The Head Constable at the desk asked if he was the brother-in-law, son-in-law or father-in-law of any of those who were being given the acid treatment. When he answered no, he was locked up for the day for creating public nuisance.

On the third day, many more convicts and undertrials for *Ganga-water* surgery were brought in from other police stations in prison buses protected with steel grilles. They were warmly received by SI Kurmi and his platoon of constables with Saligram Mandal in the lead. The constables graciously helped the older convicts get down from the high floor-board of the bus.

While Saligram was spoking the cornea of the nineteenth patient from among the visitors, a free-lancer came with his box camera and requested permission to take a photograph of *Operation Ganges Water.*

"Gladly," said the Sub Inspector. Excited at the prospect of being photographed like a minister and appearing in print, yet dutifully focused on his job, Constable Saligram tilted his torso at an angle so the photographer could get a good shot of the spoke going in directly into the cornea of Kittu Chamar, a railway pickpocket from next town whose caste was that of a lowly shoe-maker who should have stuck to his low-paying ancestral skill. Four constables strenuously pinned the man down on the floor with one hand each, brushed their hair with their fingers of the other hand and adjusted their collars, hoping that the camera would catch their determined faces. Sub-Inspector Kurmi stood behind them, smiling broadly and raising the victory-sign with two fingers. Sunlight streaming in through the bare window gave a good view for the camera. Four photos were taken from slightly different angles while Saligram kept the spoke poised in Kittu-Shoemaker's eye.

"Write in your papers how hard is our work to correct these terrible criminals." Said SI Kurmi. The free-lancer nodded. Saligram thrust the spoke into the eye of Kittu Chamar, who till then had fancied that he was lucky that he got a short acting role in a Hindi *fillum*.

Satisfied with his catch, the free-lancer scooted away without thanking the police for their strenuous effort at eliminating crime. He quickly got several prints of the photos and sent a set each to *Hindu Times, Bharat Samachar, Din-Rat Samachar* (owned by Mangat Ram, then very much alive) and airmailed one to the bureau chief of BBC in Delhi.

On that day ten more men were blinded. Once Mandal's hand slipped while pouring the acid, which flowed down the victim's face producing a soft but irritating hiss and a string of burnt bubbles down to his chin.

Next morning the news of Bhagwanpur blinding with the action photograph were splashed on all the newspapers – Hindi, English and even far-away Tamil. Opposition stomped into the well of the legislative house demanding an explanation for what they called the inhuman police brutality. The Chief Minister and the Home Minister sat beaming, knowing that the opposition was simply playing to the gallery, that they were just as pleased with the Ganges-water operation as were they.

When the speaker hammered his desk till it cracked, and the

opposition stalwarts' windpipes seemed to have lost all gas, the Home Minister got up to speak.

"Brothers," he began, ignoring the speaker whom alone he should have addressed as per protocol and disregarding the three lady-members who were present and busy knitting sweaters for their husbands, "We know what is the crime rate of Bhagwanpur district and its surroundings – a legacy from the time when opposition were in these chairs."

Members of the ruling party thumped their desks and shouted "shame, shame." Opposition stood up as if to boycott the proceedings, but sat down on cue from their leader.

"None of us is safe; not even my brothers from the opposition who fed the thugs milk and bread. (Shame, shame!). Our mothers and sisters live in perpetual fear of losing their most precious property – their *ijjat*, their honour. A woman who was raped and thus lost her precious property of *ijjat* is like a dead corpse, *zinda lash*, and like a widow, fit only to be thrown out of the society and to beg in the streets. Do we want that happen to our mothers and sisters, daughters and nieces? The railway minister in Delhi has threatened to stop all train services through our lines. The courts take twenty years and award a lame sentence after the witnesses are dead and the criminal is still at large. So, I say that operation Ganges-water should go on. If you feel that the Bhagwanpur operation is wrong, I am willing to resign."

"Then resign!" shouted the opposition leader, hoping for a reshuffle in the cabinet when he could switch parties and bargain for the seat of Home Minister.

"No, no, we are not saying it is wrong. We should blind every criminal and would-be criminal in the district till the place is safe and trains can run. Only the other day I missed a lavish wedding in Calcutta because the trains were not running. I suggest the speaker announce an adjournment so the members can witness the brave police officers in action," said the opposition leader's deputy who too had an eye on the job.

The BBC report on television the very next day was a scathing attack on the police brutality which, the report said, was common in India. Since there were only a few black-and-white televisions in the state, all of them in the houses of the rich and infamous, BBC reporter's remarks made little impact. While the *Madrasis*[60] down South expressed horror and newspapers in general wrote blood-curdling stories, they softened the effect with an equally ruthless description of the rampant crimes in the state.

In all 42 men and two women – both prostitutes who refused free service and monthly payment to the constables on regular duty in Friday Street – were blinded. Old Daulatram Rich-God, mourning and whimpering through four days on his prison floor, thankfully died and was secretly buried. When the atmosphere within the assembly and outside got overheated with the description of the brutality, SI Kurmi, Senior Police Constable Kuldip Singh (who was on leave through the four days when the operations took place) and seven constables including Constable Madhusudan Jha (Madhu-killer, remember, who was on forced compassionate leave) who had returned with the good news that his mother was hale and hearty, were suspended. The home minister promised a departmental enquiry into the circumstances of the blindings and the consequences thereof and benefits if any.

Two months later, the Deputy Superintendent who had been appointed as one-man commission of enquiry filed a report that Operation *Ganges-water*, though technically wrong, was enormously successful, that crime rate in the vicinity had come down by 55% in the district and its surroundings. In accordance with the recommendation, Constable Saligram Mandal was

---

[60] A generic term for all South Indians since geographic knowledge in the North did not extend beyond the old city of Madras.

promoted out of turn (since he had only 17 years of service in the rank of Constable) and made a Senior Police Constable. SI Raghunath Kumar Kurmi was promoted to the next rank of Assistant Inspector of Police. Other *sepoys* were simply re-instated with good remarks in their records. Constable Madhusudan Jha alone forfeited seven days' salary and received a written warning for being absent without leave for those many days.

Since then, Senior Police Constable Saligram Mandal was known as *Havildar Ram-Bann Sahib*. Saligram relished the new name with its holy connotation and the *Sahib* honorific which till 1947 was reserved for the British. He was seen marching about with a couple of bicycle spokes and a bag of acid vials in his hand even on holidays. A local saffron-clad sage proclaimed that Saligram, just as his name suggested, was an *avatar* – incarnation – of the Supreme God Vishnu himself. While fellow-Kotwals ridiculed the suggestion out of envy, small-time pickpockets touched Saligram's feet and sought his blessings before going on their rounds. His name sufficed to make confirmed criminals as well as new undertrials confess and sign or place their thumb-prints on whatever papers that were shown to them. Rarely did someone in Bhagwanpur dare spread a rumour that crime rate was the same as it ever was.

So, it was that, two years and six months later, DIG Shamsher Singh got the heaven-sent inspiration to fetch Senior Police Constable Saligram Mandal, aka *Ram-Bann Sahib*, to extract a confession from the bear masquerading as a lion-tailed macaque. Ever on the attention to take such an order, Saligram picked up a scabbard full of bicycle spokes with their metal caps, a pouch with half a dozen vials of battery-grade Sulphuric acid and a single rubber glove. He set off by rail without the need for a ticket on account of his reputation to Gandhipur Rail Station and from there took a ticketless bus ride to Gandhipur Police Station where the assassin of Mangat Ram was held.

He was received with cheers and *Jai Ramji Ram-Bann ji* calls to which SC Saligram Mandal responded with a political-style wave that half looked like a blessing. The public, this time at least half of them women, who surrounded the police station to get a *darshan* (vision) of the *avatar*, exulted and screamed

> *Ram-Bann-ji Ki jai,*
> *Bharat Mata Ki Jai.*
> (Victory to Ram-Bann, Victory to Mother India.)

Sub Inspector Rattan Pal resisted the temptation to join the crowd of lesser policemen who had collected on the veranda to greet the hero. He stayed put in his office chair. However, since his very professional future depended on the visiting Ram-Bann, he received Saligram's salute by standing up, putting on his cap and returning the compliment as smartly as taught in the training centre and never practised ever since.

"You can save our pride only," Rattan Pal said in bad grammar that was common in the local dialect.

"Oh, no, Sir, this is my duty only, humbly reporting to you only," answered Saligram with feigned modesty, and in matching bad grammar.

Kiki Macaque the monkey was no Alpha-male in his gang, but was tolerated, even treated affectionately by the leader. The chief, who was also his father, was particularly grateful that although Kiki had grown to full adulthood, he did not try to wage war and snatch away his harem. When Kiki suggested that he would go to the den of the two-legged, hairless apes, and report bear-sighting, the chief jumped up and down, banged the ground and howled like a baby macaque.

"Don't go, son, please stay. Those two-legged beasts have

fire-spitting tree-trunks and metal sticks. I heard from my cousin in Rani hills that they now have a new terrible weapon called *ganga-jal*."

Those prophetic words had trailed off behind him as Kiki Macaque hopped away, hoping to get a reward for reporting the sighting of the bear who had attacked his mother, mauled and nearly killed her.

"I'm going to be a police informer, not a banana-thief. Why would they spit fire from their tree-trunk on me," he had shouted back.

As the old ape's voice had trailed off, for some reason, the thought of *ganga-jal* gave Kiki a mild shudder. Not long ago, an aunt in his father's harem had gone to steal sweet *jalebis* – sugar-coated spiral rolls - from the forest ranger's plentiful table. Since snatch-scratch-and run was her regular routine, this time the ranger's maid was hiding in wait for her. The moment the aunt put in her face through the window, the two-legged beast threw a water-like thing on her.

"I threw *ganga-jal*, threw *ganga-jal* on the monkey," cried the maid, clapping her hands in glee. Whatever that meant, Kiki's aunt ran back howling, and fell down before she reached the home-tree. Father Macaque came down to pick his favourite wife and was horrified, the skin of an entire side of her face had peeled off; one eye had fallen off its socket and dangled. It was still sizzling and smoking.

"The two-legged beast put *ganga-jal* on me," were her last words.

Thus, Kiki-macaque knew what exactly *ganga-jal* or Ganges-water was, he had dreamed of his aunt's face several times and woken up in terror. Once the nightmare had almost made him fall from the top branch of a tree which was his favourite sleeping place.

Unable to straighten his excruciating back, Kiki-macaque dragged himself over his own congealed blood to get to the door for a clue what they could be planning for him next and what all the furore outside meant.

"No reason to worry, *Saa'b*. I've brought the tool that will get you a promotion. Even his grandfather would confess he's the killer bear. I have brought the *ganga-jal*."

A shock flashed through Kiki Macaque's broken spine. He made up his mind then and there. The pain all over the body, flattened testicles and broken bones were one thing. He did not want to die the way his father's beloved seventh wife died.

As soon as Saligram sauntered in with his confessional tools, the monkey raised a broken hand with some effort.

"I confess I'm the killer bear," he squealed.

Saligram stood stunned. Rattan Pal's eyes nearly popped out. He rushed in to the interrogation room and nearly slipped on congealed blood.

"What did you say?"

"Bring your papers. I will put my thumb-print on it. I am the bear. I do not want *ganga-jal*."

Senior Police Constable Saligram was a wee-bit disappointed. It had been more than a year since he used the spokes and the acid. He was looking forward to refreshing his skill.

Kiki Macaque the monkey, his black fur and white mane sticking to his body with congealed blood, put his thumb impression on a confessional sheet of paper in the blood that flowed from under his pin-holed nails. He offered to scrawl a signature as well, but a monkey's – he meant bear's – signature will become suspect in the Court, advised SPC Kuldip Singh. Since everyone agreed with that wise line of argument, Kiki's signature was not sought.

Town butcher Muhammad Kasab was brought in to cut off

the monkey's tail which he did with a single practiced stroke. Bleeding was arrested and the wound was bandaged by a quack who was promised safe passage to carry on with his quackery. Since a barber could not be found, Kiki's lovely white mane was cut short to fur-length and Painted black by Kamlesh Trivedi, the Brahmin who was sulking for being ignored and not trained on the *Ganga-jal* operation.

"Not a Pandit's job, I'm not a low-caste barber" he murmured while snipping away the plentiful white mane. By ten at night, Kiki Macaque minus his white mane and long proud tail was ready to be taken to a magistrate. The police doctor certified on the prescribed form that he personally examined the bear accused of killing Mr. Mangat Ram and that he found no marks of injury or signs of torture on the body of the aforementioned accused.

Since Courts do not trust a confession obtained by police interrogation, and since the courts had retired for the night, Kiki was wrapped in a gunny bag and taken to a magistrate in his house. The magistrate hid his glass of cheap flavored rum labelled Royal Whisky on the floor behind his arm-chair, and assumed the best official posture he could muster under the circumstances.

He produced an old worn-out copy of the Bhagavad Gita and asked Kiki to put his right hand on it.

"Do you, in the name of God, swear that you are a bear?" he asked.

The monkey howled a grunt when the Constable guarding him pinched a sore spot on his bottom, close to where his tail used to be.

"Good. Did you hug Mr. Mangat Ram Sharma, Son of Tangat Ram, the President of PETA and great benefactor of the poor and the needy?"

Ouch. Grunt.

"Did you leave him in the forest trail to die after the cold-blooded murder?"

Ouch. Grunt.

"Isn't it true that you were captured by the brave policemen against claw-and-nail resistance on your part, and that you had not surrendered nor gone by yourself to report to the Police?"

Ouch. Grunt. Ouch. Grunt.

The magistrate ensured that the monkey's hand was held by the *Senior Police Constable* and made to press his thumb on the confession sheet. The blood from his fingers and nails had been wiped clean earlier, so an ink pad with the regulation magenta ink was produced. The magistrate signed with a flourish that the confession was made by the accused of his own free will, and that neither physical force nor mental duress was applied to extract a confession. The medical certificate was attached to the magisterial report.

Seventeen witnesses were produced in the criminal court against the monkey who had by then begun to believe that he was a bear. They swore that they were present when the bear – yes, Your Honour, the same bear that they earlier identified in court – had hugged to death Mangat Ram Sharma, benefactor of the poor and needy and lover of animals. Prosecution did not ask the witnesses why they did not intervene. The court-appointed Defense, whom the monkey did not pay a Rupee yet and it didn't look like he would pay any, did not ask any question nor raised any objection. Since the custom demanded that Defence lawyers be beaten up by the mob waiting outside the court, the judge kindly permitted him to hide in the judges' toilet till 5 PM which was courts' dismissal time.

One of the witnesses, whom the judge recognized as one holding a frequent-witness card, testified that he had personally been attacked by the same bear a few months earlier. He showed the Court a deep scar on his exposed chest to prove the point. The judge vaguely remembered that the same witness had produced the same scar in another murder case a month or so before. In that case the accused was awarded death sentence on the strength of that scar.

One needed to go by the evidence and the Penal code, not moral code, the judge wrote while sentencing the convict to death. This is a rarest-of-the-rare case, stated the judicial order, since the bear not only committed the crime, but masqueraded as a monkey and tried his best to destroy evidence. With the possibility that he could be in line for elevation to the higher Court in mind, the judge emphasized the *rarest-of-the-rare* phrase in the sentence, which he knew was a favorite phrase with Their Lordships of the Supreme Court.

Newspapers screamed foul. One produced an old photograph with a caption, "Are you blind? How can this puny monkey who is not a bear, hug the massive Mr. Sharma to death? Do bears have trimmed and dyed mane and cut-off tail?"

Three days later, the journalist who made that report was found hanging from an iron beam on the ceiling of the only public toilet in town. A poet who wrote a soliloquy in verse on the plight of the poor and the helpless in Mother India was shot on the footsteps of his house when he came out in his pajamas to pick up the morning newspaper. The Deputy chief minister told the press that shooting the poet was certainly against the law, but all those who lacked patriotism deserved to be eliminated. The shooter was never found.

The editor of a weekly news magazine who published an article written all by himself from pirated data and photographs, but gave the names of his three data-entry operators as those who did the research, was arrested on a money-laundering case. A young woman who was named by the editor as one of the three researchers was raped in an auto-rickshaw by seven men, six of whom had earlier appeared in the witness box for the prosecution.

The Supreme Court on appeal conceded that a bear with a series of criminal records hugging a man to death was rare, that his masquerading as a lion-tailed monkey and fooling the long arms of the law and the court was even rarer. Hence the appeal was dismissed.

The Prime Minister in a nationally televised speech roared: "Let all those bears masquerading as monkeys beware. We know what you are up to. We can deal with you. For every citizen you hug to death, we will hug ten".

A canned applause rang through televisions which were on display for crowds outside restaurants and dealer shops. The screen showed a few faces showing victory signs to the television camera when they were given a sign from behind the camera.

The President, as was the custom, returned for re-consideration the cabinet's recommendation to reject the killer's mercy petition. When it came back with a request to advance the hanging date ahead of 479 other convicts on the death row, many of the waiting to be done with it for twenty years, His Excellency the President acquiesced. At the age of 87, and two more years to go for an honorable retirement with a banquet and eulogies from the Prime Minister and the press, the President did not want to rock his rickety boat.

That night the convict on death row No. 480 was given a plate of peas, a cob of corn and a cup of honey which was the regulation last meal for a convicted bear, which he did not touch, wishing he had a last meal of bananas instead. At 4:30 AM next morning he was woken, shackled, and taken to the backyard of the prison and made to stand on a wooden platform. Chief Magistrate Kushwaha asked him if he had any last words or a message for the members of his family. The convict bared his teeth though in obvious pain.

When they put the noose round his neck, it was noticed he was far too short when standing on his hind legs; he stayed suspended even before the plank was withdrawn. DIG Shamsher Singh, recently promoted to IG for his commendable services, directed Head Constable (recently promoted from Senior Constable) Kamlesh Trivedi to quickly fetch a few planks of wood or a few bricks. Trivedi couldn't find planks or bricks, so he brought four leather-bound gold-printed books from the Jail library: **Constitution of India**, **We The People** by Nani Palkhiwala, **My Experiments with Truth** with its author's name and photograph defaced, and **Animal Farm** by George Orwell.

When the books were piled on each other with **My Experiments with Truth** right at the top, the convict's paws stood firmly on it.

The hangman, who got paid Rupees 55 for each time he put the noose around a convict's neck and pulled a plank from beneath, had not been paid for the last hanging 15 years ago, grumbled that his was the only job that never got a raise during the last 125 years; that 55 rupees in *Angrez*[61] time was a fortune but less than a pittance now, and that he was only doing his ancestral duty out of patriotism. He closed his eyes, said a short prayer to his goddess, and kicked the books. The convict, still a monkey with his tail hacked off and mane cropped and painted black, shot a stream of urine that missed Magistrate Kushwaha's face. A gust of wind exploded from his behind, his legs shook for a few seconds, his head tilted and was still.

"I know the bear, and I knew the monkey", concluded Mr. Sam D'Cruz.

---

[61] English

"I believe that the depths of his sacrifice, the strength that he fearlessly revealed in the way that he lived, was not only for his political ethos. His was a way of living for the freedom of others."

- Nadine Gordimer, (Late) South African Nobel Laureate,

THE TRAGIC END OF A LOVE AFFAIR

At 6.30 in the morning, the Writer tapped her husband's shoulder and placed a cup of tea on the bedside table.

He opened his eyes, held a sleeved arm against his mouth and yawned. He nodded gratitude for the gesture, picked up the cup and took a sip.

"Up so early? What, are you on a new piece or something?

He was an art collector. Each story she wrote was for him a *piece*.

"No," she said. "We're having a visitor. The Great Man called last night. He is coming for breakfast".

"Great Man?" He paused for just one moment, stretched and nodded when realization dawned. He put aside the sheets and hopped up with the energy of one thirty years younger.

"But how? I thought he would be too busy for the next few months, if not years. And to think that he is coming, not asking you to go see him".

"He also wants to see you. He made sure that you would be around. He said that he had something important to tell us, and only us. Remember? You used to be his best friend before they took him away. I'm only a pen-pusher who sometimes writes about him and his cause – our cause."

"Maybe he liked your last story."

He began unbuttoning his nightshirt, "I thought I would skip a shave today, holiday and all. Now no choice."

"No need to rush", she called back after him as he was shutting the bathroom door. "He is a brunch man. Won't be here before 11.30".

His favourite chair in the hall had worn and had been removed to the attic. The husband found it in a heap of dust, ran a rag over it and brought it down. She got Thelma, more a friend than a servant, to dust and polish it till the grains on the wood showed. Thelma found a cushion and placed it hiding the torn back-upholstery.

The husband's chair was placed nearer to the visitor's chair; her's opposite, enough place between them for him to stretch out, and for her to place one leg over the other. He loved closeness when they talked. A small table was placed in the middle for his brunch of sandwiches, a dish made of corn and tripe that his granddaughter once told her was his favourite food, and chocolates for his sweet tooth.

They heard the car and stood up. At 11.30 sharp, his silhouette blocked the sunlight streaming through the door. The Writer noticed that the tall frame had hunched a little and the gait wasn't as sure as before. She couldn't judge the face till he came closer and extended a hand – to him first, then to her. He still had the firm grip of a close friend; fat fingers clenched under a big fist that could as well belong to Muhammad Ali.

"Ah, my chair", he said, with childish glee, resting a hand on the shoulder of the chair. "But this cushion I do not know – well, it's not bad. Good for my back."

They were glad that he didn't try to remove the cushion

which would have exposed the tears and the tatters on the ancient discarded piece of furniture. A sigh escaped the Writer.

"A pleasant surprise," said the husband.

"Surprise, yes. Not very pleasant, I'm afraid", he said, stretching a hand to hold the Writer's shoulder as if for steadying himself.

"I thought it was about your future plans, or may be about my last story which was about you," she said hopefully.

She loved his comments on her work. She knew he enjoyed adulation.

"I haven't read the story, though Thabo told me about it. Been too busy. Even without reading it, I know it would be the best ever written about me. I like an occasional praise to cancel out some of the abuses that had been heaped on me. I'm not all that modest, you know."

She knew, of course, but only smiled, resisting the temptation to nod in the affirmative.

His smile was wide, showing large white teeth. She noticed that above the natty suit and white collar, his neck had formed wrinkles; ligaments stood out like they were holding up his jaws. There were sure signs of onion rings forming under his fat cheeks; skin hung lose below his jaw bones. Age and the travails of long prison life struck even the best and the bravest. The Writer reminded herself that she was barely five years younger.

He sat down.

"Let's eat breakfast. Ah, my favourite corn and tripe. Who told you I'm still a bushman at heart?".

He laughed with them. Unlike in his younger days, his laugh was muffled, almost a pretence.

"Your granddaughter told me,"

He looked taken aback, annoyed. His voice betrayed agitation.

"What? but how...how did she know? What did she tell you?"

"About corn and tripe, not that you were still a bushman".

He looked relieved. This was a man who was given to cool calculations, logical conclusions. And now he was having the best time of his life. After all those years of accusations and allegations, now fame, Adulations and praises were coming his way – all of that which, she knew, he loved so much. Yet his demeanour was intriguing.

He bent over the small table, dropped his head and whispered a small prayer under his breath before the food. The writer, a non-believer and the husband, a neutral, sat in respectful silence.

He prodded the dish, then put the fork down and reached for the sandwich. She poured him sweetened black tea.

He picked up the cup with his left hand and reached for her husband's arm again with his right. The cup shook a little, and then steadied.

"We're parting," he said, simply

She was incredulous: "How could Oliver or anybody else in the party agree to that?"

Her voice was agitated, urgent. "All these years."

"Yes," he said. "All these years. But I'm not parting with the party, but with my wife."

The Writer really had no reason to be surprised, yet she sat stunned, while the husband kept rolling a closed fist on the cupped palm of the other. They both knew the rumours which were in the gossip columns even before he was released. Columns and columns were written about her directing a gang that killed their opponents by 'fire-garlanding' them with burning tyres. And of her love affair. Even in jail, he would not have excused her for the things that she was supposed to have done to opponents. The poor loved her for sure, but did he believe the press?

The husband sat staring at the ground, a fist still rolling in the other palm. How many times haven't he and his wife quarrelled?

How many times hasn't he threatened to walk out, and she had said that was fine with her? Yet he couldn't be without her for even a week. At one time she had famously written that she couldn't be with someone who couldn't be without her. Yet she kept telephoning him after the third day of his absence. Women, by God, women can drive you nuts.

He knew that somewhat similar thoughts were racing through his wife's mind. The man wasn't the kind who was easily driven nuts.

When the silence in the air seemed to have gone too long, the husband spoke up.

"Whatever the problem between you, it will pass. It will have to pass. Both of us have gone through bitter partings and divorces. But you are different, you're a statesman, not private people like us." He was not sure that he said the right words, not even certain that he meant them.

The Great Man laughed dryly.

Again, silence hung like a gathering storm. He lit a cigarette, took just one puff till its end burnt bright red, then just held it, moving it up and down between his fingers while taking another sip of tea from the cup in his other hand.

"She has a lover," he said with a straight face. Suddenly, his face relaxed, as if he had just put down a burden.

"Nonsense," said the husband. He wouldn't have normally used that word to the Great Man despite the friendship. The man was only confirming the rumours, but he couldn't say he and his wife knew it all along.

"Yours is a relationship that history would marvel at," he said.

"She admitted it herself – not about history, but about the lover. She wasn't joking. We don't joke about such things. Our life has been too serious. She said my remote love didn't give her the protection a woman needed. It didn't put food in children's plates when she lost her jobs."

"Don't I know," the Writer sighed.

They sat in silence, he staring over her shoulders, beyond the open window while the Writer and the husband sat awkwardly. A long stick of ash from his cigarette threatened to fall on the table, but the Writer resisted the temptation to push an ashtray under it. The clock struck twelve.

Half hour had gone. Precious time for him; he had so much to do. The corn-and-tripe that Thelma cooked with cringed nose while dressing the intestines remained untouched. The sandwich was only half eaten. His shoes kept tapping the carpeted floor; his knees were jerking up and down furiously. Nervousness so uncharacteristic of the Great Man.

"All these years." The Write mused aloud.

"All these years, yes. Lonely years for her, not so lonely for me. She had so many responsibilities, doing it all by herself. Yet never letting up her fight with the authorities till she could make those flights to see me, to bring the things I liked hidden under her clothes. Putting her palms pressed against the glass so I could pretend to feel the touch of her. Then she had to bear with those rumours, fights, accusations, all because of me and yet without me to share them, not knowing when I will be back. Even whether I will ever be back. I couldn't come around to blame her for being wild with our own people in her outbursts when people told me. How could I? Life was bl... too hard for her."

"Wasn't too cosy for you either."

"Too many sacrifices on her part. In the beginning they did put me on hard labour and sometimes threatened to hit me. But nobody did go physical on me, rarely did a guard dare man-handle me. I didn't have to go home after a day's work or fight and then find that my house had been burnt down and that the children were out on the road, crying. No one to my face threatened to rape my daughters. Not within my earshot."

The Writer noticed that his knuckles were tightening. Even his imagination fell short of the actual sufferings his wife went through.

"But," said he rather defiantly. "She was not the only wife who suffered. I survived, many were hanged. There are many still out there, never dreaming of the kind of comforts they gave me during the past couple of years. Many suffering wives you would never hear about."

"Do people know? Does the party know? The news will be a scoop for the press." The husband rose and turned to pick up the day's paper from the mantle.

"No, nobody knows yet outside the close family circle. And, of course, the lover."

He smirked at the word, leaned back and closed his eyes. "Well, he at least gave her some joy in life, which I couldn't".

"No, nobody knows. I wanted to tell you first. You wouldn't try and console me. Someday, years later, you might want to write about it with understanding. I am resigned, almost relieved, as if a part of my failures as a husband stands redeemed. Only you would understand that."

He was looking straight at the Writer when he spoke, but her husband nodded as well. He would understand too.

Yet the pain was obvious. Since he had made it clear that he would brook no advice or words of consolation, they didn't try.

"It's in the papers that you have a meeting with the Big Boss tomorrow morning," the Husband said, wanting to change subject, and pointing at the headlines. "Seems you're coming to some kind of firm arrangement."

"No firm arrangement. The Party is suspicious of him more

than of anybody else. He's a clever cheat, running with the hares and chasing with the wolves."

He braced up. "You can bet that an arrangement there will be. We will run along till the wolves tire. We hares have the stamina of having run for three centuries. Oliver is tiring a little, I am not."

"You built up better stamina through an extra couple of decades," the Writer said, half in jest.

His face clouded again with the memory. "Yes, I skipped rope for several hours a day when not called out for hard labour. I've been an amateur boxer in the school and college days, you know. That helped. Then I spent a lot of time reading smuggled books. Earlier it was hell; our eyes smarted digging in the blazing sun during the days of hard labour. When we asked for sun glasses, they laughed in our face and published in the papers that we were demanding luxury. You can't give me all the credit; I wasn't the only one... I wish she had told me when she brought those long-awaited food packets and clothes. I would have had time to adjust myself to face the public."

He laughed that dry laugh again.: "Well, *if* I ever got a chance to face the public again. Who knew then?"

"I know," is all that the Writer could say. "So many years of waiting."

"I didn't say I blamed her."

He let out a fake chuckle. "Not that it matters at my age or hers, but she doesn't come into our bedroom till I'd gone to sleep."

The writer, reputed for her understanding of human minds, wasn't sure if she should express surprise, or should react at all. The husband stared at the wall.

He stood up and took her hand. "I'm not a Calvinist like one of those man-hating missionaries, but an ordinary Methodist, often torn by doubts. Yet I do believe that some things had to happen the way they happened. maybe I will carry a broken heart for just a little while. I'm quite capable of forgetting, you know."

If he wasn't capable of forgetting, she mused, and of persuading others to forget, there would be bloodshed that could last for years.

His chin went up in a show of bold acceptance, "May be that was another reason. She couldn't forgive me for forgetting so easily".

His next words came amidst an uncomfortable wheeze, perhaps designed to hide the grief and the unseen tears.

He extended his hands. "I had to get it out of my chest before I made an announcement, but not too soon," he said. "People have a right to know. She's a fighter, and I had loved her for it. She's also ambitious. There's a talk of making me a Joint-President or some such thig. Party would agree on nothing but the President. If something of that kind happens, she wouldn't let go of me. At the moment, such things don't bother me. All that I wanted was to get it out of my chest, and you were the right audience. Thanks for making it possible. Good Bye".

"'Bye, Sir," they both said, their voices soft and hoarse; barely audible. He heard, and somewhat taken aback at the honorific, he smiled.

The great man turned around, his hand on the door handle.

"I'm forgetting my manners. Thanks for the brunch, Nadine. Sorry I couldn't do justice to it. Thanks, Rein, for the patience. Now I only hope that she wouldn't force me to wash our dirty linen in public.".

"Do justice the next time, I am sure nothing of that sort will happen," the Writer said. She walked alongside him till the gate and waited till he got in and the car reversed.

Then she watched him pick up speed as if to catch up with the rainbow that lay just beyond his grasp, not aware of a humiliating court case that would rock the nation.

"Which of these three do you think was a neighbour to the man who fell into the hands of robbers?"

The expert in the law replied, "The one who showed him mercy,"

Then Jesus told him, "Go and do likewise."

Luke 10:36-3, Berean study Bible

REMEMBERING FATHER THOMAS

I met Father Thomas when I was running an agency for garment exports. Every day a lot many promotional samples of clothing – children's, women's and men's, fanciful and ordinary, would come by courier to my office. Many of them, the merchandisers decided, were too shiny with sequins and frills for European or American taste. They piled up, filling a whole room. That was when Rita, the senior merchandiser, suggested that we talk to Father Thomas, who ran a home for the poor in the far outskirts of the city bordering a forest.

The priest landed up in a pickup truck in the same evening as I called him.

"People call me scavenger priest. Tell me what you got. I will take anything that could be of some human use."

Father Thomas was excited to see the collection of clothing I had to offer. After brooding for a few moments, he said:

"I will take them all. But to tell you the truth, I will sell some of them for money. My children don't wear fancy clothes. But to send them to school, I need the money."

The priest, I noticed, wore a robe that was clean and

shimmering white with a faint patch of blue on one shoulder. The ends of his sleeves were slightly frayed.

We met nearly every month since then, and I was greatly impressed. There was no big collection to offer every month, but his pickup van came nevertheless – sometimes with him, other times only the driver. Thomas was happy to take a table with a leg broken, and actually asked for and got a black board used in my office to display important dates for shipping. Rita frowned when I gave it away.

I told her that I was doing him no great favor. I was mostly getting rid of the unwanted at no cost.

"All but the black board which we need," she grumbled.

"You have the computer," I said. "Father Thomas needs it even more. He is doing something for the poor and needy. We'll buy a white board which is more in fashion."

When he came the next month, he noticed the new white board with blue writings on it.

"I'm sorry, but I thought the black board was not of much use to you. I believed the writings on it were mere scribbles."

"You needed it more, Father. Your needs get priority in this office for the things you do to bring some happiness into the lives of the poor."

"Oh, no. Not everybody thinks like that. Many think that I'm trying to convert people. In *Ch....* someone took a potshot at me. The only reason I escaped, I guess, was God wanted me around a little longer. I didn't go to the police; thought it would be a waste of time."

This was before Australian preacher Graham Staines and his children were burnt alive inside their pickup van.

"Perhaps you do expect a reward from your God," I said, tentatively. "Like a place in heaven."

"Heaven, who knows? Maybe Jesus used the word to make us all try and do good deeds," laughed Thomas,

Father Thomas refused to be drawn to a discussion about religion. Till one day I challenged him to explain why there were so many denominations – so many contesting churches – in Christianity. In the chapter named Revelation, God commended some churches and warned some others. Reformists said that the Pope was the living anti-Christ. Catholics worshipped the idols of Christ on the cross or Mary holding her baby, Reformists fumed that it was idolatry banned by God. How did he reconcile such differences?

"Stephen," he sighed: "No matter what we Christians say against each other, there is one thing we all agree upon. That Jesus gave up his physical body to save mankind from the result of their sins. That is the essence of Christianity. Two billion human beings believe in that truth. Two billion people are convinced of that. Two billion men and women – doctors, lawyers, writers and scientists, ministers and presidents, people from all walks of life who believe in Jesus cannot all be wrong, can they?"

I told him that two billion people were born into two hundred or more varieties of Christianity, but half of them were not sure they were right. Even Mother Teresa said she was occasionally troubled by doubts. Did he too sometimes feel the pang of doubt in his heart of hearts?

"I believe in what I do," was his curt response.

I too believed in what he was doing, I told him. I didn't tell him that although I was born a Christian, and not because I married a Hindu woman, I didn't buy the Jesus-died-for-us jargon. That Father Thomas was helping the poor *Adivasis*, the indigenous people, was what mattered. People deprived of their land and their trees, the animals they used to hunt for food, now themselves hunted by police and forced out of the forest clearings, had two options – turn radical communists called Maoists and pick up arms to kill by stealth, or convert to one form or another of Christianity and live on charity.

I said: "Let us say all two million people are true believers in Jesus. That still makes four-and-a-half million who are not – among them doctors, lawyers, writers and scientists, ministers and presidents?"

"In the seminary, we do discuss these things. A priest does not become one by just reading the Bible and willy-nilly believing in all that is written. Philosophy is one of our subjects. So is comparative religion. We have debates on the Bible. Some of them give up half way. I finished because I believe not in all the stories in the Holy Book. But in the essence of my Lord's teachings. I believe that he persuades me to do what I do. As we always say, it is your faith that will save you."

I didn't argue that there are many like him giving up the luxuries of life to serve the poor without any such persuasion from a God. I later learnt that Father Thomas had a Master's degree in Physics and had been doing a PhD on astrophysics when he was an intern of sorts in the Church – a deacon. When he was elevated to the rank of a priest and called up to work in the local Parish, Thomas gave up his scholarly pursuit and got involved in the church. That was when he came in contact with the poor indigenous people – the *Adivasis*.

On one of his later visits, I asked Father Thomas how he managed to reconcile his knowledge that there are billions of galaxies out there with the Biblical theory of God doing his work from the earth and hanging up the sun and the moon in the sky.

"The Bible and science run parallel," said the priest in his calm voice." So they never meet. Since they don't meet, there is no conflict. Haven't you heard of Father Lemaitre, a Catholic like me? It was he who proposed what you call the Big-Bang Theory. Yet he didn't denounce his faith. The two can co-exist."

"I suppose you shut one door when you open the other," I said: "Yet they should conflict some time inside your head."

"All that I have inside my head is the pang of hunger in the little children I meet. Their pleasure when I gift them a dress, their mother a new sari or the little ones a good meal topped up with ice-cream. The toothless smile of an old man when I gave him one of the colorful T-shirts you gifted last time."

I noticed that the sleeve-ends of his white robe had begun to fray even more than before.

"I will ask my tailor-master to take your measurements. Before I go, I want to gift you a couple of robes," I said. "I am closing the agency and moving abroad."

Thomas looked indignant. "Stephen, I don't live on charity. I get a salary. But you can give me the money. I could put two kids to school through a whole year with it."

I said I will give him the money, but also two sets of robes because I had the fabric and the workers in house.

'I'm sorry to know you're going away, Stephen. The people I serve will be much poorer when you're gone. But I wish you well, Keep your kind heart, Stephen. God will be with you."

Maybe, I said, if I succeeded in my plans, I could be of more help to his noble work.

He didn't collect the money before he said goodbye and left. I wasn't sure how much a Catholic Priest's robes would cost if he bought them from the market or had them made by a tailor. So I sent a thousand rupees to his office before setting off for the job abroad.

Ten years later when I returned, I looked for Father Thomas. The school he had started looked deserted. The new priest, an ageing man, whom I met at the door of the chapel said, "Yes,

Father Thomas. I have only heard about him, much younger than me, you know, and I find his name in our records, but don't remember meeting him. A few *Adivasis* used to come to church when I first came here. They would ask me about Father Thomas. Now hardly any of them comes."

Orphans don't go to church. I asked if he served the *Adivasis* in their secret hovels.

"I buried a couple of Christian boys among them. Also, a pregnant woman with her baby inside her – six or seven months, maybe. Shot dead in an encounter with the police. Very young. Those who brought the bodies had guns with them. They are dangerous commies, aren't they?"

Encounter, my foot. They were killed in cold blood. An informer tells the police when they would be arranging a meeting of thirty or forty people in the Jungle. When all of them were gathered together, the police or some other security force would spring a surprise, shoot down a few in cold blood while the rest of them vanished in the dark. Women with babies on their hips could not run fast enough to escape the bullets. A fleshy teenage girl or a middle-aged woman might get gang-raped and then shot so she couldn't bear witness. It was all a clean job, done with practiced skill. If among the dead a few were wanted men with their names on the rolls, the killers would get a reward and a commendation for their bravery.

"Yes," I said aloud. "Terribly dangerous when they are hungry. They steal guns from the police, but can't find food in the police stations."

The old priest got down from the steps of his chapel to get closer.

"Tell me," he said in a hoarse whisper: "Why can't these young people work for a living instead of fighting with the government?"

I laughed. Why didn't Jesus Christ find a job of a Rabbi or

take up carpentry rather than going around synagogues, chasing gamblers and toppling tables? Why didn't the pioneers give the Apaches work instead of bullets? Why didn't the British convicts give Aussie aborigines work in place of cannon balls? Asking a god's man those questions would be a waste of time.

"If you ever meet Father Thomas, he might be able to answer that," I said.

"Sorry, I didn't get your name. If Father Thomas did come by or I meet him in one of our conferences, who should I say came looking for him?"

"An *Adivasi* who found a job," I said.

"You do not look like one," laughed the old priest.

"Exactly," I said: "If I did, I wouldn't have got a job."

"God forbid, with these ideas, they could have shot you in an encounter. Just joking,"

"Father, that's no joke, and God doesn't forbid," I said. "Now that I'm back, I intend to work with these people. I could get shot or be made to languish in jail for life like a physically challenged Professor I know."

As a passing shot, while mounting my motorbike, I said:

"Your church might not let that out, but maybe that's what happened to Father Thomas."

Bhima alighted from his chariot, and glowered hard at his fallen enemy. Drawing his sharpened sword, and trembling with rage, he thrust his foot on the enemy's neck. Then he split open his chest and drank the hot life-blood.

Mahabharata, Karna Parva. Translation by K. M. Ganguli

FOUR DAYS OF TERROR

When my wife shook me out of some kind of a nightmare I couldn't quite recollect, it was 1:30 in the morning, the first of November, 1984.

"Satnam is on the phone," she said. "Karnail-*ji* has not come home."

Satnam Kaur was the wife of Karnail Singh Ahluwalia, whom I had nicknamed the Saint Sardar. A great friend of mine, he owned a shop in the flourishing electronic market and sold, among other things, the rather popular Black-and-white televisions and car radios – both cutting-edge those days – I manufactured in a small 1000-foot workshop in an industrial complex mostly run by Sikhs.

On the other end of the line, Satnam Kaur was crying.

"*Bhai-Saa'b*," (respected brother) she said, "*Gudia's Papa* has not come home. At six this evening he called me and said the market is closing because there is violence in the streets, and he would come home early. He told me not to open the door for anyone, he's got the key to the house."

Gudia was her first daughter, a lively five-year old. Her pet name meant doll. After she was born, Karnail became *Gudia-ka-papa* (Gudia's Father) in her lexicon.

Her sobs turned into a soft wail, and soon there were wails from her two children who probably didn't know what their mother was crying for.

"I'm coming," I said. Then, "no, I won't come there. You don't need to open the door. Instead, I'll call the neighbors and put a search. Maybe he had a car-breakdown. Don't worry, Karnail won't come to any harm."

"*Wahe Guru*," which meant something like praise the Lord, she said and hung up. For a moment I too laid my trust in the Guru whom the Sikhs expected to look after the world and bestow his special favor on his disciples, the Sikhs. For Sikhs, Guru, the preceptor, also meant God, or at least the pathway to God. I said a silent prayer to the image of Guru Nanak, founder of the religion, picturing in my mind his old peaceful face under a white turban, the noble head slightly leaning to the right, his right hand raised in a gesture of blessing, his long white beard flowing down till beneath the edge of the frame. A large painting of Guru Nanak – which Satnam called *photo* of *Babaji* – was what greeted a visitor to Karnail's lovely villa.

When I came out of my house, there was a small crowd of people at the street-corner. Northerners in their pajamas, South Indians like myself in *lungis* – a wrap-around ankle-length cloth, striped or plain, secured with a tuck at the waist. Dr. George Varkey, the dark, thick-set pediatrician who permanently wore a serious visage, carried a hunting rifle in his hand.

"Ahluwalia has not got home. Sandeep heard someone crying inside his house; his car is not parked outside. There has been trouble all along the way from Red Fort. Someone spread a rumor that *Sardars* were holding a party in Connaught place to celebrate Indira Gandhi's murder. It seems they intend to punish the Sikhs for the killing and for the celebration," said Kunju, the cartoonist. Being from the Press, he should know.

Sardar, literally headman, was a common tag for all Sikhs – probably earned when Sikhs led guerrilla wars against the Mughals. The appendix *ji* was a common honorific that fitted all – males, females, Hindu, Muslim or Sikh, gods, goddesses and Gurus. When you liked a Sikh, you called him *Sardar-ji*. If you were indifferent, or didn't like him, you referred to him with a mere *Sardar*.

Karnail's family was very popular with the neighbours. Though married to a Sikh and probably from a Sikh family herself, Satnam often joined the Hindu ladies who roamed the near-by streets long before dawn clanging little cymbals and singing aloud hymns in praise of Hindu deities.

"Let's move to Ahluwalia's house," said Naushad Ali, a renowned lawyer whose house was next to mine. "I think they are setting fire to Sikh houses in the village across the road. Some of them would know that there is a Sikh living in this colony, in our street."

I said: "If that's true, to crowd around his house would be a give-away. We'll wait and watch from here, not particularly looking at his house. Dr. Varkey, you better put away that rifle. It'd be no use against a mob. We'll have to use tactics, not try and fight the mob."

Varkey saw sense in my suggestion and went home to put away his rifle that probably could kill an elephant, but was not good enough for dispersing a violent and reckless mob. Uncock-load-cock-fire-uncock-load routine only got the first mobster before the rest of them got you.

At least seven of us stood in the junction where one road went to the community shopping centre, another went around the football-field-sized children's park of the colony surrounded by our middle-class villas, and the third led to the main road across which lay a sprawling village.

The village was tactfully named Indira *Nagar*. The idea was that any unauthorized colony would be legitimized if it was named after Indira Gandhi, the Prime Minister. It was a farmland before, now illegally converted into a residential place. Its owners waited for the next elections to have their plots and houses legitimized. Most promises by legislators were soon forgotten after the elections, a few others were fulfilled just before election in the hope that the bounteousness would translate into votes. They sometimes did. "One carrot every five years is enough to earn the gratitude of the donkey called the public," a cynic once wrote in his popular column.

At least a thousand brick-and-lime houses sat at arm's length from each other in Indira Nagar with narrow streets between rows of houses. Some small, some big, some even of two or three storeys. There was a Shiva temple, with a giant-sized, garishly painted and snake-garlanded God in all his fineries marking its location. Not far away from it stood the *Gurudwara*, shrine of the Sikhs. Whoever visited the temple rang its bells to wake up the God from his reverie and pass a blessing. Some went and prayed at the Gurudwara after filing his plea in the temple, hoping for double benefit. In Gurudwara they sang *Kirtans* (hymns) or read from the *Granth Sahib* – the sacred Sikh scripture– into a loudspeaker.

I never got to see the make-shift mosque though there surely was one; every morning and night you could hear a faint Muezzin's call. At other times the calls to the faithful were drowned in the suburban noises. Perhaps the Muslim houses in the village were few and were hustled together, or, being a small minority, they did not dare to put up a loudspeaker in the midst of a lot many Hindus and Sikhs. An undercurrent of tension, despite trade and friendly greetings, was part of the social setup.

Among the occupants of the village was Ex-Subedar-Major

Ram Kishore Singh – not a Sikh, but in the North, many who did not have a caste-name to pass off for his surname called himself Singh. The word meant lion. This Singh was from far-away hamlet in a Northern state. He chose to settle in Delhi after retirement with his wife, married sons and daughters-in-law. Singh was an impressive man with an up-turned bushy moustache above a bulky frame. Before retiring from the army, he told me, his job was maintaining discipline among nearly 1500 men of all ranks other than officers – among them Bengalis, *Madrasis*, Sikhs and Muslims. He kindled a sense of unity among all, he said, teaching them that all Indians were one family. His eminent record in service won him a commendation and a VSM – Exemplary Service Medal. Yet, his current monthly pension did not amount to much, he explained, which was why he sought the job I advertised.

He hinted that it would be good if I let him be known as Major *Saa'b*; after all, he was a Subedar-Major. I readily agreed. Having a Major, albeit a half-baked one, on our roll would enhance the prestige of my new factory. He even looked the part.

It was well past 2 AM, and one could hear screams from the village. Above the foliage beyond the main road, one noticed a flame leaping up– and it soon appeared to be spreading. The noise kept rising in decibels.

"I'm afraid they are burning Sikh houses There are quite a few Sardars there. My carpenter Gyan Singh lives there," said Kunju, known for his keen observation as portrayed in his daily cartoons in a popular newspaper.

I said: "Maybe there would be accusations and arguments, even threats, an occasional arson to release pent-up anger, but little more. The people there are neighbors, not a mob of strangers. What do those Sikhs in the village have anything to do with the assassination? There are a couple of army men living there. A retired JCO[62] there works for me. A sensible man. if he's awake, he would soon bring order in that place."

An hour after we set up guard, it didn't appear as though the *Major Saa'b* had brought order into the fiery village.

We noticed movement outside Karnail Singh's house. Under the faint streetlights we saw someone open the gate warily and walk past the front yard that doubled as Karnail's car park. The unsteady gait wasn't that of Karnail Singh, his brand-new latest model Maruti-Suzuki was not in sight. The figure walked uncertainly with a crouch and seemed more like an old hag with a patch of hair spread out behind.

We moved cautiously towards the house, looking around for any gang of intruders following the figure. While the person was fumbling with the keys, we reached the place.

Karnail Singh turned around to face us with a muffled alarm. He wore no turban, which he had always worn like a square crown; no mandatory comb in his hair which lay loose and partly burnt. Much of his facial hair on the left side had burned and curled up, blackening his fair skin. His clothes were torn and stank of urine or worse, sleeves shredded, ugly slits around his knees with bloodstains and black clumps of filth on his trousers.

Karnail Singh Ahluwalia, the Saint Sardar, who was always nattily dressed, his safari suit ironed stiff in summer and a crisp business suit with tie in winter, shoes polished like that of a Colonel on ceremonial parade, his starched-stiff turban gloriously worn like a crown, his beard gathered together and secured flat to his cheeks, now looked worse than a tramp who ran out from a burning slum.

Karnail surveyed the small crowd with squinted eyes.

When he recognized me, he twitched his mouth painfully for

---

[62] *Junior Commissioned Officer. "Viceroy's Commissioned Officer" before independence.*

a forced smile and sighed. "They set fire to my car, *yaar*, with me inside near the Lahori Sweet House."

Yaar, like *buddy* in English colloquy, meant a close friend.

His voice came in broken hisses, yet he drawled on like wanting to get his awful experience out of his chest. His left hand was bent and hung limp, right hand making feeble attempts to open the door.

"They stopped me and made me park towards the wrong side of the road. On the left was a huge crowd – maybe forty or fifty of them with sticks and stones. They didn't let me get out of the car after setting it on fire, shouting *Blood for Blood, Indira Gandhi will live forever*. Then a bus came by, maybe they saw that a Sardar was its driver, and chased after it like a pack of hyenas. When the last man by my side of the car was gone, I opened the door and rolled off to the edge of the road and lay like dead. Soon the heat from the burning car was scorching my skin, my body was like burning all over. I tried to roll away before the petrol tank burst, but fell into the storm-drain. *Guru* is very kind, there was no water in the drain, only wet mud and slush. For some time, I didn't know what was happening. I came to with the pain on my arm and the burning smell of my hair. I waited till all was quiet and dark, except flashes of light from the flames leaping out of the burning bus at some distance. My car must have burnt down, there was one loud bust, bits and pieces kept falling into the drain. This hand was painful and useless, my leg was in horrible pain, yet I walked, crouching, in the drain, crawling through drain pipes, for God knows how many hours. My watch had fallen off, I didn't know where I was going. Then my legs struck what must have been a man's body. If it was of a man, he was surely dead. I said, brother, forgive me, and stepped on the body to climb onto the street. I swear on the One above, I would never do that if I was in my senses. There I got my bearings. I was in P-Town. I walked through side-streets, avoiding a couple of crowds shouting *Long live Indira Gandhi*. I heard someone shouting *Ek Sardar ko maaro, Ek hazaar kamao* – Kill a Sikh, earn a thousand. Frightened, by God, I crouched in the shade and began to crawl again. Around the corner towards N-Town, I saw a house burning on the other side. I continued to crawl on my knees, hiding in the shadows till that corner over there. I never hoped to reach home. Merciful is the One above."

He spoke haltingly; his breathing was heavy. The narration took time while he continued to fiddle with the keys.

"That's enough, you shouldn't be talking at all, you need a clean-up or you'll die." said Varkey who was till then engrossed in the halting and painful description of Karnail's pathetic misadventure, as we all were. He grabbed the keys from Karnail, tried out a couple of them, found the right one and opened the door.

Satnam Kaur stood behind the door, not daring to open it herself though she must have heard her husband's voice.

"*Bahut shukriya*, Thank very much, *Bhai Saa'bs*. Now everything is all right," she told us. Then she noticed the state of her husband and, her hands to her cheeks, screamed.

"Nothing is all right, but screaming won't help," said Dr. Varkey in his atrocious Hindi. "Don't close the door. I need to take a look at your husband. And he needs a cold shower. It's going to hurt. Can't help that. Where is the phone?"

Varkey phoned his wife who took some time to answer. When she apparently did, he asked her to wake their son and send him to *Sardarji's* house with his medical bag and some bandages.

Soon enough Varkey's teenaged son came with the medical things. The doctor took it and got hold of Karnail, skirting a frightened and wailing Satnam Kaur and beckoning me to accompany him.

I told her not to worry, Karnail was in good hands. I didn't add that, given the circumstances, a child-specialist was better than nothing.

Karnail slipped from the doctor's hand and slumped on the floor. Satnam howled and tried to hold him. He was tall, but lightly built. The three of us lifted him easily enough and put him in bed. Satnam didn't flinch when we put her filthy and stinking husband on the bed neatly made with pristine white linen.

"We can't take him to the bath. Impossible. Let's strip him of the dirty clothes," said Dr. Varkey.

While we stripped the hairy body, except what I believed to be a *kachera*[63] in place of an ordinary underwear, his wife politely looked away. Removing the part of his shirt on his left side took some painful time – the deeply scalded skin and the fabric had merged.

As Dr. Varkey worked on him, and I swabbed the dirt away from his body, Karnail Singh tried to raise his back now and then, howled in pain, and fell back. Satnam first brought cold water and then warm water as the doctor ordered, her hands shaking and spilling some of it on the floor.

Their daughters, five and three, barged into the room.

"Mama, stop those uncles. They're killing Papa," bellowed Gudia, the older girl. The younger one kept rolling her fists on her eyes and sobbing aloud.

Satnam gathered both, whispered consolation in their ears and led them to the next room, closing the door.

Dr. Varkey took more than an hour treating the wounds and bandaging his arm and knees, giving him an injection. Finally,

---

[63] One of the five mandatory things a Sikh must have on his body. Kachera is supposed to represent the chastity of the wearer. More possibly, the Gurus made is compulsory as a protection of the vitals in a battle.

we dressed him, with quite some effort, in loose muslin pajamas that Satnam dug out from a wardrobe.

"He'll sleep for several hours. Don't wake him up. I gave him an anti-tetanus and a pain killer. His wounds are sanitized and bandaged; some stuck with anti-septic plaster. Keep children away. Give him these tablets, three times after food, if he eats anything tomorrow. If he's too much in pain, give him this tablet, only one at a time. If he develops fever, call me."

Varkey fished out a card from his bag and gave her.

He turned towards me. "That's a bloody brave Sardar, I tell you. Is he in the army?"

"No," I said, "he runs an electronics shop. One of my dealers. The best."

Satnam Kaur, beaming through tears, asked: "Doctor Sahib, what fees can I pay you?"

"Nothing for now," he said, pretending to survey the room. "When he's better, you can give me this house instead of money. It's a nice house. I'll take it."

Alarmed, Satnam raised her eyebrows and looked askance at me. When I chuckled, she relaxed. Varkey winked. I saw him smile for the first time.

When we came out and closed the gate, Varkey paused, closed his eyes and looked up as if in prayer.

"This wouldn't do. I gave him a strong opiate which I normally wouldn't. That Sardar would die if we don't take him to a hospital. I'll call them from home."

The rest of the crowd were in the street-corner, waiting for news.

"Will he live?" asked Kunju in Malayalam.

"Jesus, that Sardar is a marvel," said Varkey, in English.

"Can't imagine how he crawled, avoiding being seen – let's see how many kilometers? 15 or 20 from Lahori Sweet House near the Central Park? His left hand is burnt to the bones. Can you imagine crawling on all fours in a dirty drain? I hope tomorrow an orthopedic could do something about his elbow. He'll also need skin grafting, hoping that would help. He has many burn marks all over the left side of his back. His knees are in terrible shape after all that crawling. Can't understand how he did it. Surprisingly, his pulse and pressure are normal. Mr. Panicker and I had a tough time cleaning him up and treating his burns. Was a torture that I couldn't help, but he bore up, howling rarely. Pardon me, I need to go home and make a phone call."

The good doctor hurried home to call the hospital.

Sidhu, the shortest and the thinnest man in the crowd, grabbed an imaginary beard under his chin and said, "He's a Sardar, you know."

When everyone laughed at him, he said: "I'm a Sardar too, a modified Sikh. My father shaved off his beard and cut his hair. He said beard and *kirpan*[64] are for *Punch Pyaras* – five beloved Sikhs, favorites of Guru Gobind Singh-*ji*, the last Guru. That was his logic. All the same, we're Sikhs."

He showed his *Kada* – a stiff steel strap around his right wrist worn like a bangle – part of a Sikh's five mandatory wear.

Someone said: "If you're a Sardar, Sidhu, then don't tell that to anyone. Hide that *kada* or some bigot is going to get you."

I said: "Not to worry. Tomorrow police will order a curfew. There will be no attacks on Sikhs. The Government won't allow a few hooligans run amuck and burn houses as they seem to be doing in the village. Even the Punjab Government arrests Sikh terrorists and prevents much mayhem against Hindus. This is India, not Congo."

We could hear men shouting and screaming, calls of

---

[64] *Kirpan is a short dagger that Sikhs are allowed to wear as a part of their five mandatory parts of personal attire.*

Blood-for-Blood and Victory to *Bharat Mata,* forgetting that thousands of Sikhs had given their lives for the victory of *Bharat Mata* – Mother India.

Kunju raised a finger above his head. "Listen. *Khoon ka badla khoon* – Blood to avenge Blood – is a sure call for lynching. When men get worked up like that, they can be beasts."

I guessed Varkey tried all three hospitals where he worked and requested an ambulance. None came.

It was nearly five in the morning. We decided that there was no immediate danger to Karnail Singh and his family, so we'd catch some sleep. Surely the day will be one of mourning for Indira Gandhi, so no work in the offices, no school for the children and no lectures for Varkey's college-going son.

At seven in the morning of November 1, the air was eerily quiet. Rajiv Gandhi, the new Prime Minister, was on television[65].

> *"It is a moment of profound grief. The foremost thing to do is to maintain one's balance. We can and must face the tragedy with fortitude and wisdom. We should remain calm and exercise maximum restraint."*

The television made no mention of riots or killings. I sighed in relief.

My wife suggested that we go to our new factory built with massive loans and see that everything was safe there. Our children, both adolescents who were assigned the responsibility of helping out in the arrangements for the inauguration and setting up the place where the Minister would be received, were still fast asleep, instinctively knowing that there would be no school, and unaware

---

[65] Aired on "Door Darshan", India's lone terrestrial Television of the time. The name meant view from afar.

of all that happened at night or the condition of 'Karnail-uncle.' My son was a favorite of Karnail Singh who had no son, only two lovely little daughters.

We didn't wake the children. Twelve and ten, they were grown up enough to look after themselves for a few hours. There was no reason to be worried; all was quiet but for the arson that happened in the next village. The expected attacks on Sikhs, it seemed, had blown off like a bad breeze after what appeared to be the foreboding of a tornado. On television, the face of a newly inducted minister Buta Singh, a Sikh, was on frequent display. It was President Zail Singh, another prominent Sikh, who swore in the new Prime Minister Rajiv Gandhi. After his speech, there were no frequent calls for the Nation to stay calm. It meant that the Nation *was* calm.

Let's take the scooter, said my wife. She believed that my ancient Lambretta was more appropriate for the occasion than the Fiat car we had bought four years before in the black market. She reasoned that Karnail got into trouble when he was in a closed car, so an open scooter would be safer.

November had just set foot, yet there was a nip in the morning air. She wrapped herself in a light shawl, covering her head with it, and plumped side-saddle on the pillion. Her left hand holding me tight around my waist, we sailed in the morning breeze along the main road, noticing the wisps of smoke that hung in the air. In the village to our right, it was all quiet but for a swirling pall of smoke. You could hear a woman bawling, probably because her house had been burnt down – which accounted for the smoke. As we shuddered across the open railway bridge, my wife said she noticed trouble in the normally deserted rail station to our left below. She said a crowd was chasing a man, a howling woman was chasing after them. Was the running man a Sikh? She couldn't tell. Did he wear a turban? She couldn't tell either, his head was not visible with the crowd behind him. Fights and lynching were not unusual hereabouts, I told her and rolled the accelerator to get away from any sight of violence.

We rode on the road skirting the runway, which my children called Laburnum Road. A long row of laburnum trees stood on either side of the narrow driveway. Summer had gone; although Delhi had no real autumn, the laburnums had shredded their long bouquets of hanging yellow-and-gold flowers. Further up the empty road, I saw a Sikh riding a scooter towards us. When he came closer, I first recognized his brand-new Bajaj scooter and then him.

"*Namaste*, Panicker Saa'b," greeted Guddu, raising one hand.

"Is there trouble ahead?"

We stopped, facing each other.

"*Sat-Shri-Akal*[66], Guddu, all well? was the scare unnecessary?"

"No," said Guddu. His voice was serious. The young and normally ebullient Sikh worked as a handyman-cum-bill-collector for Chadda Engineering, the company that made moulded plastic suitcases and auto-parts. He looked flustered.

"*Veeerji* sent me to check if everything is all right in the new factory building still under construction. Half a kilometer from Cotton-town junction, I could hear shouts of *Blood to avenge Blood*. Something – probably a car – was on fire. I thought I heard the scream of a child. I turned around and fled back. Maybe *Veeerji* will get mad at me. But I feared I might get killed."

His knees, visible behind the scooter's forward frame, shook violently.

Veerji meant big brother. Guddu was no brother of Balbir Singh Chadda, but he was so addressed from familiarity.

How inconsiderate and reckless of Balbir Singh Chadda, I thought, to send this young man on a recce mission alone at a

---

[66] *The divine is eternal*

time like this. Chadda, the richest in the trade – at least in terms of unaccounted money – was all courtesy to customers, but hard on his employees.

"Take care, Guddu. We saw nothing dangerous on the road. Avoid the villages. Take only the main road."

As he said a gloomy thank you and rode away, I felt queasy in the pit of my stomach.

"I hope nothing happens to that young *Sardarji*. I don't think they are killing Sikhs the way they tried to kill Satnam's husband," said my wife.

I wasn't sure. I could see swirling dark smoke ahead.

At Cotton-town junction, something of a small square with a barrier-boom to check traffic, a crowd of young men had been eyeing us from distance. They signaled me to stop. On our right, on the road that led to the farm houses of the rich and famous, a heap of metal that must have been a car an hour ago, was smouldering. The three-pronged star, logo of Mercedes-Benz, shone through the smoking heap. Cars like that were owned by a few among the richest those days, they came with a huge import tax – something like twice the actual cost.

"Don't look," I said to my wife. Having known how Karnail Singh got away with his life only by sheer luck, I suspected that the occupants were not allowed to get out of the car. Were there children inside? Did they cry and plead *'uncle-ji, let us go, please don't kill us'* while the crowd stood outside and shouted

Bharat Mata ki Jai (victory to Mother India),
Indira Gandhi Amar Rahe (Long live Indira Gandhi) and
Khoon-ka-badla-khoon (Blood to avenge blood)?

Someone signaled me to stop, and I did. A puny young man moved towards us and asked my wife to remove the shawl from over her head. I told her not to resist, this was not the time. He yanked off the shawl himself, dragging her forward in the process.

Any other time I would have smashed his teeth in. She held on to my waist tightly and resisted a fall.

"The man is a *Madrasi*, the woman looks like a *Sikhni*," announced the young man of stunted growth, arrogant by the privilege of the situation.

Sikhni meant a lady Sikh. All South Indians, whether they had ever been to Madras or not, were summarily known as *Madrasi* in the North. Few North Indians believed that the *Madrasis* could have light skin. Against my Sub-Saharan skin, my wife's Aryan complexion contrasted dangerously.

An older man moved forward to take a look and judge for himself. I recognized the man. He was a carpenter from a town beyond the river, come looking for work in the new industrial complex. We had negotiated his making wooden cabinets for the televisions I would make in the upcoming factory.

"*Hum* Madrasi *hai*," pleaded my wife, shaken and defensive, in the South-Indian version of Hindi where words like *am*, *is* and *are* all merged into an *is*.

"*Arre Bhai*, this is Panicker Saa'b. Don't stop them. Sorry, Panicker Saa'b. But I'd advise you: don't go further. Madam could be mistaken for a *Punjaban*[67]."

So, they were not even sparing light-skinned Punjabi women, whether Sikh or Hindu.

Probably to make amends for the crudeness of his deputy, he turned around and said with unnecessary loudness: "You idiot, every *Gori* is not Punjaban."

The description *Gori*– white girl – would tickle the heart of any Indian woman – light-skinned or dark.

He returned the shawl. "Go carefully. Take care of *Bahen-ji*[68]."

---

[67] A lady from the State of Punjab
[68] *Respected Sister.*

I kicked the starter pedal and moved a couple of meters, then stopped and looked back. The carpenter came up to meet me.

"How many people in that car?"

He frowned. "Not people, Sardars. Does how many Sardars matter to you?"

Maybe it mattered. Karnail Singh had heard someone offering a thousand rupees for every Sikh killed.

"Any child inside?"

"Panicker *Saa'b*, you mind your business and go away from here." His tone had become aggressive.

As we moved on avoiding an argument, my wife placed her chin on my shoulder and asked: "He has become rude. Could this man be among those who set fire to that car?"

"He led the mob, a brave General directing the battle against the helpless and the unarmed."

I accelerated to get away quickly.

As we approached the state's border, the scene was one of a bombed-out market. On the right used to be a number of make-shift wooden kiosks where sales tax inspectors, Octroi collectors and, quite logically, butchers held shop all twenty-four hours of a day. Inspectors collected some tax and a lot of bribe. The two butchers in their respective shops killed goats and chicken through the day and kept a steady stream of supply to the lone *dhabba* – a make-shift restaurant – across the road. They were all closed; apparently the government had decided this was not the right day for tax collection.

Ranjit Singh, a Hindu *Jhat*[69] who owned *Ranjit Ka dhabba* which served sizzling mutton chops, curried lambs and chicken roasted on charcoal fire, apparently decided there would be

---

[69] A proud, mostly farming, people who consider themselves a distinct marshal race many of whom nonetheless demand that they be considered as backward castes and be granted reservation for jobs.

no business that day. Ranjit himself sold no booze because his *dhabba* was on the Delhi side of the border. There was prohibition in Delhi, not on the other side. Customers had to buy it from another hut which sold cheap rum and brandy in quarter-bottles across the fence.

I noticed that the booze shop on the other side had been smashed in; but there was no sign of broken liquor bottles or of liquor spreading on the road. Apparently, all stolen. I guessed the shop was owned by a Sikh. His religion prohibited use of tobacco, so the Sikhs did not smoke. Gurus had forgotten to include alcohol in the banned list, so some of them drank like fish and a few others ran liquor shops which was profitable business.

A mob holding sticks, cutlasses and sickles in their hands sat on wooden benches and bamboo cots lying about outside the closed *dhabba*. Many young men, for want of seats, simply stood around shuffling their legs and swinging their crude weapons. Their necks were strained towards the border, anticipating trucks and cars coming in from other states. A visitor with a turban and a beard meant an exciting hunt and easy kill.

My wife was right; if we were in a car, those men would not have ignored us the way they did after one look at us.

Ahead, men were unloading cooking-gas cylinders from a truck. A woman, whom I knew as Neelu who used to carry bricks on the construction site, was busy hurriedly stacking gas cylinders in a handcart. More cylinders were being handed down by her son over the tailboard of the truck.

"That's enough, you get down. Now I will take some," said an older man.

My wife gave out a howl, "Look," and then, on afterthought, a muffled scream in my ears: "please don't look."

As I turned left towards the Industrial complex, I stopped and looked. From the broken window of the driver's side, limply hung a bearded man's head. His turban had come unraveled and rolled down in a long stretch of wide blue ribbon. Blood kept dripping from his mouth. Surely his neck had been broken.

Neelu's son hopped down from the truck and came towards me, wringing his hands in glee.

"*Jai Hind*, Saa'b," he greeted me pleasantly. The phrase meant victory to India, one of the many patriotic or pious forms of greeting.

"When we tried to stop that prick of a Sardar, the mother-fucker showed his *kirpan*, challenged us to get near him, calling us sister-fuckers. We battered him in his seat with iron rods so much that his neck broke. The Sardar howled like a mad dog and died." There was no regret, only pride in his voice. In the bargain, he got a lot many cooking-gas cylinders from the dead man's truck.

A new truck was coming up from behind. Neelu began to pull away her cart; her son joined her by pushing it. Perhaps they would empty the cart in her hut in the open ground behind my factory and quickly get back for something just as valuable. Cooking gas was much in demand in middle-class houses that were lucky to have gas ovens. Neelu almost certainly had no gas oven, she would hope to sell all those cylinders in the black market.

"Let's go, let's go," urged my wife. I could sense that she was horrified from the sight of the dead man's suspended head.

We moved a few meters ahead. On our left, the brickwork of the large unfinished building that Balbir Singh Chadda was getting built for his moulding factory lay in scattered heaps. Broken bricks lay around like piles of debris. Two of the concrete columns had been smashed, their steel reinforcements stuck out like bare elbow bones of a giant. What must have been bamboo scaffoldings lay submerged in black and grey ash. Nobody was around. I noticed a trail of grey cement-dust leading to the right side of the road. Some of it piled on the pavement between two large wheel marks. It was clear that they stole cement bags and other building materials and drove them away before smashing the building and starting the fire.

"This is the construction that Balbir Singh Chadda sent Guddu to check," I told my wife.

"God, lucky he got away, the poor youngster."

I closed my eyes and said a prayer.

As we moved on, not many damages were in sight. There were few Sikh factories ahead. Sikhs did not trust the local government after the state partition between their state and this. Perhaps the local state government did not like allotting plots to Sikhs after the *Khalistan* terror movement was orchestrated by a Sikh leader.

My wife noticed that the long road to our factory had been spruced up, that they had placed colorful potted crotons along both sides.

"So nice to see the government beautifying the industrial area," she said. The site of plants and trees always cheered the woman who hailed from a farming family. Perhaps red-and-green croton leaves temporarily erased the horrifying vision of crimson blood pouring out from a half-disconnected human head and forming a puddle on the bitumen below.

I said: "These plants are for the pleasure of the minister who would come to inaugurate our factory. When she goes back, the same plants would go to please some other VIP."

We turned left at the sprawling and walled-up plot of a politician who was close to the dead Prime Minister.

Then I turned right and was overcome with the urge to flee. The large *pandal*, a marquee being put up for the inauguration, stood burning. As fabrics and poles collapsed, flames crackled and hissed, rising high. I could feel the heat a hundred meters away.

Since my factory building did not have a hall big enough for the inauguration ceremony, a friend who owned the plot across the road allowed me to make arrangements on his open plot. Multan Tent House, owned by an ageing but a sprightly Sikh – Kartar Singh Bhuller – had taken the contract to make arrangements for the platform and the podium, long and wide white canvas roofing, colorful fabric festoons, carpets, flower arrangements, chairs, a front row of sofas for the VIPs (since the Very Insolent Persons considered it an insult to be made to sit at the same level as the hoi-polloi audience), microphones and speakers, the works. I had shelled out an advance of Rupees 200,000 for the arrangement. Kartar Singh also brought in large cauldrons, glasses, crockery and cutlery for serving snacks – as sumptuous as a lunch – for the invitees. For food and service, I was to pay later according to the number of plates passed around.

I gasped at the sight of a guard in Kartar Singh's employ, a middle-aged Sikh with greying and blood-stained beard, lying sprawled on the sand at the make-shift Arch. Blood that flowed down from his mouth had congealed like a thick string which flattened into a dried pool on the sand. His body lay twisted, his long white shirt bore marks of blows. His turban lay, torn and flattened, a foot away from his disheveled hair; around the round patch of his bald pate outlined by bloody scratch-like hairlines, thin bunches of hair were glued together in congealed blood. The side of his face bore a deep cut, blood clotted like jelly around it.

I closed my eyes. "Killed last night," I whispered.

My wife didn't get down from the scooter.

"Let's go back. I am going to faint," she mourned, her voice a soft shiver.

I felt a nausea coming up my throat.

On the opposite side of the road, a crowd of men jostled outside the door of my factory building. Some were bringing out and sharing among each other the blankets and transistor radios I had purchased on credit. Two youngsters stood aside, with some of the stuff safely between their legs lying on the ground, one ready with a cannister of what I imagined to be petrol or kerosene. The other one had in his hand a rod with its ends wrapped in a bundle of cloth, obviously to torch the building after all the booties were taken out. He kept swinging it up and down in excited anticipation. From inside the workplace behind the office, I heard sounds of hectic activity and hammering. It was a well-orchestrated raid, planned to rob all that they could and finish with arson.

Among the marauders was the Gurkha I paid for guarding the building. He held a transistor radio in his hand and a rolled-up blanket in his armpit, urging others to hurry up,

"Gosh, what are you doing? Why are you doing this to us?" screamed my wife, her feeling of faint suddenly gone. Not mindful of the risk in her frenzy, she rushed in through the crowd.

"Madam, keep away. This is Gurcharan Singh Rekhi's factory, not yours. We are setting fire to the *haramzada*[70] Sardar's building."

I recognized the man who said it. He was Ramcharan who owned and drove the pickup van that carried bundles of the same blankets and transistor radios for me from Delhi.

A case of Hindu Ramcharan versus Sikh Gurcharan. I was in the crossfire.

"Ramcharan, this is *my* factory. Rekhi was my contractor. I fired him for stealing the scaffoldings he hired on my account and using them on another contract."

"That's not what he told me. He said he owned the factory and that you were his manager," said Ramcharan.

Rekhi often borrowed my car supposedly for bringing in building supplies. One saved sales-tax scrutiny and the need to bribe at the border by bringing in small things like electrical and

---

[70] Ill-begotten.

toilet fittings in a private car. I always used my scooter to save some cost of petrol. So, I guessed, the impression had stuck that Rekhi who drove the car was the boss, I on my old scooter his humble manager.

There rose a series of sounds of smashing of glasses and bursts of implosions from inside the workplace. Of broken glasses showering down on the hard floor.

"My picture tubes and testing instruments are being smashed. I imported them on letters-of-credit with the banks," I cried: "I'd have to run away or go into hiding."

"Stop it, you mother-fuckers," shouted Ramcharan, straining his head towards the workplace door beyond the office.

The last piece of glass fell and shattered; suddenly there was utter silence inside. A couple of young men emerged from inside, swinging long iron rods in their hands.

"What happened, is the Sardar *haramzada* dead?"

Quite a few of those who got one or more transistor radios and blankets dispersed hurriedly.

"Sahib, I told them that you are a Hindu, that you are the owner, to these people when they came. I told them that it was you who paid me for my rice and lentil – my salary. They wouldn't believe me." Pleaded the Gurkha.

Rice and lentil were the Hindi equivalent of bread and butter.

"So, you began to steal with them. Thapa, I had believed that Gurkhas are honest and brave. You should be ashamed."

All Gurkhas were summarily known as Thapa but apparently not all of them trustworthy. Times had changed.

Ramcharan ordered his gang to stop the plunder and put away the can and the unlit torch.

"Everybody brings the radios and blankets back," he shouted.

He raised hands in the direction of those who were running away and called out to stop, but the loud command made no impact. Those who gained some distance speeded their pace, blankets in plastic packs, transistor radios in cardboard boxes held tight in their hands and under their arms. Many held more than one set.

"Don't bother, Ramcharan. There's going to be no inauguration, no distribution of blankets and radios to poor war-widows. I do not want those things back. The vendors won't take them back; if I keep them, they will keep reminding me of that poor Sardar lying out there, an honest man doing his duty killed like a mad dog while my own watchman survives and benefits by stealing with you."

A few more men who were standing around walked away with what they got. Ramcharan didn't insist that they return the stuff.

"Panicker Saa'b. forgive us. We believed Rekhi, that son-of-a-bitch Sardar. Now *we* will protect your factory."

He made my name sound like panic-ker. He was right; I felt. Helpless, cowardly and panic-stricken.

My wife walked in beyond the office and into the work place.

"Come, look," she screamed.

I didn't go in to look. I didn't want to witness the scene, the graveyard of my dreams, of my relentless hard work, of the hard times she and the kids went through.

Instead I turned around and pointed at the ground across the road, the white plastic poster screen-printed with Multan Tent House still in flames and crackling. Bhuller had named his enterprise after Multan in Pakistan in memory of his childhood, where in 1947 his father was hacked to death and mother was ravaged and then let go, cradling little Kartar in her arms and dragging herself along the dirt roads to India.

"Do you know how much it cost me to get that *pandal* put up?"

"We are sorry. We made a mistake. But we do not feel sorry for that sister-fucker Sardar Kartar Singh for his loss."

"You don't need to feel sorry for Kartar Singh Bhuller. I have paid most of the cost. Things will cool soon enough. Sikhs are like cats, trust me, they have seven lives. Fight is in their blood, don't you worry. So is money, black or white. You cowards gather into mobs and lynch lone or sleeping Sardars – trust me, that wouldn't be the end. When blood-for-blood is complete, there will be no blood left. Kartar Singh will come and collect the balance from me some day or beat me up. If somebody like you killed him, then his son or brother or nephew – someone would find me and collect or kill and dump me in a drain. Unless I had committed suicide in the meanwhile."

I realized I had been sobbing shamelessly. My wife, traumatized by what she saw in the workplace, stood stoic, touching me lightly on my shoulders, trying hard not to give in to tears and lose her feminine dignity before the crude strangers.

I pointed across the road.

"Who killed that Sardar lying there?"

"Who knows? He tried to resist my boys, so they battered him with hockey sticks. A *Sala* Sardar dying is not the same as our Mother Indira Gandhi dying."

As if his words were a cue, one of his underlings who still stood around screamed "*Khoon ka badla khoon.*" A few others pumped the air with their fists and repeated the words after him aloud as a war-cry. An eye for an eye. Indira Gandhi must get her revenge even in death. Let the whole world go blind.

"*Indira Gandhi Amar Rahe*". Long live Indira Gandhi, shouted the slogan-leader. The few others who remained repeated after him.

"That Sardar lying there did not kill Indira Gandhi. Two mad bigoted Sikhs did, cheating on their duty. So, you killed a helpless Sardar who was honestly doing his duty. The Gurkha who abandoned his duty and joined the looting spree got a blanket and a radio for reward."

Ramcharan lowered his head, pretending to feel remorse. The Gurkha slunk away.

My newly installed telephone rang inside the office. I went in and picked it up, refraining from looking in through the open door to the workplace. Prasad, the faithful supervisor in my Delhi workshop, had the new number. While getting a normal phone connection took several years, this one was installed within a week after I filed the application – the magic of a minister's promised visit.

'Sir, they killed our Harkishen,' said Prasad, choking through his words which hit me like a bolt of lightning.

Harkishen Singh, maybe in his early thirties but looking no more than a sprightly 18, employed as a wireman on the recommendation of Mr. Mantri, Member of Parliament. The thin and wiry Sikh had scanty hair on his chin which he embellished by pulling down bunches of hair from under his turban and sticking them with glue on his cheeks and under his chin. The Sardar didn't disappoint me. Though he kept entertaining the girls with constant prattle, his productivity was amazing. Most of the work on the assembly line was repetitive, so his chatter didn't affect work. He had a huge store of Sardar jokes to regale the girls with. This didn't surprise me; I had heard Milkha Singh the famous Flying Sikh reeling out Sardar jokes – somewhat like Irish and Scottish jokes by the British – in the Golf Club of Chandigarh. Milkha told a couple of them even about himself. Khushwant Singh, the agnostic writer who wrote the *History of Sikhs* and an emotion-packed novel about the 1947 Hindu-Muslim massacre, *Train To Pakistan,* also wrote Sardar jokes.

As the jovial and almost adolescent face of Harkishen Singh Bedi flitted through my mind, I gripped the handset hard.

"Harkishen? No! How?"

"We were travelling together in a bus to *Phoolvali* junction. On top of the new bridge, a gang of men stopped the bus. A kindly woman who knew what could happen told Harkishen to crouch under her seat. She sat with her legs over him, her sari spread out to hide him. She motioned me to sit beside her to avoid attention.

"Some twenty hooligans barged into the bus with knives and sticks. "Any refugee bastards in the bus," asked one.

"The stupid driver first nodded yes, and then no. They combed the bus seat by seat – not for refugees, but for Sikhs. One of them looked beyond me and noticed the bulge under the fat woman's clothes. They pulled me out, kicked her aside and dragged out Harkishen. One of them slapped the old lady for trying to save him. Poor Harkishen kept screaming and pleading for mercy while they dragged him along the floor of the bus and carried him to the parapet of the bridge. I kept telling them that he was not a refugee, but a citizen. I tried to run after them, but they didn't let me get down from the bus. As we watched in horror, four of them held each of his limbs as if they were playing a game, swinging him in the air like a fishing net. Then they let go, flinging him over the rail. His cries were chilling, sir, you can't imagine how. I got down at the next stop and ran back. When I reached below the bridge, I saw his face smashed against the rail track. He was dead. There were many people standing around, but only one old man helped me get him out of the track. He is still lying there"

Prasad began to sob. I waited without urging him on. I could hear the pounding of my own heart.

"I ran looking for any shop with a telephone, but all were closed. I'm making this call from the police station. I first tried your house, and then this phone."

Prasad lowered his voice; I could picture him masking his mouth with a hand. He spoke in Tamil: "I reported Harkishen's murder to the *Havaldar*[71] at the desk. I said I could recognize the killers. I knew at least two of them – both from P-Town. The *Havaldar asked* me if I was the keeper for all Sardars in Delhi. Another one said the Sardars killed Indira Gandhi; now they will have to face the consequences."

"What buck-buck are you saying in *Madrasi*? Get out, you *Sardaron* ka *Gandu*."

That was a voice from behind Prasad. *Gandu* meant a willing victim of sodomy. There followed a sharp crack which I felt sure was a slap on Prasad's cheek. The phone was banged down. Not by Prasad. He would never bang down a phone on me.

Prasad could not understand why the killers called Sikhs as refugees. During the 1947 Hindu-Muslim bloodbath, the Sikhs as well as Hindus who lived in many cities of what became West Pakistan after partition were either killed or escaped to Indian side while the bulk of Muslims from North-Indian cities– those who were lucky to survive – went over to Pakistan. Those who fled to India were mostly farmers and businessmen who lost their everything and many of their relations during their flight for life. The enterprising Sikhs and other Punjabis took advantage of government munificence. New industrial towns and residential areas were allotted for a pittance to the lucky ones. The Bhakra Nangal dam, over Sutlej river, completed soon after independence, helped in the irrigation of thousands of hectares of farms and brought prosperity to their land.

Sikhs who chose to live in Delhi took to trading, shop-keeping and building small-scale industries. Many enlisted in the military, much of which they got to monopolize with their courage and readiness for battle. Within a few years, the refugees became

---

[71] *A Head-constable in the state police force.*

affluent land owners, farmers and businessmen, military officers and men. Yet many of them took pride in declaring "I'm from Pakistan," reminiscing over their lives in the towns and villages they hailed from.

On the other hand, the Hindu refugees in the East who were driven out from East Pakistan had no such luck. They lived for years as destitutes; some never recovered. Many women fled from the *Bhadra Lok* – secure Hindu middle-class – status in the Muslim Bengal became prostitutes in Calcutta streets to support their families. Punjabis attributed their prosperity to their inherent industriousness; others believed that they got undue favors from successive governments. When in anger, envy surfaced – people from further East – Uttar Pradesh (Northern Province) –and Bihar called them refugees. The word amounted to something despicable, an abuse.

I put down the phone, wishing, without much hope, that the constables who slapped him didn't give Prasad the standard police treatment of punching with elbows on the small of his back and knee to his testicles. Feeling crushed, I sat on my haunches on the floor since chairs had been flung around during the loot. My wife stood beside me, not asking who was on the phone. She knew it would be bad news, and didn't want a share in it.

I hoped Prasad, if he was well enough, will have the good sense to inform Harkishen's wife or parents. Hoping he would find them alive.

We came out on the road, not bothering to look for the lock to shut the building door, not caring to look at the small crowd of killers at the gate still holding the gifts that would have heartened some poor war-widows. I hoped none of those widows would come to the place two days later, trusting the invitation letter I had sent them, only to return disappointed. It had taken Subedar Major Ram Kishore Singh quite some effort and his practiced military strategy to get their names and addresses from the Ex-Army men's Association and the local military pension office.

The thought of the Subedar Major, the responsible and efficient manager, made me wonder why it never occurred to him to come and check if the factory he was supposed to be managing was safe. At least he could call me.

As we sat on the scooter, the horizon ahead of us and on our distant right appeared to be in flames and black smoke. I didn't want to ride ahead and risk her life, but my wife prodded me on. "Think of our children," she said.

Three trucks and a jeep stood burning at the border. The truck with the human head suspended from a broken neck still was there, but not on fire yet. Behind it was a truck on dying fire. Below its driver's window lay a half-burnt body of a man, one of his legs sticking up stiffly in the air. Another couple of trucks that had evidently tried to turn back some distance away from the border after sighting the danger also were burning. Five or six men with iron rods in hand, ran after a short, stocky man who jumped out from another truck and ran. I couldn't see his face, but it was clear that he wore a turban. That Sardar had no chance, I said to myself, every strand of hair on my forearm standing on their ends. There was nothing I could do.

After a few moments, as I was clearing the last of the shuttered kiosks to my left, there rose an agonizing scream. I knew they got him.

Past Cotton-Town junction, and the narrow boulevard that was Delhi Road, one breathed kerosene smoke and smelled death. As we came up in line with the runway, An Air India Jumbo was descending so low that my wife feared it would hit her head. I explained that the runway was just a few dozen meters ahead; its touch-down point may be a couple of hundred meters more.

The sight of the aircraft made me recall that at least once

before, Sikh terrorists had hijacked Indian Airline flights involving more than a hundred passengers and half a dozen crew. Not by good luck, but more by the tact of the handlers and international pressure on the government of Pakistan, none was killed. I was no clairvoyant to anticipate that in seven months yet to come, Sikh immigrants in Canada would time-bomb an Air India Jumbo mid-flight that bore 329 innocents – many of them of nationalities that had nothing to do with the pogrom on Sikhs. That their bodies would burst and scatter in mid-air in the stratosphere over Ireland. Or that only 24 of them would be Indians, 35 of them Sikhs – mostly Canadian citizens.

We turned right on to the deserted airport road and spotted a body that lay, head and torso dangling down towards the low ground some two feel below, legs spread on the sidewalk. I slowed down and noticed that one of his legs was twisted, broken. His one hand lay limp by his side, gripping a tuft of grass. The steel *kada* on his wrist sparkled in the bright sun.

"My God. Please move on. It's not your friend Guddu," whispered my wife in my ears. "There's no scooter near him."

"If it is Guddu, they would have taken away his scooter," I shouted back into the wind. "Behind every murder there's a loot."

I didn't tell her that it indeed was Guddu, that I recognized his trousers, that they broke his leg to prevent him from running, that I noticed a long and bloody tear in his trouser where he was struck probably with a twisted steel rod, breaking his calf-bone before they killed him. A young man with a wife and a baby waiting anxiously for him to get back home was killed brutally and in cold blood. Only a month ago Guddu had distributed sweets when his first child was born.

The children greeted us at the gate.

"Where did you go? Did you hear that you must not drink

water? *Sardarjis* have poisoned all the water tanks in Delhi." That was my twelve-year-old son,

"Who told you this nonsense? At least a tenth of Delhi's population are Sikhs. Won't they have to drink water too?"

"I don't know. They are going around and announcing it over the loudhailer."

"Making one more excuse to kill Sikhs."

"Dad, why are we killing Sikhs? Isn't Karnail Uncle a Sikh?"

"Yes, they tried to kill him too, not we, not all Hindus, a few blood-thirsty idiots prodded on by their leaders. My last conversation with Prasad makes me suspect that the police – even the government – might be in league with the killers. One excuse is that two of her Sikh guards killed Indira Gandhi. Another that the Sikhs celebrated her death somewhere in Connaught Place. Now they lie to us that Sikhs are poisoning drinking water. These are triggers, not causes. There were Sikhs killing Hindus before – not the ordinary Sikh, but those goaded on by a man named Jarnail Singh Bhinderwale, maybe for the last ten years, Sikh extremists pulling out Hindus from trains and buses and killing in cold blood; Hindu-Sikh riots in places. The mutual hatred has been building up in Punjab and Haryana after they separated. Delhi has become the battleground after Indira Gandhi's death. Like you can't fight a flood, Sikhs are overwhelmed by the sheer number of the killers. The government has not come to their rescue, Sikhs in Delhi and everywhere other than Punjab live in isolated clusters. So, there is no fight, only killing. Like Ghori and Ghasni on Hindus so many centuries ago."

My ten-year-old daughter stared at me with her mouth wide open.

"That couldn't be," she exclaimed. "My classmate Kulbir is a *Sardarji* with long hair, *chota* (small) turban, *kada* and all. His parents are Hindus. They took a vow after they had three daughters that if they got a son, they would make him a Sikh. Can his parents kill him now because he's a Sikh?"

They will not, I told her, but they might hide him or cut his hair, giving in to defeat. Many families are a mix of bearded Sikhs and beardless Sikhs who worshipped the same Guru, and prayed at the same Gurudwaras but the beardless would be spared since nothing marked them out as Sikhs. Many Sikhs were not averse to worshiping in Hindu temples. So many of them bore the names of Hindu deities – Ram Singh, Kishen Singh, Gopal Singh and so on. Harkishen had a twin-Hindu name – Hari and Kishen. Their sacred book had verses written by Hindu saints and poet Kabir – the ancient social reformer who tried to bridge Hindu-Muslim differences with his verses. You couldn't tell who was who, so for now the beard and long hair has become the marker for the target of hate.

Somebody had to be informed where Guddu's body lay. Not Chadda, I decided with bitterness.

I called Balwant Singh, president of RMA – Radio Manufacturers' Association, and told him of my meeting with Guddu of Chadda Engineering, and how on my return I found that he had been killed, and the location where his body lay. I couldn't pick him up, I said apologetically, I was on scooter and my wife was with me.

The Association had all Sikhs except for a Sindhi Hindu – Jagdish Mithawani and myself, a Madrasi from Palghat, among its members.

"Chadda, the bastard, worms will eat him in hell," growled Balwant and rang off.

It just struck me, I didn't know Guddu's real name. Guddu was a child's pet name he was known by in the small trade circle.

On television, the Prime Minister was speaking, as stoic and emotionless as before.

"Disgraceful incidents of loot arsons and murder have taken place. This must stop further forthwith. The government will ensure the safety of life and property irrespective of caste, creed or religion. As Prime Minister of India I cannot and will not allow..."[72]

Must stop further forthwith? So, it was all right so far, now that the message of revenge has gone home to Sikh community after innocents like Guddu were killed brutally? Why didn't he say that the murderers will be punished according to law?

The phone rang. It was Dr. Varkey.

"Mr. Panicker, too many killings outside. I keep getting calls all the time, but feel helpless. Last night the hospital couldn't spare any ambulance. I think we need to take that Sardar to a hospital without delay. His wounds could get infected. He may lose his left arm if he survives at all."

I had always imagined Dr. Varkey as a kindly doctor but a distant man, never overtly friendly. His teasing Satnam Kaur about taking her house as doctor's fee showed another side of the man, a new persona. He was a child-specialist who practised in several hospitals by turn. In the evening he ran something of a general clinic for children in his modified garage. A very busy doctor.

"Yes, doctor. I'll see that Karnail is ready. It would be easier for you than me to get an ambulance."

"Not to worry, leave that to me. I have an idea. I don't want his wife and children accompanying him. It could be a dangerous trip. Men are roaming the streets, stopping vehicles and pulling out anyone with a beard, even people whose tan on the face shows that they were Sardars who hurriedly cut their hair. This afternoon, they say, some thousand men barged into that big Gurudwara —what's its name – and killed the Sikhs there."

---

[72] *Rajiv Gandhi, on 'Door Darshan' television, November 3, 1984. On public domain.*

"You mean Gurudwara Rakab Ganj or Bangla Sahib. That's terrible. I'll go with Karnail."

"Tell you what. Don't be shocked. I will hail a hearse, not an ambulance. That would be safer. Sounds horrible, but that could save the Sardar's life. I'll wait for you in J- hospital. Come straight to the casualty. But wait. The attendants know the extent of danger. They will cover him with a shroud even though he would be secure inside the vehicle. The casualty people would know when you arrive. They won't send the Sardar to mortuary, don't worry."

I hesitated, but agreed. The ride could cost me my life if they discovered a living Sikh under the shroud. There was no other way.

It took quite some knocking before Satnam Kaur opened the door a little ajar, saw me, and let me in. Evaporated tears had marked greylines below her eyes. Her nose dripped a thin liquid which she wiped with the back of her hand, a gesture that would have shocked me at another time.

"How's he?"

"Still sleeping. Doctor Saa'b sedated him too much, I think."

"When he wakes up and begins to howl from pain, you'd think he should have sedated him much more. Satnam, I've come to tell you that we're taking him to hospital. He needs much more attention that we can give him here."

"I will come with you. Children can stay with Aunty and your children."

My wife called the younger Satnam by name after she said she preferred it to the formal Mrs. Ahluwalia. She called my wife Aunty and me Uncle-ji. Salt-and-pepper hair got extra respect.

"No, you won't. Even those traveling in an ambulance are being searched. And you look too much of a Sikh lady. We'll be taking him…. never mind how we will take him. He'll be safe. The children and you could stay with aunty Panicker and children. You don't seem to have eaten anything. She will make *iddli-sambar* for you."

Punjabis mocked South Indians as *Iddli-sambar* people just as Australians call Indians *Curry*. Yet all of them loved the delicious combination of soft and grainy fermented and steamed rice-buns and lentil curried with assorted vegetables.

She plonked down on the sofa, her hands on her face. Her body heaved in long spasms.

"Uncle-*ji*, what has my poor *Gudia-da-Papa* done? Did we kill Indira Gandhi? Why are they doing this to us? Are we not Indians, just like Hindus? Didn't our Guru Tej Bahadur die to save Hindus? You know my two brothers are modified Sikhs. If they know what happened to Karnail-*ji*, they would come running."

She gave me the phone numbers of her brothers from memory. Mohinder and Maninder Makhija. I phoned Mohinder and as briefly as I could, explained the situation to him. The man was shocked that nobody, not even Satnam, had told him.

"Mohinder Saa'b, your sister was not in a state of mind to call anyone. We're taking Karnail to J-hospital. He will be under good care. Satnam and children will stay in my house till things clear up. I will give your phone number to the hospital. You could call them and keep checking on his progress. If there's something you could do, they will call you. You can even visit him sometime later."

"Please tell Maninder, my younger brother. I won't have the heart to tell him myself. His brother-in-law in T-Town has been killed. Tomorrow was to be the wedding of his daughter to Rajan Malhotra, a Hindu."

When he began to sob, I put down the phone. I didn't have the heart to call Maninder Makhija.

A moment later, Satnam's phone rang. I picked it up. It was Mohinder. Under the impression that his sister was on the line, he spoke in Punjabi.

"Please tell your neighbor that I'll pick you up and children. We don't want to risk their safety."

I told him it was an unnecessary concern, but it was OK if that's what Satnam wished.

A van, with a morose and loud HEARSE written on its sides arrived. Two men who came with it brought out a stretcher and picked up Karnail Singh, who only grunted. Not wanting to let his wife or children know the type of vehicle he was going to ride, I made sure that neither she nor her children came out of the house. They covered Karnail with a shroud as if the one under it were dead, and closed the door. I sat with the driver next to the medical assistant who shuffled in his seat to give me space. We drove off.

Dr. Varkey received us at the Casualty gate. He shoed me off after he took over the injured patient.

"Your wife has been calling my home. She fears you might get into some kind of trouble, and probably suspects I'm the cause of that trouble." Varkey smiled.

When I returned home, Satnam's two brothers had already taken her and children away. Their door and the gate were locked.

Rumours came trickling in from neighbors, the vegetable man with his handcart and, more persistently, the colony gossip, Mr. Gupta.

Sikhs were being pulled out of trains, buses, even houses. The gossip said there was not a single Sikh left in M-town and K-Nagar. T-Town, he said, was looted, ravaged and set ablaze. Killer mobs were being brought in from nearby towns and supplied with Kerosene cannisters and hockey sticks. They pulled out men at night from their beds, broke their legs, and then killed them. Women who tried to fend off the attack on their husbands or brothers were molested, a few were raped. A young bride, being made up by a beautician for her wedding, was carried away while her father and grandfather were beaten and set on fire. In the Indira Nagar village across the road, all eleven Sardars were looted and killed, their houses set on fire, their newly built Gurudwara was gutted. Most women ran away with their children; a few were gang-raped.

It was difficult to believe what was true and what was not. I had seen enough brutality for a lifetime that morning, yet things couldn't be all that brutal as Gupta described. Gossips like him found satisfaction in making up gruesome tales.

Balwant Singh called.

"Panicker Saa'b, we are meeting the Station House Officer Inspector Bawa tomorrow. Would you like to come, or are you on the other side?"

I noted that the Saa'b part marked some distance between us, which did not exist before. He always called me by my first name, Madhav, or Panicker. Never with a Saa'b.

"Don't talk nonsense, Balwant. I'll come. Tell me when."

"We're only one percent Sikhs in India. Would they want us all to be wiped out?"

"Balwant, don't lose heart. Sikhs cannot be wiped out. You guys are forged from hardened steel."

If the compliment impressed him, it didn't show in his response.

"You know how we campaigned for Mantri, the mother-fucker who said he was not a leader, but a servant of Indira Gandhi? Every Sikh in our association had donated thousands to his election campaign. Chadda also paid for his vehicles, campaign posters and leaflets. Four years ago, we had believed that Indira Gandhi was our saviour. She attacked our Harmandir

Sahib and got hundreds killed. Now her ghost is killing us. The son-of-a-bitch Mantri, who was proud to be her eunuch servant is directing the killing. That man with an English name, the mother-fucker's own mother is a Sikh. He's in it too"

"Balwant, these are rumors. This is mob fury. Not an organized crime. Mantri cannot be in it. My Harkishen, who was killed this morning, was recommended to me by Mantri."

"The political bastards will recommend any stranger if there is a chance of a vote or two. What did he lose?"

He had a point.

"Not an organized crime? It is a war on us Sikhs, not mob fury. Kerosene is on ration. Yet freely given away to arsonists. Who gave them so many kerosene cannisters, batons, hockey sticks, even guns? They issue twisted steel rods from construction sites, cut to size"

I remembered the gash on Guddu's broken leg.

The industrial complex where most of the small-scale manufacturers had their factories was a virtual Punjab where Sikhs had their workplace below and houses above, had not been attacked. At least not yet. Station House Officer Ramesh Kumar Bawa had his police station right at the edge of the complex.

Balwant Singh said he would meet me in Bawa's office at 10:30 in the morning. Bawa had promised to be there.

I said I would pick him up.

"No need. If hundreds of Sikhs can die in one night, I am not a coward to be traveling by hiding in your car. I'll be there at 10:30. So will other Sardars be."

That evening, it was decided that there will be no night-watch since Karnail and family, the only Sikhs in the street, were safe and away.

We were wrong. A little before midnight, a mob with rods and crowbars broke open Karnail's house, not bothered about the noise they made. When I heard the commotion and came out, they were picking up the refrigerator, washing machine, stereo, safe and all that was worth looting from the house and stacking them into a mini-van. The fancy stereo was a gift I made on Gudia's fifth birthday.

Instinctively, but stupidly, I shouted at them to stop.

"Don't come near, you *Sardaron*-ka-*gandu*. You will die the death of a dog."

To prove that I was an assole for Sardars and deserved to die like a dog, one of the looters flung a heavy stone in my direction. It fell a dozen meters away from me. Perhaps he had instructions only to frighten, not to kill Sardars' Hindu assoles.

I went inside the house to alert the neighbors by phone. The looters drove away after setting fire to the house. I called the fire station. Quite some time passed before a voice emerged from the ear piece. Sorry, all fire tenders were away on duty. Give the address, the voice said, if one of the fire tenders came back, it would be sent it your place. Sorry, too many fires in Delhi tonight.

I wasted nearly half an hour on the futile call. The fire had spread.

I woke my son who readily sprang up and joined me to collect buckets of water. He went out shouting fire, fire! and ran around the street. Good boy. Soon most of the men of the colony were out, running in with buckets of water. Sandeep Joshi, who had the nearest house to Karnail's kept his bathrooms and kitchen open for replenishing the buckets. A couple of bold women, one of them Sandeep's wife, and the other, wife of Lawyer Ali, stood at the turnings, looking out for danger. A red-painted fire hydrant stood helplessly in the street. We had no hose that could fit the hydrant.

It turned out to be a useless exercise against Karnail's magnificent two-storey house. After a couple of hours of struggle, attention was turned to preventing the fire spreading to Sandeep's own house and Swaminathan's house on the other side. We kept working all through the night. By sunrise Karnail's house, fitted out with much woodwork, had collapsed into a heap of debris. Fallen blocks of brickwork crushed burnt-out windows and doors. Columns, supporting caved-in slabs stood stuck out like memorials to our wasted effort. The solitary neem tree in his small garden stood with a few remaining black and brown leaves. The yard was slushy with drenched ash.

Nine-thirty television showed a sombre Rajiv Gandhi leading the pall bearers who were bringing out his mother's flower-decked body. My daughter observed that even in death Indira Gandhi seemed to hold her dignity and that her aquiline nose towered over the flower-outlined face. Many women who were following the stretcher were crying. My wife had tears in her eyes.

I had lost respect for the woman after she declared emergency instead of honorably giving up the chair when a court ordered her election void. My wife argued that the stifling emergency brought about a semblance of order in the Country. That was nonsense, yet the sight of her body washed away much of my hard feeling. Once a young ideologist, political realities hardened her heart, and raised her survival instinct as it happened to most politicians in power. She had been advised to remove the Sikh bodyguards after she ordered the attack on their holy temple, but refused to pick and choose according to religious leanings. The last bit of ideology which remained in her heart was her undoing. I felt sad, even angry.

It was Indira Gandhi and her party that nurtured the Sikh bigot Bhinderwale to begin with – she used him as a counterpoise for the powerful Sikh political party – *Akali Dal* – The Timeless Party. Bhinderwale turned out to be a Frankenstein's monster within a short while. He was a gripping orator in his native Punjabi. Sikhs, young and old, loved him reeling out the greatness of the Sikhs and how they had been betrayed by Hindu India. Some did know that he meant trouble for the community, but youngsters were energized and indoctrinated. As he grew bolder, he gathered a horde of men whom he brainwashed with the idea of terrorism. He extolled Sikhs to kill 30 Hindus each, and caused the death of a well-known editor and attacked a breakaway cult of Sikhism.

When Indira's Government got hot on his heels, he holed up in Sikh's sacred shrine, the Golden temple, with a few hundred accomplices. Money poured in from Canada and England, warlike weapons from Pakistan. His men carried out attacks on ordinary Hindus and assassinated senior politicians and a senior police officer. As the menace grew, an exasperated Indira Gandhi ordered the army to surround the temple to frighten the terrorists and smoke them out. When it didn't work on the hardened Sikhs inside the shrine; on a day auspicious to Sikhs and hundreds of worshippers had gathered in the temple, the army chose to launch a direct attack with armored vehicles and machine guns. What followed was a full-scale battle, resulting in the death of Bhinderwale and 300 of his henchmen, but also of several worshippers – many say several hundred – in the temple. Army claimed that it lost 83 soldiers and that some 200 were injured, but Sikhs boasted that hundreds of soldiers were among the dead.

Sikhs in the street were furious at the daring attack on their sacred shrine which they believed to be unassailable. Even those who were admirers of Indira Gandhi and members of the Congress Party – except those who enjoyed high power under her patronage, among them the President and the Sports Minister, raised voices of revolt. Many Sikh soldiers deserted their posts.

On the fateful 31st October, Beant Singh, a junior police officer who often boasted of his ten-year-long closeness to the Prime Minister and Satwant Singh, a young recruit to her security setup, shot her dead in her garden while she was on her way for an interview with Peter Ustinov. Most Sikhs exulted that she had it coming and were pleased at the killing of the woman by two Sikhs, Hindus thought it was an unforgivable act of treason; some of them decided to take revenge on the Sikh in the street. He was a sitting duck, an easy prey.

When I started out for the meeting with the police officer, the television was showing the hunched figure of Mother Teresa walking somberly among the jostling crowd towards the funeral site. Four years before, while she was being awarded India's highest award, *Bharat Ratna* – Gem of India – Indira Gandhi had shed tears reminiscing her services to the downtrodden. None of our services would measure up to the Mother's, she had said. The Mother hadn't forgotten.

Ten Sikh businessmen, French-bearded Jagdish Mithawani the Sindhi and the beardless me were escorted by uncharacteristically courteous constables into the office of the Station House Officer – Ramesh Kumar Bawa, no doubt a Punjabi Hindu. Nearly all ten Sikhs defiantly wore over their shirts *Kirpan*, the dagger Sikhs were authorized to wear as a religious symbol, but normally worn inside their shirts by a few, and not at all by most. One Sikh, whom I couldn't place, chose to stay away. Surprisingly, as if in defiance, their beards hung untied below their chin. Under normal circumstances, only the extremely religious Sikhs did not tie and glue their beard to the chin. I noticed the bulge of what I believed to be a revolver in Balwant Singh's pocket. Perhaps a couple of others carried their revolvers – licensed or illegal – in their pockets too or under their long shirts.

Station House Officer Inspector Bawa, the commanding officer of the police personnel in the area assigned to him, greeted the Sikhs with a *Sat-sri-akal.* God is Eternal Truth. He looked at Jagdish and me with a frown. Only a couple of the Sikhs returned the greeting with a low murmur. They stood opposite his desk, their fists resting on its top. Defiance stressed the room. Bawa gestured all to sit down on the chairs precisely arranged for 13. Balwant and Chadda sat in the middle, other Sikhs on both their sides. Only one chair remained empty. Mithawani and I sat together at one end.

"Why are you here, Mr. Panicker?"

I felt slighted. The idiot knew I was a manufacturer and a member of the association. He had collected at least two expensive radio-tape recorders and a car-radio from me in the name of local magistrates. He never paid for them. Policemen never pay. Perhaps magistrates don't pay either.

"Did you expect me to be in the mob killing our Sikh brothers?"

Bawa frowned, but didn't come up with a wisecrack. Perhaps he too took me for an *assole* for the Sikhs.

Bawa opened the discussion with: "Look, I am trying my best to see that no murder takes place in my zone. None of you has been attacked, and God willing, none will be. I know there has been a couple of attacks in M-Town. I have increased the beat in that area. And there has been no incident after that."

"Not just attacks, but murders. But you didn't catch the killers. They are still roaming around, looking for more Sardars to kill and their houses to loot. You sit there and tell us that *we may not be* killed. You know we could be – some of us tomorrow, even today." Balwant Singh's voice was hoarse from unconcealed anger.

Almost every evening SHO Bawa would visit Balwant and share pegs of the duty-free Johnny Walker whisky of which Balwant always held a stock. His brother-in-law was a frequent visitor from Toronto, Balwant himself often flew to Hong Kong or Tokyo for negotiating imports.

Balwant continued in his agitated voice: "Who gave you the

order not to interfere with the killings in your area, Bawa? Jagat? Mantri the ingrate? Kumar? That half-caste Tailor? Or right from the top – Rajiv?" As he reeled out names, his decibel rose.

Inspector Bawa, accustomed to shouting at and beating up visitors to his office and not being shouted at, appeared strained while trying to control his temper. Perhaps Johnny Walker Black Label generated a feeling of obligation. He sat drumming the table and rubbing his well-shaven chin. Under the table his feet kept tapping the floor.

Balwant hadn't finished. "You say you have put extra beat constables in M-Town. There's not a single constable anywhere in M-Town, I tell you. You say you're taking care of this part of the town. I don't see any constable on the beat in any part of this town either. Why isn't the army instead of spineless policemen be protecting us? OK, if the army is not allowed to fight with civilians, why aren't the reserve police force be called in? Tell us, SHO Saa'b, place your hand on your heart and tell me, were you ordered to send all your constables on leave? I know that you have at least two Sardar policemen here in your station. Where are they? Have they been killed?"

Bawa's voice was calm and dejected when he said, "Balwant-ji, matter of fact one of them, Hari Singh, was killed. Not here, not in my area, but in *Pathankot Express*[73]. By 31st night, we knew that things were getting dangerous for Sikhs. Hari Singh was paranoid, he was newly married. He put a leave application on my table at night and went to catch a train to Jalandhar assuming he would be safe in Punjab where he had his family. He was stabbed and thrown out of the train just before Karnal. He had worn his uniform hoping that no one would harm a policeman. The beasts

---

[73] *A daily train service from North to a town, Pathankot, at the threshold of Kashmir valley.*

didn't care. We are making a collection among ourselves for his family."

The Sikhs offered five hundred rupees each. So did Mithawani and I. Rupees six thousand was a lot of money in 1984.

Everyone sat silent, the tragedy of one more young man, a policeman, cast a deadly gloom.

Balbir Singh Chadda spoke up. "Balwant, Bawa Saa'b, there's no point in our blaming each other. We're sorry about Hari Singh's death. May *Babaji* take care of him and give him peace. On the morning after the Indira-killing, they killed my Guddu. He's not my son, but dear to me like one of my own. Killed like a dog on the airport road. Panicker Saa'b here informed you, Balwant, not me, because, he told you, that he was mad at me for having sent the young man to the border at a time like this. Honestly, by God, I did not know how dangerous the situation was."

Kuldeep Singh Sony, the man to whom I owed the cost of a hundred transistor radios, said: "Chadda Saa'b, I am surprised you did not know. President Zail Singh-*ji*'s car was stoned in the same 31st afternoon even before they announced Indira Gandhi's death. They started the killing and dacoity even as her son was taking oath. At 8 PM that very same night, they set fire to Karnail Ahluwalia's car and killed him. My man Sunder watched the happening in horror, but there was nothing he could do. They burnt Karnail alive in his new Maruti car. That *Sardarji* died without a whimper. Then they stopped a Punjab Roadways bus coming in from Patiala and set fire to it too. They allowed the passengers to get down, but not the *Sardar* driver and another two or three Sardar passengers, broke their legs and threw them in the fire."

I chipped in: "That was terrible, but I have some good news for you on that incident. I didn't know about the massacre in the bus though Karnail told me how his would-be killers ran after a bus after setting fire to his Maruti. That was what saved him. Karnail is not dead and, God willing, will be fine. Sunder did not see his escape because he rolled away after opening the door of the car on the other side. Fortunately, they had made him park the car on the wrong side of the road, and there was a drain on that side, and a wall beyond it. He fell into the drain and crawled in it most of the way home. He is badly, but in a hospital under a Christian doctor's care. His wife and children have gone to Punjab with her Hindu brother Mohinder Singh Makhija."

I didn't want to spoil the good effect by telling them that Karnail's dream house was burnt down the next night. For a moment, the faces lit up. Jagdish Mithawani clapped hands briefly.

My fury on Chadda had not abated, I knew that he was lying; Every Sikh in Delhi anticipated trouble after the assassination and knew that it had started soon after the attack on K-Town. There was no point asking Chadda if he would have sent his own son on that morning on the same mission.

Balwant Singh's voice was calm when he said what he had told me before: "We're only a few million, you all may be seven hundred million. Though less than two percent, Bawa, you can't kill all of us. At least some of us will live and remember the happenings of these days."

Perhaps he felt what he said hurt me.

"Panicker Saa'b, I did not mean good people like you and my good friend Mithawani here. Most of the Hindus are good people. My brother's son-in-law is a Hindu. The Sikhs in the South are safe and sound. I mean the killers. Jagat or Phatak, Tailor or cobbler, we will track them down. Bawa, we are businessmen with licensed guns. If those guns are not enough, we will get smuggled ones. You try to stop us although you couldn't stop the killers. For every Sikh who dies in this area, we will kill ten."

Looking back, I feel grateful that such a threat did not happen to materialize. Sikhs were incredibly brave, but four centuries of wars and bloodshed had made them resilient.

The police officer didn't warn Balwant Singh that he was making a cognizable offence with such a blatant threat. Instead, he kept drumming on the table with his fingers. The Sikhs got up and walked out. There was no formal closure to the meeting, no summing up, no good-byes.

Bawa motioned me to stop and sit down.

"Tell them not to bring out their guns or display their *kirpans* like this. What do they have, air rifles, point two-two or double-barrels? Old army-auctioned Colts? Those toys wouldn't help against a huge mob. Killers are moving in thousands. In Gurudwara Rakab Ganj, the Sikhs had guns, swords and kirpans. Yet a father and a son were set ablaze right in front of their eyes. The manager's office was ransacked and burnt, the old man was killed. Tell them to keep to themselves for a couple of days more. Things will quiet down and there will be peace unless the Sikhs start it again."

He sounded as if there was a definite plan for the number of days the killings would be allowed.

When I came out, the Sikhs were waiting.

"What did the mother-fucking inspector tell you? Not to be with us?"

"Bhai Saa'bs (Dear Brothers), I am not a Sardar, but I lost more than any one of you. More than all my life's earnings ever."

'We have heard," said Chadda. Others nodded in sympathy.

I didn't pass Bawa's piece of good advice to them. That turned out to be a terrible mistake.

The same evening Chadda's office and factory were ransacked. Of the two guards, one a Sikh and the other a Hindu, the Sikh, who had a double-barrel gun fired in the air as he was probably instructed and was killed; the gun was snatched away. The Hindu was battered, his teeth smashed in, his right arm was broken. Currency notes stacked in jute bags and hidden among mountains of corrugated carton folds – all black money, no doubt – were brought out. The mob fought among each other for the bundles of money, witnesses watched from their windows in houses at a distance. As usual, there were no policemen in sight.

When I returned home and parked my car, children did not come out to greet me. I found them glued to the TV. There were no Hi-Dads and no smiles of welcome.

On television, the flame had died out. The pyre had flattened, the body inside had turned to ashes. Rajiv Gandhi stood with a long stick in his hand, still being guided by a priest, at the edge of the platform where his mother had been reduced to ashes. My wife wiped her nose, hissing softly.

"Was Zail Singh there?" I asked.

"Yes," said my son. "He added a stick to the funeral pyre. Dad, you won't believe it. One of those in the row of foreign leaders was Zia-ul-Huq, Prime minister of Pakistan."

"Not Prime Minister, President of Pakistan. He probably came to relish the sight of the funeral of the woman who broke up Pakistan and created Bangladesh. Zia is a *cutter* Muslim. Religious scriptures bask in stories of revenge and murder."

I was no astrologer; had no way to foresee that Zia himself would be assassinated along with many of his generals and the US Ambassador some five years later. Five years before Indira's death, Zia had engineered the execution of Zulfikar Ali Bhutto, the Prime Minister who had earlier appointed him out of turn as the chief of Pakistan Army. Governments are mafias, I had read somewhere, that in a mafia, members felt no gratitude, didn't argue and debate rights and wrongs. They arranged each other's execution.

On the fourth of November, as if on an order, all became quiet like a storm that ended abruptly. Policemen reappeared and roamed the streets, announcing over loudhailers that those who had taken away things from Sikh houses should deposit them at specified places, or the consequence would be serious.

There was no call for the murderers to surrender or that they would be dealt with seriously.

That evening, Ex-Subedar Major RK Singh landed up in my house.

"How did you like it," he asked me, beaming with pleasure.

"Like what? The killing of *Sardarjis*?"

"Not killing, but *sabakh sikhaya* – taught them a lesson. Now the Sardars will know that we Hindus can do what they have been doing. That if they are *sawah* lakh, we are *dhai* lakh." He said.

Sikhs' tenth and the last Guru, Gobind Singh, had once told his soldiers that a single Sikh can defeat 125,000 – *sawah lakh* – of his opponents. Such an encouragement, I suppose, was needed in the face of the odds that the Sikh soldiers of his time had to face in the battle field. This made many modern Sikhs fantasize that they were equal to 125,000, or at least a lot many Hindus or Muslims. I knew a Sikh in Jammu whose name was Sawalakh Singh (one who could fight 125,000). There were names such as Hazara (thousand) Singh, and Lakhon (Hundred-thosuand) Singh. Sikh peasants who aspired their children to fight in the army named them Jarnail (General) Singh, Karnail (Colonel) Singh, Major Singh, even Sepahi (ordinary soldier) Singh.

The Ex- Subedar's *Dhai lakh* stood for 250,000; he meant that Hindus were twice as strong as Sikhs. They had the numbers.

"Major-Saa'b, I expected you to save the Sikhs in your village across the road. They had nothing to do with the assassination. I am shocked to hear that every Sikh in your village – some eleven of them were killed; that one of their women was raped. You had once told me that you cultivated brotherly fraternity among Hindus, Muslims and Sikhs in your army station. You could have done something like that to stop the carnage."

"Why would I save the Sikhs, the bastards who killed their own Prime Minister? My sons killed two of them – his clients – with their own hands. Actually, all Sikhs in the village were his clients. You know, my older son has an herbal medicine shop where he sells bottles of *Eternal Life*, supposedly an Ayurvedic medicine – no medicine, really, but some root juices mixed with pure alcohol passing off for medicine to hoodwink the excise. *Eternal Life* is much in demand in the evenings because of prohibition; most of the Sardars came to our shops to buy the stuff. Officers on the beat loved the booze; they closed their eyes for free booze-tonic and a *hafta*[74] of a couple of thousand rupees every month."

"Yet at the first opportunity your sons killed two Sikhs in cold blood?"

"Of course, they were not alone. It was a *Dharam yudh* – battle of righteousness. My sons are the offspring of a soldier, you know. Shoot to kill is a soldier's motto."

"Do soldiers shoot to kill innocent civilians? Do they kill without an order to kill? Or did they kill on your command? Do soldiers enter an innocent man's house, kill the men, rape the women and set fire to their houses? Did your sons also loot refrigerators, televisions, radios and all such things?"

The old man chuckled. "They are not that stupid. There already was a talk that police would search every Hindu house for looted stuff. Now they are doing it. While other fools were busy taking away all those things, my older son decided that they look for title deeds of properties of the dead Sikhs. They got

---

[74] *Hafta means weekly; but usually referred to a pre-determined monthly bribe, also called speed-money.*

three documents, and a fourth one of the *Gurudwara* plot, which they couldn't use, so threw it into fire. They looked for more title deeds, but most were burnt in the fire. Three are enough for my two sons and a daughter – two of them more than 3000 square feet, the one of 2200 feet which will go to my daughter. If we manage to get more, we will sell them."

"Don't you feel a tinge of guilt?"

"Why would I? They are all unauthorized plots, don't know if those bearded bastards even paid for them. We will fudge the names and get them regularized in my children's name before next year's election. Did the Sikhs feel a tinge of guilt when they pulled out six Hindus from a bus and shot them? Did they stop Bhinderwale from building a huge armoury in their so-called sacred *Harmandir Sahib*? Who but two ungrateful Sardars would shoot the person they were paid to guard? Would you celebrate and open champagne bottles even if your enemy was dead? My cousin in London phoned and said the Sardars there distributed sweets in celebration. Maybe they did it in Canada, America, wherever."

"Did the Sikhs who paid money to your sons and binged on your bootleg did any of that?"

"Does that matter? If they had the chance, they would do that too. If you know history, Panicker – what does a *Madrasi* know about our history? – you would know that our first freedom movement – 1857 – was defeated not by the *Goras*, but by Sikhs."

Gora, the white one, was a derisive term to describe the British.

"If you know history yourself, RK Singh, you should know that when the Sikhs fought the British twice before 1857, it was the same Northern and Eastern Hindus who sided with the British to defeat the Sikhs. You forget that every war that India fought with Pakistan, and the one with China, Sikhs gave their lives. You are from the army, you know about the Sikh Regiment, and so many Sikhs in the other regiments and services."

It didn't escape me that he had never before addressed me without the honorific of Saa'b. And never with the derisive *Madrasi*.

"Now Sikhs want Khalistan, just like another Pakistan, to break up India once again. They have been killing Hindus in Punjab, haven't they? Do you know that many Sikh soldiers deserted the army in protest against the killing of Bhinderwale the terrorist, not against the attack on their golden temple?"

"So, you and your sons, aided no doubt by a few more thugs, killed a dozen Sikhs – poor carpenters, blacksmiths and lathe workers, I hear – who had nothing to do with Bhinderwale except maybe listening to his audio cassettes, and nothing to do with the bus killings, or the airplane hijacks. While many of those incidents were happening, your sons were selling bootleg and sharing jokes with them. You were telling me how you taught the soldiers placed below you the need for friendly fraternity among Hindus, Muslims and Sikhs. Yet you killed or abetted the killing of those innocents Sikhs – all eleven of them in the village. Killed them like mad dogs with sticks and kitchen knives in cold blood while they were begging to be spared, probably reminding you of their friendship. You let your blood-thirsty lackeys take away fridges and televisions and gas cylinders which you knew will be confiscated by the police, but your sons were so smart that you got a few title deeds of housing plots worth hundreds of thousands, of which nobody will know, and which belonged to your neighbours whom you killed. Terrific, Subedar Major, terrific. What a military strategy."

Anger flared in his eyes. He got up and pointed a finger at me. "Why are you talking like a boot-lick of Sardars, you *Madrasi*? Who wants your two-penny job? I warn you, if you tell anyone about the title deeds, of which I told you in good faith, you will get the same treatment as those Sardars. Mark my words. My boys will know who told the police if they come searching for those documents though they will never find them."

"If I tell your killer neighbors that you and your sons made an ass of them by letting them take away the things that would be confiscated, but kept the real booty to yourselves, they would deal with you and your sons, not me."

Fear darkened his face. He got up and walked out, not omitting to clear his throat and spit, Indian way of displaying utter disgust. At the gate, he paused and turned around.

"Panicker Saa'b, that story about title deeds was a bluff. We didn't pick up anything from those Sardars' houses." His voice had taken a low, humble pitch.

"Don't worry," I said. "You don't have to try and go back on what you told me. I am not going to tell anyone. If I do, the properties will not go back to the real owners. In your world, killers are takers. Two days ago, I gave away the blankets and radios meant for the war-widows whose names you collected. The goons got them for destroying my dreams, all my life's earnings and bank loans."

Thus reassured, his aggressiveness returned,

"Serves you right. I heard Rekhi made an ass of you and cheated you of a lot of money. Ramcharan is looking for him. Go save Rekhi. He's a Sardar too."

He cleared his throat and spat again.

A new thought occurred to me like a flash.

"One more thing, RK Singh. The news of killing in your village will spread. They might not know about the title deeds, but about the decimation of a whole population of Sikhs in Indira Nagar. Did it occur to you that Sikhs can be reckless when they are furious, that shoot-to-kill is their motto as well, that a horde of them – maybe a revolting fraction from the Punjab Regiment – could descend on your village one day and kill every one of you – and take your house and all those precious 3000-foot and 2000-foot plots? That your wife and your daughters-in-law would be begging at their feet that their husbands be spared?"

A shadow of Terror passed over the old man's visage. He appeared rattled.

"Did you have to say such a terrible thing with your black tongue, you *mother–fucker*?"

I watched him walk away, shaking his head, probably reassuring himself that such a retaliation by the Sikhs on him and his sons would never come to pass, yet afraid it could.

I never saw him again. He didn't seek to collect his unearned salary from me. Whether it was bad conscience or the fear of Sikh reprisal that drove him back to his native town, I never learnt.

Just because something doesn't do what you planned it to do doesn't mean it's useless.

-Thomas Alva Edison,

THINGAMAJIG – AN OLD SOLDIER'S TALE

This happened when I was undergoing training as a Wireless Mechanic in the technical training school. I made friends with two seniors who were, like me, great radio enthusiasts and, with me, made up the sole members of the Station Radio Club. Corporal Frank Simon, by the relative elegance of his rank, was the gang's leading light. The second one, Leading Aircraftsman Samir Ghosh was undergoing conversion to Radar Mechanic, which was then a fancy and mysterious trade, and the third, a mere underdog, was trainee Aircraftman Class II Peter O'Shaunessy – a misfit in India with an unpronounceable name – myself.

We assembled stereo amplifiers and radios in the cobweb-filled room called Radio club which provided two desks, a few stools, a multimeter and a couple of soldering irons. Although for all other resources we had to fend for ourselves, when completed, most of our productions were taken by one or another officer or a Warrant Officer who wielded power. The things that were not whisked away were added to the 'Radio Club inventory.' From among us, Simon alone managed to spirit away a stereo which graced a corner beside his bed in the forty-bed staff billet.

Whether it was Corporal Simon or the underdog me who

unearthed an article in a magazine *'Electronics for All* shall forever remain an unresolved question. The magazine was a wireless enthusiast's Bible for hobbyists in those primitive days of Electronics. International communication passed through manual switchboards. The wait for new technology was long; only alternative means of communication was through Morse code which needed transcription by clever operators with dexterous fingers and skill at speed-writing. The cutting-edge technology of the time – teleprinters – were just making their appearance.

The gem of the article we discovered in *Electronics for All* described a circuit that would respond to a hand-clap or any other high-decibel sound. With the circuit, promised the article, you could remotely switch on any device by clapping your hands or making some other sound loud enough to qualify as 80 decibels. You could switch on your bedroom light by clapping your hands, or turn on the radio by shouting at it. Such a remote control was indeed cutting-edge. Or so we felt. Things like infra-red remote control, Bluetooth or Airdrop were not dreamed of even in science fiction.

Simon, being a Corporal and on the permanent staff, had some access to resources. So, he strategized and procured most of the things required for our pirated invention – two vacuum tubes – barrel-shaped little lamps with a network of rolled-up little wires and grilles inside, with eight-pin bases, along with a few colour-coded carbon resistors and condensers. Vacuum tubes, like dinosaurs, were fossilized within a couple of decades later with the proliferation of transistors and integrated circuits, but in late 1950's they were still the rage; those fragile glass tubes (summarily known as valves) were the foundation pillars of electronics. Simon also managed to bring with him a relay that once was part of a High-Frequency transmitter which had, in any case, been cannibalized to the skin. Air Force, justified Simon, sustained itself by cannibalization of parts. I guess it still does.

Ghosh, being a Leading Aircraftsman good at workshop practices fashioned a six-inch-wide square epoxy board he scrounged from the workshop. He made the necessary number of holes for passing wires through; and precision-drilled holes for the eight-pin vacuum tube sockets as well. I, being the lowly worker in the gang, threaded wires and smaller components through those holes and soldered connections on the other side according to the circuit diagram.

Since we needed a microphone to make the device work, Simon sounded the officer in-charge of the signal section who showed only vague interest in the project. Nonetheless the Sig-O, a Flight Lieutenant, lent us, after receiving signatures from all three of us, a microphone and a small motor that we needed to demonstrate how the invention worked. The last of the connections was soldered, the vacuum tubes were put into the eight-hole sockets.

The arrangement was to be powered from the mains through a pair of wires that led away from our plastic board. Simon inserted those wires, their end insulations nibbled off with teeth, into a wall socket. The vacuum tubes blinked, and when Simon shouted into the microphone, the motor jumped into action and fell off the table. Hurray, the contraption worked. Thankfully, the fall did no damage to the motor.

When he heard of the success of our experiment the Flight Lieutenant Sig-O with an engineering degree under his belt got enthused. He invited the senior officers of the training unit to watch a demonstration. The normally irritable Senior Admin Officer (SAd-O publicly referred to as the Essay-doe, but privately known among the ranks as the Sad Officer), smiled and invited the Unit Commander, a Wing Commander. The Wing-Co was visibly impressed and congratulated the Sig-O while we three looked on as the humble coolie force who only acted according to orders. Nobody considered any incidental contribution of the Corporal and the two trainees to be of any significance.

Wing-Co had a great idea. "Can we use this *Thingamajig* to open a curtain by clapping hands?"

"We can do one better, Sir," said Corporal Simon, audaciously out of turn, trying to get into the spotlight. "We can make it open by saying aloud OPEN! Then if we say CLOSE! it will close."

The Sig-O gave Simon a withering look for speaking out of turn – not through proper channel, which ought to have been through him. Flight Lieutenants ranked several ranks and class above a mere Corporal – a Non-commissioned officer with no office – who was only to be seen in the presence of commissioned officers, not heard unless asked. Anyway, the Sig-O wasn't willing to share the spotlight with a lowly Corporal.

"We can make it open by saying OPEN. Then if we say CLOSE, it will close," the Sig-O parroted as if the idea came from himself.

The Wing-Co, being an engineer himself, was not fooled.

"Even if you say OPEN the second time, it will close. It just needs some sound, right?"

He directed the question at the Sig-O who looked at Corporal Simon.

Simon, who was sulking, did not answer for the legitimate reason that he was not asked. The silence was deafening.

"Yes, Sir, whatever you might say into the mike, once it is open, it will close. Works like a toggle switch," I said. I had learnt about toggle switches only in the morning class and was proud to put it to use. I only meant to relieve the tension, but the Sig-O, the Corporal and the Leading Aircraftsman gave me progressively harder withering looks.

"That's true, Sir," said the Sig-O, this time letting go of the proper-channel protocol. I noticed that he heaved an almost imperceptible sigh of relief.

"We could use the *Thingamajig* to impress the visiting VIP, the Defence Minister," suggested the Wing-Co with a smile.

That was when we insignificant Other-rankers learnt for certain that the great DM was to visit our school. That was also the time when the Voice-operated control, designed by an anonymous guy, published in a little-known journal named *Electronics for All*, dug out and put into life by three airmen of progressively less significant ranks, came to be officially christened as the *Thingamajig*, forever to be known by that name.

"We will put a curtain at the guardroom gate, Sir," said the SAd-O brightly.

"Not a bad idea," said Wing-Co the Unit Commander, which appeared to further hearten the SAd Officer.

While casually strolling back to his office, the Wing-Co turned around and said: "Make one more *Thingamajig* for standby. You can't trust one of that kind to work when you most need it."

Have a stand-by was one of the profound principles of the Air Force. Stand-by for the VIP Viscount aircraft that was to fly the Prime Minister. Stand-by pilots for the Pilot and Co-Pilot who would fly the Prime Minister. Stand-by Super Constellation to pick up the President if his special Air India flight got stranded in some god-forsaken place. Stand-by for the only communication equipment mounted in the Dakota aircraft. Stand-by for airmen assigned guard duty.

We had no resources for a second *thingamajig*, but the Unit Commander's was an order. Since the SAd-O had access to resources as well as money, he graciously sanctioned Rupees 200 from Station Contingency Fund and granted us the use of a jeep to go to the City Market where they sold radio parts. Thus, I had my first proud jeep-ride, Ghosh said it was his second, but Simon, being a Corporal with eight years of service under his belt, boasted he could even drive the jeep himself, at which the Anglo-Indian driver Leading Aircraftsman Jonathan Jones guffawed.

We bought at the City Market all that was needed for Rupees One hundred and seventy-four including a printed circuit board with copper-clad connections on a glass-epoxy sheet for the same circuit that we had always believed was our own secret baby. The salesman at the City Market told us the circuit was very popular among radio enthusiasts in the town; that was why he got the printed circuit board (a novelty then) designed and manufactured. With the balance of twenty-six Rupees, we healed the wounds of our pride with coffee and potato-cutlets for all including the driver who asked why we looked peeved, but was given no clue. That half the electronic hobbyists in town were making voice-operated devices to operate bedroom lights, radios and even a garage door should, we decided, forever remain a secret in Air Force records as FOE&EO- For Our Eyes and Ears Only.

We returned none too pleased, but since the bigwigs had come into picture and the show had to go on, I soldered the connections into the fine pre-printed board where the relay and other components sat firm and more stable than on the crude prototype we had made before, and it worked.

Now was the time to set up things at the Station's gate where *Thingamajig* could demonstrate its miracle, out in open, not in the hidden-away radio club. The burden of arranging things shifted to the SAd-O. Sad or not, the Squadron Leader was a capable officer.

His nickname, the Sad Officer was in bad taste; he had every reason to be a happy officer. It was he who handled all the resources in the Station while the Accounts Officer had the role of a mere bank cashier. The local Military Engineering Service reported to the SAd-O. On his command two ten-foot long GI poles were secured and put up at the main gate, twenty feet apart, and cemented firmly to the ground on either side. The hand-operated boom at the gate that normally blocked intrusion without permission was raised. The DSC – Defense Service Corps – *Jawan* (the name meant a young soldier, but this was an ageing man) – whose job it was to operate the boom on order. The middle-aged soldier was given furlough for the day.

The boom stood at an angle like one of the cranes at a seaport. A horizontal GI pipe that was procured as an afterthought was screwed on to the top of the poles, creating what looked like a very large door-frame. A blue (Air Force colour, if you didn't know) velvet sheet was procured, cut into two curtains ten-foot wide each and got stitched to size by the tailor-shop contractor of the Station. It was attached to hooks suspended from the parallel beam. Simon was called in to design and wire the setup; Ghosh made suggestions, and I stood on a stool to thread the wires through the loops atop the curtain and connect them to the fine circuit board. Our own cruder prototype was relegated to stand-by; but not even the Sig-O with an engineering degree noticed the difference. The microphone – a large silvery commercial variety – last used when a previous vociferous Defense Minister addressed officers and men six months before, was connected and slung unobtrusively in a corner.

We faced a new problem. The guard room, a wooden kiosk with little more than enough space for a police NCO to sit at a small desk with a telephone on its cradle and a couple of registers, had no electric socket to power the *Thingamajig* when it was installed at the gate. The only technical device in the whole vicinity was a glaring hundred-watt electric bulb that hung from the ceiling of the guardroom. Ghosh pointed at the bulb. Simon got the hint and ran to the signal section.

The Flight Lieutenant Sig-O, still sulking, told him to go tell the SAd-O. The Sad-O called the MES. A plumber from MES, who had never gone near anything electric before, brought a bakelite contraption called adapter that could be screwed into the lamp holder. The adapter had two pins at the top to mate like a bayonet with the original lamp-holder with a similar lamp-holder at the bottom with the addition of two plug-in sockets sticking out on either side. I screwed on the adapter to the lamp holder in the guardroom, chewed off an inch of insulation from each wire, connected them to the plug we had bought, and shoved it to one of the sockets on the suspended adapter.

"This will do," said Simon.

"Yes, that will do" said the Sig-O in the voice that befitted his authority. He must have figured that it would be he who would be called upon to explain the *Thingamajig* to the VIP when he descended on the Station in all his Defense Ministerial glory.

Many trials were held. Each time someone said OPEN loud enough, the curtains parted. A CLOSE! call closed them together. It occurred to nobody to try shouting OPEN a second time. In any case, it didn't matter. The VIP wouldn't have a chance to learn that a second OPEN command could just as well close the curtains

There was still a week to go. When the Sad-O, the Sig-O and the Wing-Co, not to forget a Flight Sergeant who was the expert Senior NCO of wireless training section certified that all was well, the curtains were removed, *Thingamajig* and its humble stand-by were safely stored away in the SAd-O's private cupboard lest someone fiddled with it, and the preparation for the VIP Inspection got underway.

During the next week, office walls received a fresh coat of

paint; plants in the garden outside the main offices were pruned, even the dusty leaves of trees were given a pressure wash. Some plants were added and some transported to lesser places. Hedges abruptly sprouted pansies and mini-daisies; clusters of yellow marigolds and red roses appeared in the CO's garden. Pots were painted with red mud-paint. In offices that mattered, the photos of the previous Defense Minister that graced the walls were unceremoniously brought down and replaced with those of the visiting dignitary – the New Defense Minister – to beam between a smiling Mahatma Gandhi and frowning Nehru. A truck with a long trailer honored with the name of Queen Mary moved around, placing potted bougainvillea pruned into the shape of domes, rose plants with flowers and multi-coloured crotons, interspersed with golden and purple Dahlias at equal intervals, all on pots painted uniform mud-red, stood in single files on both sides of the road.

The VIP, they said, would arrive at 11 AM sharp. By 6 AM on the day of the Inspection, we presented ourselves at the gate as per the order to install the *Thingamajig* once again. The roads within the Station and the one outside that led to the civilian highway shone like ebony with freshly laid and dried bitumen. A welcome arch in the name of the visiting dignitary stood mounted above the curtained frame at the gate, hiding the GI pipes. Broad intermittent white lines were painted in the middle of the road as if it were a runway. Where the road to the Air Force Station parted ways with the civilian highway, a round, raised platform outlined by flower pots appeared as if from nowhere; a Police Sergeant in white regalia, white gloves and white anklets stood on it practising traffic direction. There was much sprucing up going on in the broad square within the Station, where stood the proud flag mast with the National flag at the top and the Air Force Roundel below, already unfurled and hoisted at sunrise. The twin flags lay limp, occasionally waking up like a dozing Member of Parliament in session and waved.

First the SAd-O came along on his scooter and ordered the yellow boom with the STOP sign raised. The DSC guard was dispensed with. Two Corporals, picked for their height and good physique, armed with polished 303-rifles were installed on both sides just outside the gate. They promptly presented arms to the SAd-officer who returned the compliment with a tardy salute.

The installation was better than before, the microphone was better hidden, the circuit board, secured in a cardboard box, found its place on the policeman's desk. The police NCO, totally innocent of technology, was instructed to stay away from the box. The power cable, which was now more reliable with a two-pin male plug at its end, was shoved into the adapter socket on the lamp holder. Simon said be careful, the power is ON, I said never mind, I could handle even 2000 volts.

When done, the SAd-O stood away a couple of metres from the middle of the curtain and called out OPEN, a little louder than necessary, and the curtains promptly parted. As was the drill, he said CLOSE and they obediently glided in together and nearly snapped shut.

A few instructor-officers, even a couple of Warrant Officers and the Flight Sergeant, coming in for the VIP *Inspection*, all in their fine uniforms with colorful medals adorning their chests, got down from their respective scooters and bicycles at the gate and stared at the fancy blue velvet blocking their way. When the *Thingamajig* was explained, they spoke the OPEN! *mantra* and passed through, mightily impressed at the ultra-modern technology.

A VIP visit in an Air Force unit was known as inspection. Inspection always necessitated a kit-layout in the billets of airmen. The idea, no doubt borrowed from the Army, was to show that the men were properly kitted and fighting-fit. Airmen-trainees cut grass outside their billets, pruned hedges, cleaned the windows and swept the ceilings to clear cob-webs. Then they spread the best regulation bed-sheets on their *charpoys* – cots - with their dinner plates at the center, a mess-tin (which they never used), the cutlery (which they proudly used and pretended they had been using it all along in their lives) and a few other knick-knacks on the bed. Their parade boots were polished like tinted Ray-ban glasses and placed atop the standard blue wooden kit-box.

Although a visiting VIP seldom took a second look at the strange display, the unit discipline officer, a warrant officer who wore stiffly starched uniform and never walked but always marched like a one-man parade, took note of the boots which were not polished well enough and the displays that were deficient in kits. He would give a list of the defaulters to the Adjutant who usually let it lie and rot in a PENDING tray except when he had no better job to do.

But the kit lay-out was important for all men under the rank of Sergeant. Simon was only a Corporal though not a trainee, Ghosh and I were mere insignificant labour class who could be officers' orderlies and be washing their wives' clothes if we were in the Army.

By 9:30 that fine morning, the entire drill, meticulously planned, was rehearsed. The VIP's car would be stopped six steps away from the gate. The place where the front wheels of the car should rest was marked with white powder and shown to the driver who would, accompanied by the Station Commander (a Group Captain four ranks above an army Captain and yet whispered simply as *Groupie* among lesser beings) would pick up the Minister from the airport tarmac and bring him in. As the car approached the station's gate, the two police sergeants on white regalia atop blue -and-black pilot motorcycles would flare away to the sides. The driver, a Sergeant with VIP experience and several rows of medals on his chest would stop the car exactly as directed, and get out quickly, open the door and salute. First would emerge the Station Commander (the Groupie), and would wait, with a courteous bow, for the bulky VIP to squeeze himself out. The security jeep that followed the VIP car would stop, and Wing-Co the Unit Commander would jump out and move forward to the curtained gate, acknowledge the Groupie, but salute and receive the Defense Minister, and with just a few words, explain the automatic curtain opener made by the Research-and-Development section of the Station. The smart corporals standing by the hedges will present arms with their rifles. The Station Commander, (Groupie for Group Captain) would request the great man, in whispers, to order the curtain to open. When he obliges the curtain would open, the thoroughly impressed VIP would walk through to be surprised and overjoyed to be presented arms and a Guard-of-Honor by a contingent of the pick of trainees, commanded by the Equipment Officer who was the fairest looking person other than the unit commander himself.

The DM would walk along the Groupie who slow-marched along the length of the Guard-of-Honor where the men would swivel their necks just so their eyes would dutifully follow the dignitary. At the end of the line, the Equipment Officer would salute and smartly withdraw, and the DM would step on to a red carpet that was rolled out all the way to the Station Headquarters where there would be a briefing and tea and biscuits with the option of hot potato-stuffed *samosas* in case the VIP happened to be a glutton.

The rehearsal was conducted three times – once by the SAd-O standing in for the VIP, then the Unit Commander (Wing-Co) obliging, and finally the Station Commander (Groupie) doing a trial run without losing his dignity under his peak-cap lined with gold laurels. At every trial, the corporal-guards presented arms, the curtains obediently parted and then, on the second voice cue, closed. On one of the rehearsals, the corporal near the hidden microphone clicked his heels too loud, and the curtains opened. It was decided that the heels will be brought together without the regulation click. Firm instructions were passed around, making it clear that no one in the vicinity should make a loud noise when the VIP was in the process of negotiating the area lest the curtains closed in on his voluminous belly. The parade commander, a Flight Lieutenant from the Equipment Section, was also given to understand that he shouldn't shout his command to the Guard-of-Honor parade till the VIP was well past the curtain into the square.

The Sig-O, I suspect, expected a *Vishisht Seva* (Meritorious Service) Medal after the VIP expressed his appreciation and congratulated all the officers involved. The SAd-O no doubt decided to let in that the idea originated from him. Simon, Ghosh and I stood to a side, behind the curtain, ready to pounce into action if any snag occurred and hoping that some of the shavings of the congratulatory expressions would fall on us like coloured confetti.

By 10:45 AM, as the tension was nearing its peak and one expected to hear the warning horn from around the corner any time and for the escorting motorcycles to thrust into sight, the SAd-O noticed us three airmen, no doubt a bloody disgrace, and of suspicious motives, to be standing around in the haloed surroundings.

"What the hell are you doing here now?" he asked in anger. "Get back to your billets and make sure your kit-layout is done properly."

We hesitated, and the SAd-O said: "That's an order."

Peeved, humiliated and disheartened in the proportionate degree of those emotions, Corporal Simon, LAC Ghosh and AC II O'Shaunessy walked, heads down, heart heavy, back to our billets.

"At the double!" roared the SAd-O from behind.

We walked briskly.

That, I believe, was when the SAd-O caught sight of a patch of yellow light coming out from the guardroom window and marring the shimmering blue of a part of the curtain. The affected part looked a dull grey against the pristine sky-blue of the rest of the velvet fabric which sparkled in the white sunlight. Viewed from outside, it seemed like a faint but big patch of stain on the curtain.

He looked at the Corporal (AC2, just out of training, Acting-Unpaid) who had been standing stiffly in his starched uniform, white cross-belt holding a revolver in its holster at the hip that he barely knew to use, and a white peaked-cap with the ranker's badge on it glistening like gold.

"Corporal, do you need that bloody light?"

The young man stiffened despite being stiff enough already.

"No, Sir," he said.

"Then switch it off," said the SAd-O: "It's a bloody a distraction."

"Yes, Sir," said the young man. Though he did not quite catch the word 'distraction'. He turned off the light and, along with it, the power to the overworked *Thingamajig*.

Next moment – this is what the young police corporal told me later – the warning horn was heard. The VIP car with its Defense Minister's flag and the glorious Ashoka lions on its bonnet turned in from the civilian highway. The motorcycles flared out into the hedges. The VIP driver stopped the car at precisely the right spot, ran around and opened the door. The Group Captain gracefully and smartly came out; then did the Lion of Calcutta, the Defense

Minister, emerge with some effort. The Wing-Co alighted from the security jeep, walked up smartly, saluted, and explained, as briefly as he could, how the Unit had researched and developed this amazing technical marvel. The two corporals standing by the hedges, tall and muscular, presented arms without clicking their heels.

The DM, always a little skeptical of our military services after the China debacle, walked up and said OPEN! As he was told.

The vacuum tubes, of course, had gone stone-dead. The blue curtains only swayed a little in the warm breeze.

"A little louder, Sir," pleaded the SAd-Officer, now really feeling SAd. His voice shook.

The Defense Minister, perceptibly annoyed, repeated the order to the Curtain to Open.

The curtains disobeyed the great man's order. That their life-blood was not flowing through the wires from the light-switch, nobody had a clue.

The DM, famed for his quick anger looked at the Group Captain, who looked at the Wing Commander, who stared at the SAd Squadron Leader, who glowered at the Flight Lieutenant Sig-O who was till then hoping to lay a claim to the invention. He looked around to glower at the three bloody rankers who, he felt, had somehow let them all down with their technical wizardry. But they were nowhere in sight.

The VIP smirked, parted the curtains with his own hands, and walked in.

The Guard-of-Honor went like clock-work, Present-arms was performed with rifles hit smartly on their sides and the boots of sixty trainees clicked loud like one burst. Sixty pairs of eyes and sixty necks swiveled to follow the DM as he moved slowly to keep with the Group Captain who slow-marched as per the procedure.

The ceremony failed to impress the Minister after the opening fiasco with the curtains. He, red-faced and smarting under a suspicion that the thing with the curtains could be a practical joke played on him, was meekly escorted on the red carpet (which no longer seemed bright-red) to the Station Commander's office for tea before the 'Inspection'.

The young police NCO, relieved and relaxed, switched on the light and sat down.

In a jiffy, power flowed to *Thingamajig*.

A pale and crest-fallen SAd-O and the even paler and crest-less Sig-O, who were deliberately ignored from attending the tea with the VIP, returned to the site of what they thought to be the graveyard of their prestige, pride and good annual recommendation.

"OPEN, you bloody curtain!" shouted the SAd-O, not even bothering to get close enough to the gaily waving pieces of velvet or the microphone.

The tragic end of this story is: The curtains, grateful for the renewed supply of electricity, parted gracefully.

Then Jesus said to the woman, "I was sent only to help God's lost sheep — the people of Israel."

Matthew 15:24 (New Living Translation)

HOW JESUS SAVED MRS. FRANKSON

Syedpur is a small town with a Catholic Church and a convent, a popular Christian Hospital and separate Catholic-run schools for girls and boys – all in a row. Though a busy railway junction presided over the setup, the town's claim to fame was that Syedpur was the constituency of a former chief minister of the state who had gifted the town with a Law College before he died with boots on (battling the opposition) at the age of 92.

Around the corner at the end of the dirt road was a popular Muslim Saint's *Dargah* (Mausoleum-cum-Mosque) and not far from it a Ganpati temple – one dedicated to the elephant-headed Hindu God. The two places of worship complimented each other with reflected glory. Hindu residents and those who came from afar to worship Ganpati repeatedly struck a hanging bell at the entrance to the temple to alert the God of their arrival. This caused some annoyance to the Muslim worshippers in the mosque who had come to say their *Salat* and also to those who sat around on the parapets of the *Dargah* to meditate on Allah and His Prophet, to discuss the government subsidy for the next *Hajj* season or to relive the miracles of the long-departed Peer[75].

---

[75] Muslim saint.

The noisy nuisance of the ringing bells was forgiven when the Hindus, after filing their appeals to Lord Ganpati, went by and dropped a coin – more preferably a ten-rupee note – in the donation box at the *Dargah*. In return, for Ganpati-immersion days Muslim craftsmen fashioned beautiful images of the elephant-headed god in clay, painted them in bright colours and sold them to their Hindu brethren for bargain prices. Those beautiful images were drowned on the auspicious day in the local rain-fed lake with much fanfare. Ganpati was a benign and all-forgiving God who blessed those who drowned his effigies year-after-year and polluted the main source of water for the town.

Newly wedded Hindu couple would visit the *Dargah* to seek the blessings of the *Peer* whose grave-stone adorned the centre of a large hall. The nuns in the Christian hospital were famed for their loving care of patients and free treatment for the poor. Hindu, Muslim and Christian boys and girls studied at their respective Catholic Schools and were taught and treated without explicit discrimination. Thus, despite an occasional rumour that the church used imported money to convert the tribals and the very poor in the village nearby, religions nudged along together in Syedpur without noticeable abrasion.

One summer day it rained incessantly – not a regular occurrence. The unpaved road got inundated. Though the rain had let up by evening, people waded in ankle-deep and thick muddy water on their way home from work. I was coaxing my reluctant bicycle through the slush when I heard a woman shout for help. I stopped.

I noticed a female head under a shock of greying bobbed hair above the rushing brown water in the roadside drain. She held on to a tree-trunk, her fat arms with a single gold bangle straining to keep her from drifting away in the current. She called for help by turn in English, Telugu and local Urdu which passed off for

Hindi. All three languages were spoken in Syedpur; the last two were easily understood by all while English was for Anglo-Indians who lived in the railway colony a couple of kilometres away, and priests and nuns who worked in the hospital or taught in the schools. The students in the law college nearby, where I served as a humble junior-lecturer on the lofty subject of Constitutional law, spoke different variations of English in accents that let you guess their mother tongues.

A small crowd had collected around the woman's bobbing head with bobbed hair, arguing among each other, but not making a move to rescue her. One asked in local Urdu, "Aunty-*ji*, how did you get in the *khadda*? *Machi pakadtha, kya*? Were you trying to catch fish?". Others laughed. The woman spat and screamed curses at their callousness.

I let drop my bicycle and bent over the pit, gave her a hand, then both hands and heaved her up. I thrust a foot against the root of the nearby tree to keep myself from sliding down with chunks of mud that gave way. She weighed a ton. I suspected I might have sprained my back.

Her clothes, which must have been white with large red rose-prints before she fell, were drenched a filthy-brown. Thick chunks of mud crept leisurely down her fat legs when she stood up with a slight hunch before plonking herself on the street which was more like a swamp. She squatted on her haunches, unmindful of the dirt, her hands on her head, elbows resting on her shaking knees. Her pink skin showed through the streaks of mud and water. A thin gold chain with a cross on it caressed the valley of her mountainous bosom. You could see her teeth chattering, body shuddering as if from fear of death. Syedpur was never cold, and the rain had only cut a couple of degrees from the usual 40 in summer.

I handed her my handkerchief to wipe her face.

"Thank you, son," she said in a voice that trembled. "I could have died there, but Jesus brought you along. None of these fools, all Hindus, or may be *katuas*, tried to help me. Thank God a good Christian like you came along."

She spoke loudly to express her anger at the men who laughed at her plight. *Katua* was a derisive term you'd never expect a lady to use. It referred to Muslims who, it was well known, had the tip of their foreskin cut off to correct an omission by *Allah* during the process of creation.

"I am not a Christian, I'm a Hindu," I said, more out of defiance than any special pride in the religion of my Mother and with a lot of disdain for the religion of my father who had come to India under John Kennedy's USAID Program. He had promised to take my mother and her two children – my elder sister Rita from Mother's first husband who died from alcoholism, and his own infant son, which was me – with him to Georgetown, Denver in the United States when he would be called back after his PL-480 tenure.

Whether he meant to keep that promise or not, it was not to be. My mother caught him in the act of attempting to rape my adolescent sister and raised an alarm. The neighbours in the block held the white American and called the police. With the cops hot on his trail, the man who fathered me fled back to America when he was released on bail. After an initial display of urgency, the police did nothing to follow up. Perhaps they received orders from the government not to ruffle American feathers in those hard-up days. The local economy could hardly get by without American wheat and powdered milk.

My mother, a nurse in the big hospital with income enough to bring up us two children, and to put us through college, never trusted a man or the government since then. She made me pray at every temple wherever we went and taught me Hindu scriptures with a vengeance. I had no revenge to wreak on anyone, not even on the white man I hardly remembered except when boys in the school called me White Cockroach. Thus, I grew up to treat all religions with equal disdain.

I recalled her name – Mrs. Jennifer Frankson. I met her with her daughter at a Sunday ball that the Anglo-Indians held at the railway colony. Sometimes when the menfolk were away driving trains, scooping coal into the fire-belly of a steam engine, manning a rail station or working a shift as guard on a passenger train, the colony had more girls than men for a day-time ball they called the Jam-session. So, some of us – a couple of students and myself – from the college got to be invited.

Perhaps my light skin and unusual name (Jonathan Moore, which most people in the college pronounced as Jonthan Morray) presumably induced her to think that I could be a good catch for her daughter. She introduced herself as Mrs. Jennifer Frankson and her daughter as *Little* Lily. Even though it was mid-day, Mr. Frankson was too drunk to introduce himself, and too embarrassing for his wife to introduce him.

Little Lily was a big-made girl of twenty or twenty-one with an alluring figure and, nimble feet on the dance floor. She actually led me through many twists and turns on a Slow Waltz and taught me to catch up with the rest of the crowd during the lightning-fast *Mexican Fiesta*, which proved to be a cue for packing up and going home. We held hands a little longer than necessary while saying good-bye. Her mother looked on with a twinkle of an idea in her eyes.

That was then. Now Mrs. Frankson sized me up in disbelief. If she remembered me from the Sunday Jam-session, she didn't show it.

She said, in a voice filled with pity and genuine concern: "Jesus Christ, You're not a Catholic? That's terrible. Dear me, you look like an *Anglo* and talk like one. If you are not a Catholic, then you better become one. A gentleman like you should get baptized before the devil gets you. No matter how good a Samaritan you are, if Jesus can't save you, you will go to hell. I will tell Brother Frank to help you."

Brother Frank was a preacher I knew who was de-frocked from becoming Father Frank for the carnal sin of fathering a couple of kids with a pretty tribal woman and – gosh, can you imagine – shamelessly admitting it. Yet he was a generous man who carried a bag of sugar candies to give one to any child he met; his jeep served as an ambulance when a child in the nearby village caught measles or mumps and had to be hospitalized, or a woman was in urgent hurry to deliver her baby. The locals thought of the roly-poly man in admiration mixed with suspicion and some amusement.

"Push her back in that pit," shouted one of the onlookers in that peculiar local Urdu, He evidently understood what Mrs. Frankson had spoken in English, and his Hindu-pride was wounded: "You're going to hell anyways."

The crowd guffawed.

I laughed and moved to pick up my bicycle. A look of sheer terror spread on Mrs. Frankson's face. Apparently for fear that I was going to push her back into the drain, she jumped up with amazing agility and dashed away, her feet splashing muddy water all around. You'd scarce believe, the way she ran, that this was the same old woman of heavy, unwieldy buttocks, so clumsy in her drenched clothes, whom only a few moments ago I had retrieved from the horror of drowning in the flooded drain,

I learnt later that Mrs. Frankson went and told her folks in the Railway Colony how a terrible young *Hindu bastard* who looked and talked like an *Anglo* tried to push her into a muddy pit during the rains and how Jesus saved her. There was no mention of the same young Hindu bastard saving her from the flooded drain.

The job of saving anyone who had fallen in a dirty drain rested on a man who could not save himself from a horribly slow death two thousand years ago.

Shortly after that incident I ran into Mrs. Frankson's Little Lily in the market. She refused to acknowledge my greeting; even to make eye contact – let alone engage in the joy of the minor flirtation that we usually shared ever since the first meeting.

To my lonesome bachelor's chagrin, I was never again invited to the Railway Colony Ball.

Printed in the United States
By Bookmasters